# The Brothers Path

by
Martha Kennedy

This is a work of fiction that includes references to historical characters and events. Wherever possible, the author has followed reliable historical sources regarding their words, ideas and the events of their lives as they intersect the story.

Cover design by Martha Kennedy

Cover image, a 16th century Swiss cookie mold

Copyright © 2016 Martha Kennedy
Free Magic Show Productions

ISBN: 978-1535101295

Printed in the United States of America

## ACKNOWLEDGEMENTS

Thanks to Beth Bruno for her perceptive editing and her enthusiasm for the adventures of the Schneebeli boys.

Thanks to Lois Maxwell and Linda Hill Spencer for taking the time to help me proofread an early draft and, most of all, for loving the story.

For Lily

# Zürich, Switzerland in the 16ᵗʰ century

# Book One

## Salvation

# chapter 1

## Rudolf, June 1524

"Hugo, hurry, get Frau Beck. Tell her it's an emergency! Then go to the mill for Father and my brothers."

"Yes, young sir," said Old Hugo. He stopped his work on the woodpile and rushed to the barn to saddle a horse.

Andreas returned to his mother where she lay almost too weak to do what her body demanded of her. "Old Hugo's gone for the midwife, Mother." He sat down by Verena's bed and took her hand.

"Andreas," she said, "get Hannes."

"I can't leave you alone, Mother. Where is everyone?"

Before Verena could answer, the baby tried again to enter the world. Verena screamed and squeezed Andreas' hand until he wanted to scream, too. Then she fell silent, exhausted.

Andreas wiped her brow and prayed, "Heavenly Father, please get the midwife here in time. Please don't let my mother die."

Verena slept. Andreas waited.

The previous night seemed like a lifetime ago. Andreas had listened to Pastor Zwingli talk about teaching people to read so that all could know the word of God. "The Scripture is clear to everyone," Zwingli said. "No one needs a priest or a bishop or the Pope to tell them what it means." By the time the sermon had ended, the city gates were closed. Andreas spent the night at the home of Felix Manz, inside the city walls.

"Missus?" The midwife appeared at Verena's door. Seeing Verena's wan and harrowed face, Frau Beck crossed herself. "Surely not yet. Surely not." She took off her shawl and set down the basket that held the implements of her trade.

"I don't know, Frau Beck. I got home just a little while ago. There was no one home except Old Hugo. I don't know where Elsa is, or the children, or Little Barbara, the maidservant."

"She must have been well when she woke up this morning or she would not be here alone. She should not..."

"I know, Frau Beck."

"Last time..." Frau Beck stopped and held her peace. Last year, when Verena had miscarried, Frau Beck had warned Old Johann, but he would never believe that by loving his wife and doing what God had ordained, he could hurt her.

Verena awakened and, for a moment, seemed not to know where she was. Then she remembered. "Andreas? Has the midwife come? Has your father come?"

"Frau Beck is here. She's gone to the kitchen. She'll be right back. Father has not come yet."

"Hannes?"

"No, Mother. He will be here." Then Andreas felt his mother squeeze his hand hard again. "Frau Beck!" he called out. "Hurry! She's..."

Frau Beck came in with a basin of water and all the clean linen she had found. She lifted Verena's knees and spread them. "The baby is on his way. It is too soon, far too soon." She crossed herself, fearing she'd accidentally willed the little one dead.

Verena cried out again, and, in one final painful spasm of blood and life, the babe came into the world, blue and far too small.

Frau Beck cleared the baby's mouth, tied the umbilical cord, washed the little one quickly, and was about to give him to Verena but changed her mind. "Take him, young sir," she said. "Your mother is too weak to hold him, small though he is. You'd best baptize him. I doubt he'll live long."

Until this moment, Andreas, at nineteen, had been the youngest Schneebeli boy. He held his tiny brother in his arms and took a deep breath, knowing he would not baptize him. Zwingli's words on that question were fresh in his mind, that children should be baptized only "...*after a firm faith had been implanted in their hearts and they had confessed the same with their mouth...*"

"Will you name him, Mother?"

Verena whispered, "Rudolf."

Within minutes, the baby was dead.

"I'm sorry, young sir. Give him to me. I'll take care of his little body. A pity he died before you could baptize him."

His heart empty of all save sorrow, Andreas sat down beside his mother and watched her fall asleep. Frau Beck washed the baby with great tenderness, and then swaddled him in a linen towel.

\*\*\*

"Verena! Where are you? What's going on that you had to send Hugo after me?" Old Johann shouted from the front door. Seeing Frau Beck rushing toward him, he shivered in fear. "What has happened?"

"The baby, sir. He has come before-time," said Frau Beck.

"My wife?"

"She's very tired and very ill. The baby took everything out of her, sir. I..." Frau Beck stopped.

"What, woman? Speak up!" Old Johann yelled in Frau Beck's face.

"I told you last year if she became pregnant again, it was likely to kill her. She's sleeping now, God bless her." Frau Beck crossed herself. "It would be a kindness to her if you would leave her sleep. She's in God's hands."

Old Johann's face reddened. "You're telling me she's dying?"

Frau Beck nodded. "Yes, sir. It's likely. She knows it. She's been asking for Hannes."

"She has not asked for me?"

"She knows you were sent for, that you would come home. Her fear is for the safety of her soul. It's natural it would be so."

\*\*\*

Hearing Old Johann's voice, Andreas walked out of his mother's room and into the private courtyard that opened onto to the orchard. He could not bear to see his father or be anywhere near him. Anyway, the baby needed a coffin. Andreas walked between the late spring apple trees, with their bright leaves and fading blossoms, and opened the door to the apple shed. On the floor was a neat stack of boxes used for apples that were too good for cider. He found one that was clean and new and dusted it with an apple sack. When he returned to the house with it, his brothers, Heinrich and Thomann, were standing in the courtyard.

"Mother asked for Hannes," Andreas told them.

"I'll go." Thomann, six years older than Andreas, most resembled Verena physically. He was short and sturdily built with red hair and changeable eyes. "It's best you stay with Father, Heinrich."

"Hurry," said Heinrich, feeling a chill up his spine. The oldest, Heinrich was already in his mid-thirties, his father's right-hand man at the mill and the father of four children. Thomann took off running in the direction of Angel Mountain Abbey.

"Where's Father?" Heinrich asked Andreas.

"Gone to look in on Mother. I hope he will leave her be. She's dying, thanks to him."

Heinrich gestured toward the apple box. "What is that for?"

"Rudolf."

Heinrich looked at Andreas, not understanding.

"Our brother."

Heinrich crossed himself

"Where was everyone?" Andreas asked. "Mother was alone!"

"It is Little Hans' name day," explained Heinrich. "Elsa took him and the other children to celebrate with Hannes. Mother was fine when we left this morning. We had no idea..." They did not notice that their father had joined them.

"It would have changed nothing," Old Johann snarled at his sons. "Nothing."

Andreas turned his back on his father and went back to his mother's room. He lined the apple box with clean linen and gently placed tiny Rudolf inside. "There, little one," he whispered. He set the box out of the way on a table near the arched window.

\*\*\*

"Where is Hannes?"

"He'll be here, Father," said Heinrich.

"Why didn't Thomann take a horse?"

"I don't know. He should have."

"Pray God Hannes gets here before it's too late." The old man crossed himself. "I won't have Verena damned because Thomann has dawdled."

Thomann appeared at the bottom of the hill, running. Hannes was close behind him, lifting his long, white monk's robes so he would not trip. Elsa and the children came soon after.

"Go to her!" said Old Johann to Hannes before he'd even reached the courtyard. "There's no time to waste."

Hannes, panting, nodded and hurried inside. He looked quickly at the tiny baby. The midwife sat beside Verena's bed, her face red with crying. "Frau Beck," said Hannes softly.

"She's been asking for you, Father Hannes." The midwife stood to give Hannes the chair. "I'll be outside, Father."

Verena was wavering between two worlds. "Mother," Hannes began, but his voice caught in his throat. He shook his head to regain himself, then placed her rosary in her hands. "Do you sincerely beg our Lord for forgiveness of your sins?"

Verena nodded.

He opened the cross-shaped, silver box he wore on his belt for the services of Last Rites and took out a small vial of Holy Oil and a wafer that had been blessed by the Holy Father in Rome. With the oil, he traced the shape of a cross on his mother's forehead and placed the wafer between her lips. He knew she could not eat it, but it would protect her from Satan, who could take her soul at the last minute.

"May our Heavenly Father pardon you whatever sins or faults you have committed. In the name of our Savior, Jesus Christ, his holy mother, Mary, St. John the

Baptist, St. Joseph and St. Verena, name saint of our sister and my mother, Verena." He made the sign of the cross over her body. It was not long before she followed little Rudolf in death.

Wiping the tears from her eyes, Frau Beck returned to care for Verena before Hannes invited the family into the room. "I'm sorry, Father Hannes," she said as she closed Verena's eyes. "We will miss her. It is a shame, at her time of life. She might have lived to enjoy her grandchildren. God rest her sweet soul." She laid the apple box with the small babe beside Verena on the bed.

Hannes could only nod.

"Shall I call them in, Father Hannes?"

"I'll do it. It's all right, Frau Beck. Father, Heinrich, Elsa, Thomann, Andreas, you can come in."

"What of the baby?" Hannes asked his father, "Did you baptize him?"

"I wasn't here. Only Andreas was here."

"Andreas?"

"No."

"How long did he live?"

"Minutes."

"And you did not baptize him?" Hannes was stunned. Surely it was the right and obvious thing to do to ensure the Kingdom of Heaven to their tiny brother. "Then he cannot be buried with Mother. In the few moments of his life, the Evil One might have captured him. He will go to Limbo with other unbaptized infants and remain there until our Lord returns to judge the living and the dead. We must have prayers said for his soul so that on that day, he will join Mother in Heaven."

"Such a little thing as he died in the state of grace and innocence as all small children too young to know good from evil. He went immediately to Heaven and waited there for our mother," said Andreas, disgusted by his brother the monk "If you spent any time outside this valley and that monastery, you would know that there is nothing in the Bible about infant baptism. There is no

'Limbo' or 'Purgatory'. Those were made up by the Church to steal money from poor, sad or broken-hearted people, even guilty people such as our Father."

"Andreas, you could have baptized the baby for our father," said Thomann gently, though he, like Andreas, followed the new thinking coming from Zürich.

"Are you serious? How would that be 'for' our father?" Andreas turned to his brother in astonishment.

"The baby could be buried with our mother. That would mean much to Father," Thomann said softly.

Heinrich nodded. How could it matter to anyone more than it mattered to the old man? The baby was doomed from the start. A purely practical man, Heinrich couldn't see it as a religious question. "Thomann is right, Andreas. The baby couldn't live. What difference would it have made for you to have said some words and blessed him? All this God talk has made you blind."

"Me?" Andreas turned to Heinrich. "What of Hannes? It is Hannes who says Rudolf cannot be buried with Mother, not me. Where were you, Hannes, if it is so important to you? You knew her time was coming."

"Not for two months, Andreas. You know that full well."

Heinrich's wife, Elsa, sighed. "I wish I had been home with her. But she seemed fine when we left this morning. There was no sign of anything."

"Why were you here, Andreas, and not at the mill?" asked Heinrich.

"I spent the night in Zürich after listening to Zwingli. Mother was in a bad way when I got here. I wasn't going to leave her here alone and come down to the mill. I sent Old Hugo to get Frau Beck, then after you and Father. By the time you got here, the baby was dead. If you'd been here, Heinrich or Father, you could have done whatever you wanted. I wouldn't have interfered."

"I have a mill to run," sputtered Old Johann. "It is short-handed most of the time with you up in Zürich, and yet you're paid? Now my little son will spend eternity in Limbo just because you..." His face reddened, his grief buried in rage. He did not think how much worse it would have been if Andreas had not been home.

"There should not have <u>been</u> a 'little son', Father, but you could not leave our mother alone." Andreas, torn from the loss of his mother and anger at his father, spoke from his heart. "Now you've killed her."

Old Johann raised his hand to strike Andreas, but Andreas ducked and stomped out, leaving his brothers to contend with their father's anger and sorrow.

\*\*\*

Verena was buried in the Schneebeli/Lunkhofen section of the abbey cemetery beside the graves of the first Andreas, who had died of measles when he was two and little Oswald who, alone in the family, had succumbed to the plague five years before. He was ten years old. Verena's husband and three of her six living sons, Heinrich, Hannes and Thomann, each in turn threw clods onto her casket. Conrad, of Old Johann's sons the closest to Verena, refused to attend the funeral out of anger at his father.

\*\*\*

As prayers were said over Verena's grave, Andreas was digging a hole in the orchard for his little brother. When he finished, he sat on the pile of dirt and waited for Thomann.

"You should have come to the funeral, Andreas."

"Very likely," Andreas admitted. "I just don't know why the old man couldn't let our mother be."

Thomann nodded. "She should have been past her time."

"But she wasn't. Father should have known that and considered the dangers."

"Perhaps he didn't know."

"My God, Thomann! They lived together for more than thirty years! He must have known. Last time, when she miscarried, just last year, he was told! You were in the room yourself."

"Yes. But, the old man has his way. You know that and I know that. We get nowhere like this, Andreas. Anger can never be God's will."

"No, it can't." Andreas sighed.

Thomann lifted the apple box. "Poor little one," he said. "Never to see this beautiful, beautiful world." The petals on the apple trees had shaken free in the wind, covering the spring grass in white and pink. A few had fallen on the baby. *There is your baptism, little brother,* he thought.

They slid the lid over the box and gently placed it in the hole. Because Andreas had done the work of digging, Thomann took the job of covering Rudolf.

"There," he said, tamping down the dirt with the back of his shovel.

"We should mark it somehow," said Andreas. "Here." On the ground nearby, he found a stake used for supporting young trees and handed it to Thomann. "Pound this in. We can come back and put up a cross."

Thomann set the stake at the end of the box where Rudolf's head lay and pounded it in with the back of his shovel so only a few inches rose above the ground. "That should do it. Say a prayer, Andreas. You're better at it than I."

"Heavenly Father, who knows better than we the reasons for things, please care for our little brother, Rudolf, who spent only a few minutes in this world, not long enough to harm anyone or anything. In Jesus' name, amen."

The brothers stood in silence for a few minutes before brushing the dirt from their leggings. They kicked their clogs against a tree, startling the mud from the bottoms, and walked down the hill to join the neighborly meal that traditionally followed a funeral. When they got to the courtyard, people were seating themselves at long tables.

Andreas and Thomann sat down with the family, expecting an angry look from their father, but Verena's death, and his part in it, had taken something from Old Johann. He was suddenly an old man. He stood up slowly.

"Thank you for being here. Thank you for standing with me at the funeral of my wife, Verena." A lump rose in his throat. He had loved Verena from the first moment he saw her when she was barely 13. She was just 14 when they married. Within the year, their first son, Heinrich, was born, then poor Andreas the first, who died at age two, and then one boy after another over the years, nine in all, counting little Rudolf. He knew his sons could not understand why he, an old man, and she, an old woman, still desired each other. He hoped that their lives would give all of them a similar love.

He took a deep breath to make the memories disappear. "Our family has, for generations, recited a psalm every morning before beginning our work. I would like to share it with you and with my sons who are here and perhaps, too, with Verena, my poor dead boys and the small Rudolf whom the Church said could not be buried with his mother. Perhaps they hear us and know that we love them."

None of Old Johann's sons could believe what they were hearing. Was this the same hard old man, the strict father who met backtalk from his sons with a hard slap across the mouth?

"My sons." Old Johann motioned for them to stand up. "Everyone." Heinrich, Hannes, Thomann and Andreas stood. Old Johann began, and they recited together, *Bless The Lord, O my soul, O Lord my God, Who coverest Thyself with light as with a garment; who stretchest out the heavens like a curtain, who layeth the beams of his chambers in the water; who maketh the clouds his chariot, who walketh upon the wings of the wind."*

The old man sat heavily in his chair, his mind filled with questions. Andreas said that Rudolf was in Heaven; Hannes said he could not be. Who was right? Old Johann had chosen to ignore the changes filling his world, but now change had been laid on his doorstep.

***

"Father, come," said Thomann, offering his arm to Old Johann after all the guests had gone. "I'll show you where we buried Rudolf." The two walked slowly up the hill behind their house to the apple orchard, which had helped support their family for generations.

"Would that Andreas had cared for his soul," he said, his red eyes rimmed with tears.

"Father, Rudolf is with our mother in Heaven, even if he is not beside her in the graveyard. You do not need to worry about his soul."

"How do you know that, Thomann? Hannes says the baby is in Limbo."

"Andreas is right. There is nothing in the Bible about Limbo. There is nothing to say that a baby who has not been baptized will not have eternal life with our Lord."

"The Bible? And you have read the Bible?"

"Pastor Zwingli speaks on the Bible every Sunday and reads from it in our language," Thomann replied. "Others, too, speak on different questions. Many are very interested in this question of baptizing infants. They say it's wrong, sinful. They also say that demanding money for prayers is theft. They tell us how the church in Rome is very rich from preying on the superstition and fear of well-meaning people."

"The Church has been with us since time began. How could it be so wrong? And tell me, why is your Pastor Zwingli just finding out now?"

"The Church has been in trouble with itself for a long time. Even Conrad's old songs tell of the Pope taking our money and leaving us poor. Here it is, Father." Old Johann looked down at the small mound of earth.

"Did you at least say a prayer for him, Thomann, you and Andreas? Or does your Pastor Zwingli say prayer is no longer needed?"

"Yes, we prayed for him. God hasn't gone anywhere. He's where He has always been. Shall we say a prayer for Rudolf together, Father?"

Old Johann nodded. "Help me down, boy." With Thomann's help, the old man knelt on the apple-blossom covered earth of the orchard. "Oh Lord," he said, "forgive me."

# chapter 2

## Conrad, 1524

A well-traveled trail known by everyone as "The Brothers" ran across a ridge through the forest between the Schneebeli home and the old von Lunkhofen castle. Centuries earlier, the trail connected close friends, Sir Heinrich von Lunkhofen and Squire Adelbert. Duty had bound them to join the Emperor's Crusade against the Ayyubid Sultan in Egypt, where they witnessed the end of the siege of Damietta, a horror so beyond anything imaginable that when Adelbert returned to Affoltern, his coal black hair had turned pure white, earning him the nickname "Schneebeli," snow ball. Over the generations, the nickname became the family name.

Back then the trail also connected lovers, Sir Heinrich's son, Rudolf, and Squire Adelbert's daughter,

Gretchen. In his turn, young Rudolf had gone on Crusade, returning after many years to marry Gretchen. Local legend said that Sir Rudolf was saved from death by a desert-dwelling angel who tended to his wounds.

Sir Rudolf and Gretchen had three sons who used the trail constantly, running or riding between the von Lunkhofen castle, where they lived, and the Schneebeli home to visit their grandparents, and so, the trail was ever after known as "The Brothers."

***

On this well traveled ancient trail, Andreas rode in the mist of early dawn. He loved his brother, Conrad, who was, in many ways more his father than was Old Johann. When Andreas was a boy, it had taken only two quick slaps across the mouth from the old man for him to stay out of range. He kept as far away from his father as he could, and though he worked in his father's mill along with Heinrich and Thomann, he lived with Conrad and Christina.

"Where's my brother?" he asked Old Stefan, who was sweeping the stone courtyard.

"With the horses."

Andreas dismounted and led his mare down the hill to the stables.

"Ah, Andreas! How was the funeral? I couldn't come. I would have killed the old man."

"He's not the same. He got a hard lesson."

"He was warned. Never a good listener, our father." Conrad sighed.

"No," Andreas agreed.

"What's the news of your Brother Zwingli?" Conrad changed the subject. It was hard for him to think that he would never see his mother again and talking with Andreas brought every feeling he had to the surface.

"I wish you'd join me and Thomann."

"Andreas, you know I don't -- this is my world, this is enough right here. The horses, Christina, you rushing up here to save my soul from Satan, Hannes running up here from the monastery to save my soul from Satan. It's wonderful, all the attention given by my brothers to my soul. Why do you both think that God doesn't care every bit as much as you?"

"Don't joke. Nothing is more serious than your immortal soul."

"I'm not joking, Andreas. I'm always amazed that you and Hannes both think so little of this omnipotent God that you must do his work for him!"

"Now you're joking."

"No, I'm not. Our brother, Peter, sells himself and the bodies of his men to the Pope, the Holy Bastard. The Holy Bastard orders these servants of his to fight against the most Divinely Ordained Christian King of France. And these armies are all bought and sold to this or that Divinely Ordained Christian King or Holy Father! They fight men just like themselves, equally bought and sold by a well-born younger son looking for a fortune, someone like our brother Peter. Maybe some Sachsen, maybe some Hessian or some Lombard or a Venetian lord are moved around like chess pieces on a board. Any one of them could become a king. It has happened. The battles? You cannot imagine. For that you must thank your God. However you do that, I do not know, but thank Him. Boys, farm boys, mostly, go into battle against other farm boys. They slash at each other with pike and halberd, slice off heads and legs only because their leader has been paid so that they will kill each other."

"Brother Huldrych is putting an end to mercenary armies."

"That's a nice line, but do not believe it. He cannot succeed. It's a very unpopular idea. Where are people to get money if they do not sell their sons? And what of the sons who want to go?"

"It will be illegal for boys to be bought and sold."

"That will work well with the poor farm family led by some horny bastard like our father whose main winter activity is rogering his wife, who, because the church says it is her duty, sends forth armies of sons from her tired loins." Conrad wiped a tear from his cheek with his rough glove. He banged his fist on a post. He'd trade his father for his mother any day. He knew he would miss her every moment for the rest of his life.

"Conrad!"

"Well? If there were no armies, how would these families feed these sons? Where would they get the money they need to buy what they cannot grow or make themselves, or to buy seed, or medicine for their animals and children? They are grateful for the mercenary armies. They relieve these families of mouths to feed and bring in an income. Many a peasant family worked its way into the gentry by sacrificing its sons and selling off its daughters as servants or worse."

Conrad brushed the gray gelding harder in his fury. The horse stepped away, whinnying in reproach. "Sorry, Prince. It's not you. God knows," he crossed himself, "that your kind have also died uselessly in battle."

The days of the noble knight on his powerful destrier were gone. The Swiss army relied more on foot soldiers carrying pikes, hackbuts and halberds than it did on mounted knights or even on an infantry armed with bows. Conrad had even accused his brother, Peter, of being nothing more than a shining bauble riding in full plate armor on a black stallion. "Ornament? I am the leader, the inspiration to my troops."

But when he wanted to marry and had no money, Conrad joined Peter's army as an officer. There Conrad learned that Peter was ruthless and completely selfish. He also understood that no war leader could be any other way. Peter's unquestioning confidence in himself helped him transform the ragged group of farm boys into a fighting force. Peter —because of his unwavering self-love — easily convinced others that he indeed deserved to be the center of attention and respect, and his troops duly adored him. Conrad no longer regarded the silk and armor clad Peter as a mere ornament, but as something powerful, deadly and without conscience.

"I wish your Brother Huldrych all the best in that quest, if he is sincere, but I think he is simply shrewd enough to know that with a third of Zürich's population killed in the last plague, the people have no sons to send away at any price. And those who remain? They stay home to work."

"You're saying he's lying?"

"No, but change and compromise go hand in hand."

"He doesn't mean what he says?"

"Did I say that, Andreas? I'm sure he is a smart man. He's done well in his life so far, as Preacher of Zürich at a young age and a leader of the church. And now? He has the confidence of the magistrates and of the people. He will do whatever he wants."

"He wants to follow God's will, Conrad."

"And he knows what that is? Most of us have to wait to see how God's will unfolds. Your Brother Huldrych knows ahead of time?"

"From the Bible, Conrad. God's own word." Andreas put up his horse and went inside to see Christina.

Conrad had seen in his brother's face the same bewildered look Andreas' had worn hundreds of times as a small boy. He remembered how his mother often said, "Don't tease your little brother. Don't forget there are twelve years between you. He is not old enough to understand your jokes. You hurt his feelings."

The memory brought all of Conrad's feelings to the top of his heart, and his eyes filled with tears. "To think, Prince, I'll never see her again." He brushed old Prince's coat absently, remembering the night he had gone to visit his parents to tell them of his betrothal to Christina. Conrad had no interest in the mill and avoided his father, whom he saw as a bully and a tyrant. But his news was too important not to share, and he wanted so much to tell his mother. Events unfolded as they usually did between him and Old Johann.

"You'll be working for me in the mill, then," Old Johann said. "As you are to marry, you'll need the money."

"I'll make my own way," Conrad told his father. "I have enough money now to marry Christina. We'll live in grandfather's old castle, and I'll breed horses."

"Nonsense," said Old Johann. "You'll work in the mill. That's where your fortune lies."

"Not *my* fortune, Father, with all due respect. Yours."

"You think Christina will want to live in that drafty ruin of a castle? She's used to much better." Christina was the daughter of Verena's cousin who lived in Mettmenstetten. The cousin was a wealthy landowner with the hereditary right to collect tariffs and tolls on the road leading from Zug to Zürich, part of the way to the Gotthard Pass.

"Grandfather did."

"Your grandfather did nothing to keep it up. The place was more run down when he died than when he moved there. I'm sure Christina will have no part of it."

"I'll build Christina new rooms, Father, if she wants them."

"How will you buy your horses then?"

"With Christina's dowry."

Old Johann had imagined Christina's large dowry going into improvements on the mill, and he was now even angrier with Conrad.

"You steal food from the mouths of your brothers, Conrad, and the future from their children."

Conrad laughed. "Father, how you exaggerate. You have the first penny you ever made! Besides, I am marrying Christina. You're not."

The old man's face had turned bright red in fury, but Conrad was too old for him to slap. Conrad got up from the table and prepared to leave, but seeing the anxious look in his mother's eyes, he sat down again. Verena had never been a great beauty or a great wit, but she was very good and was absolutely dedicated to the welfare of her boys. Conrad was her favorite; he knew it and he adored her.

"Sing something, son," said Verena, deflecting Old Johann's attention. "One of the old songs."

Conrad went to get the lute from the wall in the hall. He ran his fingers across the strings. "It's badly out of tune, Mother," he said, returning to the table.

"No one plays it."

"It needs playing if it's going to keep its sound. Why not you, Thomann? You could play."

"Father..."

"There is that." Conrad laughed somewhat ruefully. He plucked the strings one by one, listening carefully, adjusting the pegs and listening again. He strummed a chord. "No, not quite that, not quite." He turned the pegs slightly and strummed again. "Almost there, almost there." He adjusted them slightly again, in reference to each other, and struck a chord.

Seeing Old Johann get up from the table, the servant came in and removed the plates and left a pitcher of cider, a board with cheese, and a bowl of dried figs and walnuts. Conrad strummed a chord and hit a pitch. "Sing with me, Mother."

"Oh, Conrad, no! Not my old voice."

"Come on. It is only us. Sing a round with me, Mother. You too, Thomann, Andreas. Heinrich? Elsa?"

*Comes May! Comes May!*
*Its many different tender flowers*

*Give new life to all that winter's violence spoiled.*
*All creation rejoices,*
*Creation rejoices, all creation rejoices.*

Song soon filled the room. Try though he might, Old Johann could not stay away and stood at the door adding his bass to the varied tones of his family.

*Days long gone now,* Conrad thought, wiping tears away with his sleeve.

He looked up to see that Andreas had returned. "Supper's ready." Andreas wrapped his arms around his big brother. "I know you miss her, Conrad. Take comfort that she is with our Lord in Heaven."

"That is no comfort, Andreas. She should be here with us."

# chapter 3

## Hannes, 1524

Old Johann and Verena had dedicated the life of their second son, Hannes, to the Cistercian Order at the Angel Mountain Abbey. At the age of seven, he went to live with the monks. He studied the languages, scripture, the commentary and polemics of the Church Fathers. He learned rituals and sacraments and the lives of the Saints. At thirteen, he was tonsured and took the vows of chastity, charity and poverty then donned in white robes of the Cistercian Order. He served God and the Prior who was like a father to him. During the plague, Hannes became the Prior's close assistant, walking and riding around the countryside helping the sick and giving Last Rites. The dark days passed, and Hannes continued in his role of ministering to those who lived farthest from the abbey. The horrors of the plague, the hopelessness, the numbers of dead, had aged the Prior. Hannes, more and more often, said Mass.

Everyone trusted Hannes. He was patient, conventional and friendly. His family was one of the oldest in the valley, its history inextricably linked to the valley's history. When his familiar form came up a lane or along a narrow forest trail, everyone knew that even if a tragedy was at the end of his journey there would also be comfort. In winter Hannes might come pulling a sled (on which he might ride back down to the abbey after his visit).

Hannes was happy. The decision his parents had made for him suited him perfectly. He was intelligent and liked learning. He had no quarrel with the way the Brotherhood taught the word of God. He gave and accepted the sacraments believing, completely, that God would forgive all who asked. The dissatisfaction fomenting in Zürich did not touch him, and he had no idea from where it sprang. That the Mother Church needed money was only logical to Hannes. He did not imagine that anyone took their vows with less sincerity than did he.

Andreas had called Hannes naive. The sad issue of the unbaptized Rudolf was Hannes' first real glimpse into the intense debates that would soon shake his world, privately, professionally and spiritually.

\*\*\*

Easter came and confessed parishioners streamed into the abbey chapel to share in the body of Christ. As the choir sang an antiphon, and the air was rich with cleansing incense, Hannes felt the Holy Spirit everywhere. Spring sunshine came through the colored glass windows. Winter was finally, really, over. Everyone in the valley was returning to the labors that yielded the crops for which they would be grateful when winter returned. For now, the world was young. The blossoms of the apple trees were on the verge of opening, and Hannes felt that the same was true of the hearts of the men and women in the sanctuary this morning.

Hannes said to the people of his congregation, "Behold, the Lamb of God, behold Him who takes away the sins of the world. Blessed are those called to the supper of the Lamb."

"Lord," said the people in the sanctuary, "I am not worthy that you should enter my roof. Only say the word and my soul shall be healed."

Hannes took Communion. Then, in a State of Grace, he gave communion to the people that they could participate in the miracle of bread becoming the body of the Lord.

The faithful women of his congregation knelt before him. "The body of Christ," said Hannes to each one. The last was a young girl on the threshold of womanhood. "The body of Christ," he said. The girl opened her mouth so that Hannes could place the wafer on her tongue. Hannes' skin felt hot and tingly, and he wondered if he were coming down with the flu. A stream of cold perspiration ran down his back. *"I must be ill,"* he thought, and shook off the moment of unease before giving the Host to the next woman.

\*\*\*

It was nearly full summer when Conrad's servant appeared at the abbey, red-faced from running, demanding Brother Hannes.

"Old Stefan has taken a fall. He cannot talk, and his eyes look off in two directions."

"Wait. I'll go back with you. I must tell the Prior." Hannes vanished for a few minutes and came back carrying the instruments he would need to offer Last Rites to the old man.

"Do you think..." the servant crossed himself.

"Only God knows, but it's best to be prepared so that Old Stefan will not spend eternity in Purgatory for lack of my being ready."

"No, Brother. That is right."

They walked quickly up The Brothers Path in silence. Conrad met them at the bottom of the road that led up the hill to the castle, a stone-paved road shaded by blooming linden trees.

"What happened, Conrad?"

"Old Stefan forgot he is old. He climbed a ladder to reach the upper branches of an apple tree beside the courtyard wall."

\*\*\*

Old Stefan's room was at the bottom of the old castle tower, facing the grassy pasture and hillside. He lay on his cot, a linen bandage wrapped around his head. A crimson stain betrayed the spot where the old man's head had hit the wall. His tongue lolled out of his mouth, and he did not seem to know anyone.

"The doctor?"

"Come and gone." Conrad feared to speak in front of the girl who sat beside her grandfather, holding his hand. "Vreni, will you leave us for a moment?"

"I want to know," she answered calmly. "He is my grandfather. I should know."

Conrad looked at Hannes, then at the girl. "The doctor says Old Stefan may live a while yet, but never in his mind again, and he may die soon of bleeding inside his head."

"Do you want me to give him the sacrament, Conrad?" Hannes looked up at his brother.

"Ask Vreni. She is his only family."

Vreni's blue eyes filled with tears. Hannes felt he was falling into them. He shook his head quickly to dispel the dizziness, but he still saw her dark hair in loose strands around her face, her nose and cheeks red from crying. The hand resting on her apron was red from washing pans. Hannes' heart was suddenly in his throat.

"Vreni," he said softly, "even if your grandfather stays with us longer, he may never recover his reason. Do you want...?"

Vreni nodded.

"You should leave the room. The Holy Spirit may lead your grandfather to confess before he dies."

"Please, Brother Hannes, no, God forgive me." She crossed herself in apprehension, for fear of sin. "If my grandfather awakens, I want him to see me, so he will not feel alone."

"Vreni, the Rite is very clear that the Priest and the dying should be alone together."

"Let her stay, Hannes," said Conrad. "Would you not have Vreni here if her grandfather recovers his mind?"

"It may keep him from unburdening his heart to the Lord, Conrad. It may put his soul in danger."

"You mean if I am here my grandfather could go to Hell?"

"If he cannot speak freely to God and ask for forgiveness."

The girl stood and attempted to release herself from her grandfather's hand, but the old man held fast.

Vreni looked at Hannes in panic and helplessness. She did not want to leave her grandfather, but she wanted him to be with the Saints in Heaven, not, because of her, condemned to Hell's eternal fire.

"Come on, Hannes. Surely God knows everything already. Old Stefan raised her. He's been both parents to her," said Conrad. "Besides, do you really think he will suddenly become conscious? He's been in this state for hours now."

"There is nothing for it. Sit down, Vreni," Hannes said. "God forgive us. Have pity on your poor servant,

Old Stefan. Have pity on this girl who this day may lose her grandfather, and with him all her family."

Hannes gave the old man Last Rites, and, before he was finished, the old man's soul left to join the souls of his daughter and his wife.

"Is my grandfather in Heaven, Brother Hannes?"

"Yes, Vreni. He is safe now and out of hurt."

As Hannes prayed for the old man's soul, he wondered what angels in Heaven could equal this one beside Old Stefan's corpse. When morning came, Old Stefan's body was buried in the family cemetery beyond the castle's broken walls.

\*\*\*

Hannes walked back to the abbey, exhausted and deeply perplexed by his emotions. He'd visited Conrad many times before, but had never, that he recalled, seen Vreni.

What would Vreni do without her grandfather? Conrad and Christina would doubtless arrange a marriage for her. To some peasant boy? Or some old man whose first wife was dead and would have another? Some rough handed lout would stroke Vreni's soft cheek in the firelight. Hannes shook his head. What demons were these? "Heavenly Father, forgive me." He crossed himself. "I do not know where these thoughts are coming from."

\*\*\*

"Father, I wish to confess. I'm..."

The Prior looked at Hannes' haggard face. This calm spirit was clearly troubled. "Of course, Brother Hannes. Now?"

"If you have time."

"I do."

Hannes knelt before the Prior and began, "Father, I have sinned. I seek your intercession with the Holy Mother who understands all our weaknesses and faults."

"Yes, my Son. Go on."

"I sat at the death bed of an old servant at my brother's home. His granddaughter, Vreni, was with me. He was her only family. I felt strange, Father. She..."

"You felt attraction, my Son?"

"Yes." It felt good to have his feelings fenced by words.

In a way, the Prior was relieved. The sin of Sodom was a problem in the church, and the Prior knew this. And Hannes? He had been a beautiful boy when he came to the abbey, with bright blue eyes and golden curls. He was now a handsome man. His curls had turned dark blond, and his eyes were still bright blue; he had a sweet smile and a gentle manner. Well, sin was sin.

"You know this is a sin, my son. You have taken vows of chastity and you know that to feel desire for this girl is, in the eyes of God, the same as having slept with her."

"I know, Father. What should I do?"

"Avoid your brother's house. Soon, I'm sure, they will find a husband for her. Then you will not need to worry."

Hannes had a sudden urge to keep his fears secret, but he took a deep breath, and said, "That's what troubles me. Who will they find? Some rough boy or an old man with children already who needs a maid-servant and whore?"

"Brother Hannes!"

"I know these people. I've lived here all my life and they are, that is..."

"Yes, my son, they are and it is that way. Women do not have it easy in this world. Childbirth often kills them. Their lives are hard; they are—as God wrought— the servants of their husbands. Still..."

"I..."

"Son, surely you know that a great many priests live a family life, though they cannot marry. These reformers, the first thing they do is marry the woman with whom they already have children. That renegade in Zürich, Zwingli, and his friend, Jud, both sons of priests, mind you, are now married. For a long time priests have argued with the Holy Mother church that it is against the nature God gave us to remain celibate." The Prior sighed. "They are right, of course. And worse, you know, worse. Some priests, well, never mind."

"I cannot make Vreni my concubine, Father, even if I were a secular priest. Could we not be married secretly?"

"You wouldn't have me do that, Brother Hannes. It would add sin on sin, making a liar out of me and our Order." The Prior's soft voice was stern.

"Father, I want to continue serving God, serving the people. I do not want to stop doing this work. I believe I help you. I believe the work is important. And blessed. Blessed work."

"So I believe, also, Brother Hannes. But your situation now is complicated. You can give up this idea and stay with us here, honoring your vows. You can do as many others do and take Vreni as your concubine and live away from the abbey with her and work as a secular priest. You can leave us, join your father and brothers at the mill, and marry the girl. You must search your heart and pray to know if what you feel is love or pity."

"It is not pity, Father. I..." Hannes took a deep breath. "Vreni attended Easter mass. I..." Hannes stopped, then, "I felt my face flush, my body... I thought I was coming down with the flu, but I was not ill. The signs of illness lasted a few moments and were gone. But I sometimes remembered and felt the same discomfort, confusion. At her grandfather's bedside, I understood, so I am here."

"Ah," said the Prior. "Pray, Brother Hannes. You have a big decision. You will need God's help."

"What penance do you give me, Father?"

The Prior thought the confusion Hannes suffered was penance enough, but he knew that the structure and familiar authority of the Order could help Hannes clear his thoughts. "You will say 100 Our Fathers each day for the next three days between Morning-song and Evening-song. You will keep silence during these three days except for prayers. You will, on your hands and knees, clean the floor of the Kreuzgang each of these three days."

"Thank you, Father."

"Find peace in God's will. In the name of the Father, the Son and the Holy Spirit." The prior made the sign of the cross over Hannes, and, for a moment, Hannes' heart felt free again as it had before he had looked into Vreni's sad eyes, pleading for more time with her grandfather.

\*\*\*

Hannes' peace did not last long. Searching his soul to find God's will, he found himself in a labyrinth, and he did not know which way to turn. Hannes thought of what he'd heard of Zwingli. He was married. The Priest of Zürich. Part of the changes Thomann and Andreas had spoken about. Zwingli would perform the ritual. Zwingli, the renegade.

Could he do that? Could he marry Vreni, pretending to the Prior he had not, going on day-by-day as he did now but with Vreni, his wife, living all alone, somewhere in secret? His heart sank. How would that improve her station? How would that be any protection for her? He could only leave the Order. What would he do then? Serving God was all he knew. And what if Vreni did not want to marry him? It was possible. Hannes felt a new fear. What if he left everything, left the Order, made that decision -- right though it seemed -- went to Vreni, offered his hand to her and she turned him down?

He would have nothing. *I could talk to Vreni first, and remain as I am if she refuses me*, he thought. *But what a hypocrite I would be!*

"*NOW you need faith*," his heart spoke to him, very clearly. "*This is your test.*"

"Yes," he spoke aloud to his own heart. "This is my test."

He decided to walk through the forest, up The Brothers, to Conrad's house. He wanted the kind of thinking he found only in active solitude. He wanted to see Vreni. He needed to know he had not just been carried away by the moment -- even though in his heart he knew he had been carried away and that there had been two moments. He wanted to see if there was any chance...how could he know that? He was a monk. Brother Hannes. They called him Father and took the communion wafer from his hand. They asked his blessing -- or God's blessing through him. They sought him for confession. In their eyes, he was not a man. He was God's servant, the vehicle of God's will on earth. He was struck by the fact that even he had never known himself in any other way.

\*\*\*

The woods were damp with morning. Everything proclaimed summer: the dew strung spider's web, the bright green full-grown leaves, the small apples pushing their way into the world, the fading linden blossoms.

Where the abbey path to the forest ended, and a wanderer could turn onto the Brothers Path, right to the house of the Schneebelis or left to the old castle, was a shrine to the Holy Virgin. It was tenderly cared for, partly because it was the most public of the shrines along the path, but also because it was the most loved. Centuries of rain and snow had smoothed her features, and a fall sometime in her history had broken off one of her outstretched hands. A devotee had built a wooden shelter over her and planted roses at her feet. The years had made her a special destination for young women who hoped to become pregnant, and they believed the fruit from this rose bush, made into tea, would make them fertile.

*"You call it faith? Superstition! That's all it is."* Andreas' words echoed in Hannes' mind. *"These people go to church, you give them fifty Our Fathers and tell them not to sin any more. They go to God as if they are debtors and God a bill collector. Salvation for them is little more than a bargain combined with a bushel of good luck."*

Though he often feared for Andreas' soul, Hannes never disputed with his younger brother other than to say, "The Holy Church is more than one thousand years old." Hannes believed that Divine Word interpreted by the Holy Church was beyond the reach of simple human understanding, and the first requirement of faith was that it be without question. But this time Andreas had struck a chord. How often had Hannes thought something similar? Who was HE to forgive anyone, anyway, when, for the most part, their sins were the natural result of being human?

And now he was in the thick of it, himself, his own soul, his own struggle against -- what was it? Human nature or temptation? He really did not know. Both? *It could be both*, thought Hannes. *Human nature must be subdued to the will of God.*

He dropped to his knees before the shrine. "Holy Mary, Mother of God, like you, I never imagined to be in such a bind. Help me find guidance. Intercede for me with our Heavenly Father to show me the way. In the name of the Father, the Son and the Holy Spirit."

Hannes continued up the trail, stopping to offer a small prayer at each broken shrine. First he met St. Martin. Clad in old-fashioned mail armor, he was barely standing. He held the hilt of his sword in his right hand though the sword itself had been lost in a battle with time. His out-stretched left arm would have held a cloak in offering to the poor wanderer, but it, too, had fallen away, taking the hand with it. Next up the trail stood a headless St. Lazarus. The staff on which he would have leaned had vanished long ago; the dog at his knee stood on three legs and, though he might have wagged his tail at this poor man as he licked his wounds, he no longer had a tail to wag. Farther along, John the Baptist, brought down by the fecundity of earth, reclined in a thicket of holly. Hannes felt a surge of compassion looking at these broken friends. He'd heard how in Zürich the images had been thrown into the streets and squares, broken and burned, and how the beautiful old frescoes in St. Peters and the Grossmünster had been defaced. "Idols," Andreas called them.

Hannes thought of the saints only as reminders of men and women who, like all men and women, had to contend with the Evil One and to accept the will of God. Both St. Lazarus and St. Martin stood beside The Brothers to teach compassion. Whatever long-ago lord had placed them here thought this lesson was important. It was important to Hannes. "These three abide, faith, hope and charity, but the greatest of these is charity."

He reached Conrad's house just as the household began its day. Everyone was standing in the courtyard, reciting, "*Bless The Lord, O my soul, O Lord my God, Who coverest Thyself with light as with a garment; who stretchest out the heavens like a curtain, who layeth the beams of his chambers in the water; who maketh the clouds his chariot, who walketh upon the wings of the wind.*" Hannes joined them. The short recitation had become an echo of humility and faith across the generations, recognizing the miracle of morning.

"Hannes!"

"Passing by, brother." Hannes saw that Conrad knew he was lying, so he closed his mouth. He'd have to tell Conrad, but he didn't know what, and he didn't know how. He had come to see Vreni. That was all. He'd seen her at prayer, following the customs of his home, as if she were his wife. Nothing within his heart had changed. The Prior was right. He would have to make a choice.

"Will you stay for breakfast, Hannes? A meal in the morning strengthens us all."

Hannes nodded.

Hannes sat down to breakfast with the family and servants at the big trestle table in the courtyard. The warm loaf of bread was passed around and hot tea poured into the pewter mugs. As Vreni ladled applesauce and porridge into his bowl, Hannes, his mind trained to allegory, found the tables had been turned. Where he had given her the body of Christ, she gave him warm milk, porridge, applesauce, bread and butter. He had offered her the next world and now she offered him this one. Which was worth more? Hannes no longer knew. He'd planned to talk to Conrad and then return to the abbey, but he was suddenly taken with the idea that he should just go to Zürich. He was no longer Brother Hannes of the Angel Mountain Monastery, no longer walking on the familiar earth, through the world he'd known all his life. His journey had become one through the world of signs and allegory.

*** 

Hannes had never had much business in Zürich, and the recent plague and religious upheaval had made it even more remote except from his prayers. His brothers went to Zürich often; Andreas and Thomann made the trip to hear Zwingli speak, Conrad to buy and sell horses, and Heinrich served on the town council.

The steeple of St. Peters rose above the city, not far from the Ketzistürli, the gate through which Hannes entered. Hannes took the proximity of St. Peters as a sign. He chose that course and walked directly to the recently denuded church. He entered, looking in dreamlike amazement at the empty altar and the walls, whitewashed over the brilliant old frescoes. How would the people get the word of God without the pictures, the stories painted all around them? Unwittingly, he crossed himself. He did not know if, in the new religion, this gentle gesture of humility were sacrilege or not. His brother's word, "Superstition!" echoed in his memory.

"Brother?"

Hannes turned. "Ah, Brother...?"

"Leo. Leo Jud. Pastor here and, well, before. Parish priest before. Are you looking for something?" Leo Jud looked at Hannes' white robes. "You come from the Angel Mountain Abbey?"

Hannes nodded.

"A good walk."

Hannes nodded again. He was completely lost. He had not come with any resolution, any decision. He knew nothing, not even why he had come.

"I'm ..." he halted.

"I'm sure you have many questions. Just ask."

"How will the poor find Jesus if they cannot see the story?" Hannes was surprised at this question, yet something inside prompted him, something he had to trust.

"The times have changed, Brother. It has happened quickly. No one could have imagined this in our father's time. Is it a wonder that the first book printed was God's holy word?"

"No, no. No wonder."

"And with that, more men read. They do not need the pictures to tell them what to think, how to imagine God, his Son, to turn them into idols. They can read the Holy Word themselves and understand His will. As Brother Huldrych has said, God's word is clear to all. The people do not need anyone to explain it to them."

Hannes shook his head. Well, this accounted for the endless disputations. With no Holy Mother Church to explain things, men would struggle over the meanings of the words, each having its own meaning to this man and to that. "I fear mankind is contentious by nature. I fear people will simply argue."

"And so they do, but is that wrong? For so long the Church has told us what to think. It is only reasonable that we should now contend to find our own way. But to help with that, we have a school, called the Prophezei, where everyone can come and learn about the scriptures. Clerics such as yourself are being taught, as well, that they do not need to leave their flock or abandon their calling."

Hannes' ears were suddenly alert. "How does that work, Brother?"

"We meet at the Grossmünster each day. Brother Huldrych and I conduct lessons using the new Bible we are translating. Come join us, Brother Hannes, at the Prophezei. We are working through the Gospels together, praying to understand them correctly, teaching and learning from each other how to lead our pastorate. Along with the Bible we are teaching how to preach the new message. It will not be long before all the churches -- even your abbey -- will be converted to the new way."

His own abbey. How would it come? With disputation? Fire and sword as it had come to other places, even this place? "Perhaps something needs to remain of the Old Church for those who are too old to endure such changes," he said, thinking out loud. In his mind were the old women and men in his own parish whose lives were comforted by his visits and their faith in the Church.

"God's will is God's will, Brother Hannes, and we cannot compromise righteousness. Here in Zürich the change has been peaceful and life is generally better for all. The bondsmen and women are now free workers. People were starving and freezing in the Kratz while not fifty yards away rich nuns languished in ornately paneled rooms, cozy in silk and wool, warm fires glowing in their stoves. How is that God's will? Now the poor live in the abbey and are fed and warm."

Hannes' mind returned to The Brothers, the broken St. Martin, and the headless St. Lazarus. Was this why that ancient lord had placed those statues there, that each passerby would be reminded? "Charity does not come easily to us. It is for this the Holy Mother Church offers forgiveness of sins for those who practice charity."

"Forgiveness is not the business of the church, but of God," Jud replied.

"The Church is God on Earth, Brother."

"I do not believe that the church has been Godly in many long years. It has grown rich on the backs of the poor. We have even sold our young men into the service of the Pope's army until, between war and plague, there are few left to till the fields. We are returning the wealth to the people in the form of schools and hospitals and direct aid to the deserving."

Hannes had no reply. Nothing Brother Leo said was wrong. He agreed with it. Silence fell between the two.

"How can I help you, Brother? You came here for some reason."

"You are right. I..."

"Something is troubling you."

"Are you married, Brother Leo?"

"Yes, I am. It is natural for men and women to have families. That vow of chastity drove men to dishonesty."

"But brother, surely a vow is a vow."

Jud nodded. "Tell me, Brother. How many men and women come to you with stories of carnal desires and sin? And how many of those are members of your own order?"

Hannes answered honestly. "Everyone does. Everyone."

"It is our nature. The Bible tells us to go into the Earth and be fruitful and multiply."

"After The Fall, Brother Leo."

"Can we ever find that Divine Garden again? I don't think so. If it were God's will that we could regain that lost innocence, we would have. Can we force ourselves back inside now? We've all eaten of the fruit. Haven't you, Brother?"

Hannes blushed. It was why he had come to Zürich and had, unconsciously, sought this man, this conversation.

"You have then."

"I'm here because of her. To see, but now I see it would be wrong."

"You want me to perform a marriage that you will keep secret?"

"I see it would be wrong," Hannes repeated with a sigh. "You see, my life was dedicated to Christ's service, by my father and mother soon after I was born. I was raised by the Prior. It has always been my world. It isn't only that it is familiar. I believe in it. I awaken joyful every day to be serving God. But maybe God has other plans for me."

"You do not have to be a monk or a priest to serve God, Brother. I'm sure you know that."

Hannes went on as if Leo Jud had said nothing. "I grew up in that valley. My family has always been there. It comforts the people when they are ill to have me by their bedside, someone they know, who knows them. Especially the poorer people, the working people, people who may never even have traveled here, to Zürich. My brother says..." Hannes stopped.

"Your brother?"

"Andreas. He and my brother, Thomann, follow Zwingli. They have spent many nights and days listening him speak, and you, too, no doubt. And to the disputations."

"I know them. What do your brothers say?"

"Andreas? He says the people have no real faith, only superstition."

"That is probably true."

"How can you know what they have? How can I know what they have? It seems to me that if they believe their Our Fathers said as penance please God and they are forgiven, they are freed from a burden too heavy for them. Most of their sins are small. They lie. They take some eggs from the neighbor's hen who has wandered too far from home. In their minds these small sins are as large in God's eyes as if they had committed murder."

"Aren't they?"

"Isn't it written in scripture, 'all have sinned and come short of the glory of God'?"

"Romans 3:23."

"Yes. These people are unsure, uncomfortable with the invisible. A few words spoken at intervals during the day, to remind them of our Heavenly Father. Yet, my brothers tell me this is wrong and the people will not attain salvation that way, no matter what they think."

"Your brothers are right. Salvation has nothing to do with deeds, but with God's grace."

"Ah." Hannes realized at that moment that his faith was a matter of pragmatism. His goal as a priest was to stem the irresistible tide of human suffering. Was this his ancestor's message to him, reaching out with broken plaster and clay across three hundred years? How often had he taken the coins offered him by some poor woman attempting to purchase her soul or the soul of a loved one a few days reprieve from Purgatory? He'd often wondered, *does God really want this woman's money?* His explanation was that God valued the willingness of the faithful to put their eternal lives ahead of their earthly lives. More often than not the hard won coin went into the poor box from which came this same woman's daily meals. The abbey kept an open refectory for the poor of the valley, serving a midday meal to all who came.

"This woman you love, Brother Hannes? What will you do? Is she, uh . . ." Brother Jud hesitated.

"No. She doesn't even know my feelings. In her eyes I am Brother Hannes. That is all."

"Good. You need time to think this through. It will be hard for you to leave behind your calling. I can see that." Jud paused. "Join us. As I said, all of the canton will have to join us sooner or later."

"Have to, Brother Jud?"

"Well, yes. It would be most unkind of us to allow our neighbors, our brothers and sisters to continue on the road of sin, not knowing our Lord and Savior, in thrall to superstitious idolatry, believing they can buy their way into Heaven."

Hannes began to fear for the abbey, the men who lived there, the prior, the beauty of the chapel sanctuary, the statues and the paintings. His heart beat a little faster imagining these black-clothed men, as impassioned and intense as Andreas, descending on the abbey, forcing conversion on everyone in it, burning books and statues and liturgical robes. Hannes shuddered. But what if it could happen in some other way?

"Thank you, Brother. You are right. I have a great deal to think about, more than I imagined."

"Prayer, Brother Hannes. Trust in our Lord. Ask for His help."

Hannes nodded. He could feel his whole future pressing against his heart. His eyes filled with tears. *Thy will be done.* He felt the words; he did not speak them.

"I hope you come back, Brother Hannes. Bring the young woman."

Hannes turned and walked to the door after kneeling and genuflecting to the empty altar.

\*\*\*

It was early summer and evenings were long. The city's street smells, lingering at the end of a hot day, assailed Hannes' nose. Sausages and bread, beer and animal dung, held inside by Zürich's fortified wall. "No wonder the plague settled here and stayed." His only desire was to return home to the abbey, to the beautiful painted chapel, the bright gold and silver candlesticks and chalices. That most people did not have them added to the wonderment and the miracle of the Mass.

"This new religion does not seem to value the belief that Heaven is filled with beauty. Even St. Augustine wrote that the beauty of earth is a dim reflection of the beauty of God. What beauty, otherwise, do people see?"

The abbey chapel was a simple chapel, not a grand cathedral, and the White Friars had, by and large, remained simple monks. They spent their time in work, prayer and service. Still they had lands and earned an income from them. The monks worked much of the land themselves; only a few parcels were let to tenants. They had their own orchards and the cider press, too, and a monopoly on cider requiring most of the people in the valley to bring their apples to the abbey. That was true. The cider press was very profitable. Hannes suddenly saw that he lived not like an abstemious monk but as a wealthy man. Hannes liked the idea of schools and a hospital because, yes, they would make life better, but he wondered. Were the poor better served through daily meals, kindness in times of need, a familiar ritual and a companion at their deathbed?

"*For ye have the poor with you always, and whensoever ye will ye may do them good: but me ye have not always,*" the Lord had said. There was need, Hannes thought, for communities of pious men and women. But even the Prior admitted that not all such men and women were as they should be. He, himself, was not as he should be. Hannes sighed.

His long day, his walk, his own heart, all had exhausted him. Unthinking, he found the nearest haven, appearing again at Conrad's house just as the long summer day surrendered to darkness. Conrad was with his horses. "Hannes! Where have you been all day? They sent a messenger from the abbey looking for you."

"Zürich. I walked to Zürich." Hannes blushed, and then took a deep breath. "My whole life has been shaken."

"Not by Andreas and Thomann and their irksome cant?"

"No. Well, maybe. In a way. Conrad, I want to marry."

"How on God's green earth will you do that, Hannes? *BROTHER* Hannes?" Conrad was about to burst into laughter at the thought of his white-clad, naive, sincere and pious brother embracing a buxom girl, but seeing Hanne's face in the lantern light he did not laugh. "Who, Hannes?"

"Vreni."

"OUR Vreni?" The story became even more extraordinary.

"Yes. Your Vreni."

"You must be starving, brother," said Conrad changing the subject. "Come on. We will find you some bread and cheese at least." The brothers went to the house and Conrad searched the larder for something Hannes could eat, returning with some ham, bread, cheese and cider. "Here, now, eat something."

"I have no appetite."

"That is beside the point." Conrad cut a slice of bread and wrapped it around some cheese. "Now, eat and drink your cider."

Hannes gave in to Conrad's good sense.

"You want to marry Vreni," said Conrad, shaking his head. "In Heaven's name, how has this come about?"

Hannes took a drink of cider. "I saw her first at church, or noticed her. I suppose she's always come to church."

"She has."

"It was Easter. I gave her communion. Normal enough, but somehow I looked at her differently as she took the wafer. I saw — felt! — her sweetness and her beauty. Her youth, too, I suppose. I was enchanted and terrified at the same time."

"I can well imagine."

"How can you, Conrad? You have made no vows like mine."

"No. Not like yours. But Hannes, we all make vows, we take huge oaths with great seriousness and we believe them, but none of us knows what fate has waiting in the road ahead."

"The idea is that we surrender to God with our vows."

"Vows are not surrender. It seems to me they can put us completely at odds to God's will, but I'm no scholar of these things."

Hannes sat, silent. This was an interesting thought. He first thought of taking it to the Prior, but he realized that when he returned to the abbey he might no longer be a monk. He honestly didn't know. Where once there had been complete certainty, nothing was certain.

"Look at you," Conrad continued. "Father and Mother vowed to give one son -- you -- to the abbey to grow into a monk, serving God and the people. They did this without knowing you or what the future held for you or the world itself. They did this selfishly, for the forgiveness of their own sins."

Hannes nodded. "That's what the prior said. That perhaps the monastic life had never been my nature."

"You spoke with him?"

"Oh yes."

"He said?"

"That I need to decide."

"Ah. Have you asked Vreni?"

"No, no. It would be a shock if I stood in front of her in these robes and offered my hand."

"She may say no. You should speak to her before you decide to leave the abbey."

"I have to leave the abbey no matter what she says. Yes or no, I can no longer be a monk."

Conrad saw tears in Hannes' gentle eyes.

"When I started out this morning I just planned to walk and think and pray. I can never see our faith as 'superstition,' but maybe Andreas' words stuck in my head. I know the Prior's did. In Zürich, I talked with Brother Leo at St. Peters. I do not understand his ferocity or everything he said, but... He showed me a way to serve God and marry Vreni. I do not have to choose." Hannes' tears flowed freely now. He seemed not to notice them at all.

"Stay the night, Hannes. You are exhausted. Tomorrow we can talk more. Maybe things will be different, maybe the same. But you may be clearer in your mind."

"My mind is clear."

"You look very tired, brother."

Hannes could only nod.

"In any case, you need to talk to Vreni."

"That terrifies me."

"Should I talk to her for you? It would not be strange, as I am her guardian."

"I'm afraid she will feel to blame for my decisions. But all that's happened is that God has shown me who I truly am."

"I will talk to her, Hannes. You don't even need to see her tomorrow if you don't want to. I will speak to her after you have left."

Hannes nodded. "That might be best."

\*\*\*

Hannes was up and walking down The Brothers long before the family awoke. He thought of Conrad's words. *"We all make vows, but none of us knows what fate has waiting in the road ahead."* What is the meaning of a vow, then, if fate has its own plans? Hannes wondered. When even our most earnest vows or passionate acts of will or any energetic thrusting at the future or even all our prayers cannot control what happens? He knew he would find some comfort in familiar routine and maybe, even, some answers, though inside his heart he knew he had only one remaining question: Would Vreni have him?

He stopped again to pray at the shrine to the Virgin. She was important to his order and, it seems, to the mysterious ancestor who had set her here. Hannes had heard that the new religion viewed her as an idol, though Huldrych Zwingli had called her a model of humility, of surrender to God's will. Even so, among the first images to be thrown into the flames had been statues of the Holy Virgin. But who else could help him with his plea, that God forgive him for abandoning his vows, for loving Vreni, for speaking with Brother Leo, for all that had happened?

"Holy Mother of God," he whispered to the faded broken image placed beside The Brothers so long ago, "help me accept these new times. Help me face my destiny with some of the courage with which you faced yours. Ask the Heavenly Father to forgive me for not being able to keep my vows to serve Him as a monk. I pray it is Vreni's heart to love me in return, but if she cannot, give me the strength and patience to accept God's will. In thy Holy Name." He crossed himself, feeling intensely that he was practicing a gesture that would soon, with this statue, be cast into the flames. He longed to drape his cloak over her, to protect her and hide her from the future.

After spending some moments in prayer, Hannes saw what he had to do. He did not know enough to decide anything. He did not know about Vreni; that was true. He did not really know what Zwingli and Jud would have him learn, what the duty of an Evangelical pastor would be compared to his life as a monk, a priest. He needed to know these things before he decided anything. What if it were, as he understood it to be, heresy?

# chapter 4

## The Prophezei, 1524

There was a momentary shuffling of feet as the men standing on the hard stones in the barren, broken-walled sanctuary of the Grossmünster prepared to listen. Most were priests and monks, but not all. Men like Andreas and Thomann stood in the crowd.

"Yesterday, brothers, I spoke to you about becoming the true shepherd, to empty yourself of all save Christ's will for you as did Jesus' disciples and to allow the Holy Spirit to fill you until there is nothing inside you but God. Once you are filled with the Holy Spirit, you will see yourselves for the sinners you are. You must, then, repent of your sins. You may feel afraid, but do not be afraid. Your armor against the enemy is your fearlessness. As our Lord said to his disciples, '...

have peace in me…for I have overcome the world.' Christ calls us to go forward in his work though we may be faced with troubles. Trouble is the nature of the world, and the world cannot be anything different to the shepherd. But our certain comfort is that in his resurrection, Christ is the victor over the world. And if we are his loyal servants, then he will overcome the world's afflictions for us. Be joyous rather than afraid."

Pastor Huldrych Zwingli's speech was captivating, energetic, and passionate. The joy of which he spoke seemed to rush from him to his listeners. His power as a speaker was the great gift that had led him from the Priest of Glarus, to the great abbey at Einsiedeln, to becoming the Priest of Zürich at only thirty-four. Hannes, too, was captivated. Yes, Christ's love should inspire joy, not fear.

"One of the great dangers in the world is presented by the false shepherd, a wolf who appears to be God's servant, but who really serves the world, himself, or Satan. Brother Jud will pass out a paper on which these points have been summarized so that you can have it with you and commit it to heart."

Jud moved among the gathered men, handing each one a paper on which was written a list of characteristics.

"We would all be true shepherds, leading our flock to salvation. But what differentiates the true shepherd from the false? The first characteristic of the true shepherd is that he is a teacher. A pastor's most important work is teaching the word of God. Those who do not teach are nothing but wolves, though they might be called shepherds, bishop, or king. Look around you. How many of the bishops teach anything?"

There was shuffling and nodding among the assembled group. Yes. Brother Huldrych spoke true.

"Then, among those few who teach, many teach their own ideas rather than the word of God. Such are also wolves. A true pastor teaches the truth of the Bible, by the grace of God. Other wolves, more difficult to spot, may teach the word of God, but not to the honor of God, but for themselves and for the Pope, for protection of their high station. These are harmful wolves, coming in sheep's clothing."

Hannes had heard from Andreas and Thomann that the great men of the Holy Church were not men of the church in any real sense. He thought of his own Prior and his teachings. Throughout Hannes' life, the prior had stressed care for the poor, mercy for the weak, respect for the ritual and the Mother Church, and forgiveness. Where was God missing from that? Hannes wanted to interrupt Pastor Zwingli, to ask, perhaps to challenge, but it seemed Zwingli anticipated the question in the next point.

"Those who teach already and teach even with the word of God, but do not, however, disturb the greatest aggravators, the leaders, but allow their tyranny to grow, are flattering wolves and traitors to the people. Those who do not practice with works what they teach with the word of God are nothing among the Christian people, destroying much more with their works than they build with their words."

Hannes wondered. Was his abbey guilty of this? The abbey was not immune to the dissension all around, but how could simple men such as himself or the Prior be expected to challenge everything they judged to be wrong? "We will serve the good," said the Prior to the monks in his care in the face of growing discord all around. "We will study God's word, follow God's will, and in this way, the good will prevail. Life is a constant battle against darkness, won best by moving toward the light. Honor the sacraments, confess when you know you have fallen short of God's will for you, seek forgiveness, and do better." Hannes wondered in what way the Prior had ever NOT practiced what he preached.

"This man makes a generalization," thought Hannes, and he decided to take what he heard with a grain of salt. If Pastor Zwingli believed the Mother Church should be criticized, scrutinized and held to task, should not this new church be also?

"Further," said Pastor Zwingli, "those who do not pay attention to the poor but let them be oppressed and burdened, are false shepherds. Many use their position in the church to accumulate wealth on the backs of the poor. Those who wear the name of shepherd, yet rule in the worldly sense, are the most evil werewolves. Many of these 'princes of the church' are true werewolves, gathering riches, forgetting Christ's words about the rich man who cannot enter the Kingdom of Heaven."

*Ah*, thought Hannes, *charity is Christ's charge to us. But the poor? How has the mother church not worked to serve the poor? It is the main mission of the abbey.* He knew that many bishops amassed great wealth for themselves and their orders. It was easy when the remission of sin could be bought with gold. Who would not buy a few years less in Purgatory or eternal salvation for the transfer of property? Maybe the ideal was that, as men of God, they would use their wealth to alleviate the suffering of the poor. Hannes knew very well that didn't always happen. Look at the Abbess of the Fraumünster. Who in Zürich had more wealth than she? Yet around the corner from the cloister was Zürich's poorest quarter, the Kratz, where Zürich's impoverished people lived in shacks and tents, and women sold their bodies to buy food for their children. Zwingli had cleaned that up and those poor people now lived within the safe walls of the Fraumünster. They were fed, sheltered and schooled with money that had come from melting down rich ornaments. Hannes nodded. The Evangelical faith — and even Martin Luther in Wittenberg — had found no basis in the Bible for Purgatory and opposed the selling of salvation.

"Last, those who do things with doctrine other than undertaking to plant the knowledge, love and childlike fear of God among the people are false shepherds. They must soon be removed from tending the sheep or they will devour them entirely."

"All of these I have described may seem to do God's work on earth, but they are false shepherds, leading the people into darkness. You are the true shepherds, charged with bringing the word of Christ to the people, leading them to repentance and salvation. Your first duty, always, is to rightly teach the word of God."

*** 

Hannes walked away form the Prophezei that second day wondering about the new ideas as well as the explicit criticism of the life he had always known. The tall spires of the Grossmünster still reached to Heaven, but the heart of the church was changing. Pastor Zwingli had delivered a harsh judgment, seeming unconcerned about the natural failings of men, and priests were men just like others. Was that not the Evangelical's argument for marriage? It was true that many bishops had become very wealthy, and many sought high positions in the church for prestige and riches. No one denied that. Even Conrad's old songs had verses of how the greed of the Church in Rome was stealing the bread from the people in the northern countries, and those songs were hundreds of years old. Nothing here was new. But the church itself? It held the people together. No one needed convincing; it was part and parcel of the daily lives of men and women everywhere and had been for a thousand years and more.

*** 

The next day in the Prophezei, Pastor Jud talked about the organization of a proper Evangelical service. While it was not wholly different from what the people were used to, its central feature was the sermon delivered by the pastor, the educational message on which everything turned. "The greatest challenge to those of us who have been priests and monks, who may have served God and the people, but never with teaching, is the sermon. Here are the essential points to remember. First, you are the host. Welcome your flock as guests to God's house. Second, follow this with the prayer taught us by our Lord Jesus Christ. This gives your flock the reverent sense they need before receiving God's word. Following the prayer, read the scripture that is the center of your sermon. This gives context for the teaching in your sermon. Follow your sermon with the confession of sin. It is the duty and obligation of every Christian to admit to his sins. God already knows where we have sinned and has already forgiven us, but by asking for forgiveness we acknowledge God's power and his mercy. Your flock must fear God and humble itself before God in this matter of confession. We ask forgiveness through the Lord's Prayer. Follow this with the business of the community, remembering those who have died in the interval since the last meeting and offer prayers for the poor. Conclude your service with a blessing on the community."

"Two points of scripture and faith that cannot be stressed too much. First, we cannot serve two masters. We can serve God or we can serve the world. The world is filled with idols that people worship when they should be looking to their savior, idols such as wealth, power, desire, illusion. Second, we are all sinners. Salvation comes to us by the grace of God, not by works. Salvation can come to us only if we let the Holy Spirit into our hearts and choose God, not the world. You must impress upon your flock how important it is to choose God, that God has offered us hope in the form of his Son who died to redeem our sins."

The simplicity and directness of the service seemed to Hannes as barren of wonder and mystery as the denuded walls of the Grossmünster sanctuary.

Would the people understand it as a worship service, or would it seem to them as just a meeting in the chapel?

About the sermon, Pastor Jud was right. It was the most difficult for those he taught, especially as the Evangelical church required meetings twice each day. Hannes wondered what he could find to say in two daily sermons. *How will I care for the people in my parish if I'm writing sermons all the time? I am no Zwingli. Pastor Jud says the sermon depends on scripture, but I think Zwingli's great success has come from the power of his speech. How can I do that?* Hannes thought. A voice in his heart answered, "If you want to marry Vreni, you will have to do that." Hannes felt suddenly cold. Who was his God after all, his Heavenly Father or Vreni? Then it struck him. The first act of many of the Evangelical leaders had been marriage.

*** 

While Hannes studied in the Prophezei, he lived in the Grossmünster dormitory and ate in the refectory with others like him. Often there were debates. Many of Zwingli's earliest followers, it seemed, disputed changes Zwingli had made to his own tenets of faith, most notably on the subject of infant baptism. Zwingli had once insisted that there was no Biblical support for baptizing babies. He had stated his beliefs clearly, saying that only a person who'd reached the age of reason could experience real baptism. Zwingli supported his ideas by showing how Christ himself had been a man when he went to John the Baptist and asked to be baptized but he later retreated from his own adamantly expressed statement.

"What do you think, Pastor Hannes from Affoltern?"

"I don't know. It's a doctrinal question beyond me. If we are saved by God's grace, then is baptism even a question?"

"But we are not all saved."

"No, perhaps not, but the choice is there for all of us. Baptism of infants in the old religion protected the child against damnation if it died. Heaven would see the babe belonged to God and allow the little spirit entry. Maybe, as is said, that is illusion, just a story, and all children belong to God, but if that is so..."

"Zürich magistrates were infuriated by the idea of abolishing infant baptism. If he'd clung to his belief that infant baptism is wrong, Zwingli would not have won that disputation against the Bishop of Constanz or won the support of the magistrates. It was . . . what do you call it?" asked a young priest from Wald.

"A necessary compromise," said a Zürich lawyer. "After all, Zürich records births at the moment of baptism. Without infant baptism, how would we know who to tax, who lives where, how many to a family and so on? The church has always kept those records. That is what upset the magistrates."

"But what has that to do with God?" asked a bookbinder from Kloten.

"Shh," laughed the lawyer. "You don't want to be mistaken for a Re-baptizer and end up in Wellenberg."

\*\*\*

Hannes left the Prophezei prepared to take on the new role of pastor. He planned to return to the abbey and slowly make the changes to transform the abbey into an Evangelical community. He believed in most of the changes; he was sure the Prior would, too. What could be wrong with a simple service the people would understand, spoken in their language? What could be wrong with converting the wealth of the abbey to schools and housing for the poor? Everything he'd learned fit his conscience, except that he loved the beauty of the old ways. *Vanity*, he thought, *this love of beauty. Vanity and habit.* Carrying a bundle of pamphlets in one hand

and his clothes in a bundle in the other, Hannes headed home, crossing the bridge leading to the Fraumünster. He thought of the abbess, who had, for centuries, controlled the city. Now, even the she had turned to the new teachings and had married!

He stopped halfway to look at the tower that stood in the middle of the river. Wellenberg Prison. "Heavenly Father," Hannes whispered, "keep Andreas and Thomann in your care during these perilous times." The Prophezei had also taught him who Huldrych Zwingli's enemies would be and they were not only the Roman church. Hannes sensed that the unresolved issue of infant baptism could prove explosive.

# chapter 5

## Andreas, 1525

For months, Andreas had spent most of his time in Zürich. Thomann joined him whenever he could get away from the mill. The disputes had continued, not only between the representatives of the Bishop of Constanz and Zwingli, but between Zwingli and some of his followers. A group emerged that insisted that Zwingli had compromised his beliefs in exchange for the support of the magistrates of Zürich.

Everything they stood for was expressed in Zwingli's simple statements, "The Bible is Truth. Anything not in the Bible is not truth." And yet? He'd given up his original position opposing infant baptism and the separation of divine and temporal authority — in spite of what the Bible said.

Felix Manz, one of Zwingli's oldest friends and supporters, objected, quoting Zwingli back at him, saying, "Did you not say yourself, Brother, 'A man who is inconsistent in his speech is not to be trusted...'? And now you change your mind on these vital points?"

Manz and his friends argued that infant baptism was a Popish practice that claimed to cleanse an infant of "original sin" and assure the child a spot in Heaven if it died. It did nothing but prey on the superstitious, ignorant fears of parents. They believed that there was no such thing as original sin as none was ever mentioned by Christ. A true Christian would do as Christ had done and seek baptism when he could understand what he was doing. Baptism should be an affirmation of God's grace and individual salvation, experienced by men and women old enough to choose. For this they were called twice baptized, Re-baptizers, Anabaptists.

Zwingli had invoked the Old Testament and drew a parallel between circumcision, which identified a child forever as Hebrew, a follower of God. He claimed that infant baptism was but a gentler method of making the same statement, setting the child apart from others as a member of the community of Christ.

The decision came down from the Zürich magistrates. At the end of the disputation, the council decided in favor of infant baptism. They had their reasons. The census depended on church records of christenings and deaths. Manz, Blaurock and Grebel -- the leaders of the "Anabaptists" -- were told, "Obey the law or leave the Canton of Zürich." Others who were with them, and who were not Zürich citizens, were sent away and told never to return.

The group reassembled later in the home of Felix Manz. Some argued for giving up, others for continuing. Finally, George Blaurock passed around a plate of bread and said, "Whoever will be counted as belonging to our community should eat of this bread." Some, carried away by the importance of the moment and intense spiritual feeling, asked to be baptized into the new life.

With their hearts and minds filled with these events of drama and irrevocable changes, Andreas and Thomann headed home, baptized with the spirit and water, and drunk on God. When they reached the old castle, Andreas stopped. "I'll stay with Conrad. Tell Father."

Andreas had a new sense of himself and his importance in the world. He was ready to convert everyone, starting with his own family. He wanted to tell Conrad and Christina everything he'd learned, seen and heard, of the great change that had taken place in him, to share the beautiful paper on which was printed the word, "Freedom." He wanted to baptize them right there in their house, and their servants with them, to join all his family in the family of free Christian hearts.

Thomann continued down the mountain, past the broken saints and the Holy Virgin belatedly sheltered on The Brothers path. In his pocket was a small volume of scripture Manz had published in Zürich. Thomann hoped to read and to learn, to discover just what God wanted from him, and, as always, he was ready to wait until he fully understood. Thomann was not interested in changing anything. A quiet, stolid and predictable middle son, Thomann had gone largely unnoticed between the brilliant Conrad and the beautiful Andreas. He learned his lessons because he studied hard. He competed at games with his brothers, but with no ferocity or desire for victory, and he seldom won. Old Johann trusted him to keep the records at the mill in the same way he trusted the millstones and the flow from the canal over the big wheel that made everything work. Though his blue eyes were as calm and untroubled as the Zürichsee, Thomann had inside of him a channel as deep as that of the River Reuss.

He stopped at home only long enough to eat, wash and change his shirt. He was late at the mill. His father would be angry, an anger that would only barely cover his fear that something had happened to his sons in Zürich, traveling as they did during these perilous times.

***

"Brother, let me tell you! The most amazing wondrous things have happened to me, inside, in here." Andreas tapped the space above his heart. "I have been baptized."

"I know, Andreas. I was there. Andreas, listen. Do you know Katarina?"

"Conrad, I'm not speaking of the false baptism of babies with no conscience or awareness, sinless babies, but the REAL baptism with the Holy Spirit."

"What are you talking about?"

"Last night. At the house of Felix Manz and his mother."

"Felix Manz? Who is Felix Manz?"

"He and others, and a man called Grebel, stand against Zwingli. They were sent away from Zürich. Others, too, who are not Zürchers, and they can never return."

"Why were they sent away?"

"For saying publicly that Zwingli has sold his soul to the magistrates of Zürich, gone back on his word, prostituted his beliefs, abandoned his friends -- LIED, in short -- on the subject of infant baptism."

"Ah. This can't go well, Andreas. I fear you're on the wrong side."

"God's side is never the wrong side."

"No, I suppose not, but how do you know what side God is on?"

"The scriptures. There is nothing in the scriptures about baptizing babies. Christ himself was a grown man when he sought baptism from John the Baptist, but the real baptism was his crucifixion."

"There are multiple baptisms, then?"

"You're mocking me."

"Yes, I'm mocking you. Fanaticism leads to bloodshed. The only thing good about it is the price of horses goes up until some army starts stealing them."

"Conrad, take me seriously. This is important. Your soul is in the balance."

"I have heard that all my life. If I do not confess, my soul is in the balance. If do not properly honor my idiot father, my soul is in the balance. If I want cousin Lunkhofen's mare, my soul is in the balance. There is nothing new to me about my soul being in the balance. Right now, my peace is in the balance. I came out here to get some peace and quiet because, wait. *Do* you know Katarina?"

"No."

"She is Christina's sister. Her father left her here for the week he's on council in Zürich."

"Is she a little girl?"

"Would that she were." Conrad shook his head.

"Why, then?"

"Christina's father wants Katarina to marry one of my brothers. There are only you and Thomann, and I've decided on Thomann, and Christina says Thomann won't do."

"Why?"

"Apparently the girl has romantic notions of a hero on a brave charger. I can give Thomann a horse, if that's all it takes. That isn't it, though. She wants a hero from the songs. Probably a dragon, too. I have no idea. But I pity anyone who marries her, that is certain."

"Pity, Conrad?"

"In Katarina's world there is only Katarina."

\*\*\*

Katarina sat on a tapestry-covered chair, her opulent skirts spread to their best advantage. Her pale blond hair, fashioned in a thick braid, lay over her shoulder under her starched, lace-trimmed, linen cap. Her linen apron, trimmed in lace and embroidered quite elegantly, covered her skirt. As was the fashion, she was laced very tightly. Her full, round breasts showed above the lace of her bodice. She held a needlepoint that she never finished, but which kept her from appearing to others to be as idle as she actually was. It showed off her small but graceful hands and gave her somewhere to look so that her long eyelashes cast shadows on her perfect cheeks.

Conrad entered the room with Andreas and was immediately sorry.

Katarina looked up, turning the full force of her large brown eyes on Andreas.

"Katarina," said Conrad, "this is Andreas, my baby brother. Andreas, Christina's sister, Katarina. I believe you've met before. She was a child then, and perhaps you were a child, too."

"I would remember meeting such a beautiful girl, Conrad."

"We met at my sister's wedding to your brother," said Katarina softly.

"You would have been a little girl."

Katarina looked down again in feigned modesty.

"Come outside, Andreas," said Conrad suddenly. "Help me with the horses."

"We just left the horses."

"That is neither here nor there. Come outside." Conrad grabbed Andreas by the arm.

"I suppose I must go," Andreas said, as he was pulled out the door.

"Stay away from her," said Conrad through clenched teeth, once they were outside. "Katarina's not for you."

"What's wrong with me?"

"You? Nothing is wrong with you. It's *her*. She would not make you happy."

"We just met, and you have us betrothed already."

"I know you, Andreas. I know your passions. I saw the expression in your eyes. She's beautiful, beautiful like those red-capped mushrooms in the dark shadows of the forest. Poison. Pour your love into Katarina and you'll never see a return."

"Do we love to have a return?"

"This is not one of your Brother Huldrych's famous disputes, Andreas. This is no theory of God. This is your daily life forever, and she would be the mother of your children."

"Still, the question is a good one."

"Love that is not returned is a wound that never heals."

"How do you know that? You have not had that experience."

"No, I have not, thanks be to God." Conrad crossed himself. "I know others who have. And that girl in there? A mother? To forget herself in the care of a helpless creature? Never. Katarina would simply be annoyed."

"This is not your business, Conrad."

"You are my brother. It is my business."

"I'm of age. Her father will arrange for her, no doubt. You said he wants one of your brothers as a husband for his daughter."

"Yes, I suspect he does, but the man for Katarina is not you. She will break your heart, Andreas. I think Thomann is more suited."

"Thomann has a heart, too."

"That is true, but Thomann is less likely to be swept away by feelings. His feet are on the ground. You, my little brother," Conrad reached to ruffle Andrea's blond curls, "your head is in the clouds."

# Chapter 6

## Katarina, 1525

Katarina first saw Andreas as he stood in the doorway, lit from behind. She could see his well-formed legs, his broad shoulders and that he was taller than Conrad. When he took off his cap, the sun lit his golden hair, making a halo around his head. He stepped into the room and she saw his blue-green eyes, his bright smile and the gleam of sudden infatuation.

He was not Peter, but he was not a red-bearded troll like Thomann or an old man like Heinrich or a grump like Conrad.

She looked down, knowing it would make him want to see her face. Then she slowly lifted her eyes to meet his, just for a moment. She saw the effect.

At that moment, Conrad had grabbed the arm of his younger brother and pulled him from the room. Katarina could imagine what Conrad was saying. She knew Conrad didn't like her. Oh well.

Anyway, Andreas was not Peter.

She had seen Peter only once, at Christina's wedding to Conrad. At thirteen, she was already beautiful, the early promise of the woman she would become. She was visiting her sister. Because the Alpine passes were closed, and there was nowhere for his armies to go, Peter had come home to visit his family. He rode up The Brothers in the falling snow, his black horse prancing along the untrodden trail. Horse and rider wore the bright blue and white of Zürich and the gold of Peter's army. His cap was topped with a gold feather; his black leather boots were turned down at the top, revealing a red lining. His silver spurs jingled and gleamed. Just at this moment, Katarina happened to be standing outside, and, against the dark pine and lacy frost-clad branches of winter trees, Peter appeared to her to be a glorious creature, a hero.

"And who are *you*?" he'd asked as he turned into the courtyard, dismounted, and handed the reins to Old Stefan.

"Katarina, Sir." She curtseyed.

"Katarina, Katarina."

"I am Christina's sister."

"Why haven't I seen you before?"

"You have, Sir. When my sister married your brother."

"That was eight years ago."

"Peter!" called Conrad, coming up from the horses; at that time, he had only Prince and the little roan mare. "You are home!"

"Not by choice," Peter answered. "The snow has closed the passes."

"Come. I'll show you the new stable."

"Will I see you later, Little Katarina?" Peter never missed a chance to make a conquest.

Katarina blushed.

"She's staying here, Peter. Of course you'll see her again. That *child* is Christina's sister." Conrad, knowing his brother, put very special emphasis on the word "child."

"Until later then, my lady." Peter bowed low before the girl, flourishing his hat. Katarina felt as if she were a noblewoman in an old painting or one of Conrad's songs. In just this way, Peter won her heart.

At supper, Katarina kept her head down, but the way her pink cheeks flushed each time Peter spoke betrayed her feelings, at least to her sister, who watched her with wry curiosity.

"She's in love with Peter," Christina told Conrad that night, as they lay side-by-side, holding hands.

"She'd best get over that soon."

"She won't," said Christina. "She never moves when she wants something." She had vivid memories of Katarina's temper tantrums and her parents' inevitable surrender. "Katarina gets her way."

"Not this time. Peter is on his way to see his bride."

"Will he marry soon?"

"Ha. Not if he can help it. But the girl's father pours money into Peter's army, so it will happen sooner or later. Poor little Katarina."

"If her heart is set, and I believe it is, and she is doomed to be disappointed, as you say she is, yes. Poor little Katarina."

Katarina rose early after a sleepless night, ready at thirteen to declare herself, but Peter was gone.

"Where is Peter?" she demanded with tear-flooded eyes. "He did not tell me good-bye!"

"Why should he tell you good-bye? He's on his way to his betrothal," said Christina, hoping to stop the fire before it burned too bright in Katarina's young breast.

"Betrothal? You must be mistaken, sister. He did not speak of it at supper. A man who is going to be betrothed would be excited and happy. He would want to speak about it to everyone!"

"You're very silly, Little Sister," said Conrad. "Marriage is business. Peter needs money for his army, and Old Wyder is rich and needs a husband of a decent rank for his daughter."

"So he does not love her."

Conrad wished he could take back all he had said. Better by far Katarina believe Peter married for love. "Don't forget, little sister. Peter is a soldier. To speak of such things would be girlish, silly. I must watch what songs I sing when you are here." Conrad sighed. "Of course people marry for love. I married for love. Your sister did, but it was not easy. I had to have a fortune of my own before your father would let her go. Fine by me, else it would be said I married her for her dowry, shaming us both — and a lie."

"Peter must not feel very much for her. He's clearly a passionate, brave man."

"How many words did you exchange with him, Katarina? Four? And you know this?"

"I know what I feel."

"You are too young to feel much," laughed Conrad. But he was wrong. If anything, the young feel more. The burning sentimental infatuation of teenage girls and the racing unreasoning desire of young men make up the madness on which the human race is based.

# chapter 7

## Andreas, 1525

Conrad's warning made Katarina's charms more
intriguing. Sitting across from her at supper, Andreas
forgot Brother Huldrych, Felix Manz, his own baptism
and all he had heard in Zürich. His world was filled with
Katarina's creamy complexion, her soft brown eyes, her
moist, pink lips, and her rising and falling breasts. He
felt he could sit there forever just watching her breathe.

Their courtship was swift. When Katarina
returned home from her visit to Conrad and Christina,
her father told her that Andreas had already been there
and had asked for her hand. The old man also had letters
from Conrad and Old Johann on behalf of Thomann.
This was what he had hoped, that one of the Schneebeli
boys would court his youngest girl. He was half in love

with her himself, she was so much the image of her mother before she had grown fat and shrill.

"Conrad and Old Johann both speak highly of Thomann. They praise his steadiness and honor. He and Heinrich are now running the mill. His future looks to be very prosperous, very bright. Certainly Heinrich will inherit the mill, but Old Johann says that Thomann will have a large interest in it. Why would you have the other brother? Thomann is the better match. You will be near your sister and near us."

"Thomann? Lord no!" she said, crossing herself. "He's red-haired and short. He has nothing to say for himself. He's dull. I do not mind the family, Father," she said, thinking of Peter, dashing and brave, "but I could never marry Thomann."

"Thomann is no fool, nor is he, as you say, 'dull.' He does not waste time in idle conversation or foolishness. I know he will care for you as I have cared for you. You will want for nothing."

She remembered Andreas as he stood in the doorway. Andreas was at least tall, well built and handsome. And he was in love with her. She knew that. He would do whatever she wanted. If she had to have one of the two for husband, she would have him. Her father should be happy enough.

"Not Thomann."

"Truly, Katarina, though Andreas did come and speak for himself, I..."

"Andreas."

"What does he have? Old Johann says he cannot even be depended on to do his job at the mill. He's unsteady, flighty. They say he has joined the Radicals in Zürich, those Re-baptizers. If that's true, he is playing a dangerous game. Zwingli is quickly becoming the most powerful man in Zürich. He will not suffer the disobedience of the Re-baptizers, even men who were once his friends."

Katarina looked at her father in bewilderment. She had no idea about anything happening in Zürich. Her life was limited to her dresses, her home, her wishes, her dreams. "Whatever are you talking about, Father?"

"Your Andreas. They say he... Never mind."

This made Andreas more interesting to Katarina. If it were true then he, like Peter, was a brave warrior.

"Andreas may not work as steadily at the mill as Thomann, but why should he? His family is rich."

"You are sure, my little one?" sighed her father.

"Yes, Father. I would have Andreas. Please not Thomann." By then she was kneeling beside her father's chair, looking up at him through her long lashes. What could he do?

Katarina's father let it be known that his daughter would have Andreas, if her dowry were met by an equal portion given by Old Johann to Andreas. Old Johann made the bargain, telling Andreas he must work off the investment by attending to his duties at the mill. Andreas sold his freedom for Katarina's beauty.

Their wedding was held in the small church in Mettmenstetten, and they made their home in Old Johann's spacious house. Andreas did not even object to a Papist ceremony since, at the end, this beautiful girl was his wife.

# chapter 8

## Andreas, 1526

"No, Andreas. Please."

"Katarina?"

"I need to know you, Andreas. You are a stranger to me. Let us wait until we know each other."

"We will grow to know each other this way, Katarina. Sharing our bed, sharing out bodies and our love for each other, planning our future. Sweet one, I will not hurt you." He reached to untie her gown, thinking of the plump beauty of her breasts. He leaned forward to kiss her cheek. She pulled back from him as if he were made of fire.

"No! Andreas, for pity's sake! No!" Katarina began to cry.

He dropped the ribbons of her gown and left her alone in the spacious ground-floor room that Katarina's mother, Heinrich's wife, Elsa and her little girl, Gretchen, had decorated with all of Katarina's trousseau and beautiful hangings carefully preserved through several generations. The room was the most private in the big house, with high, leaded windows. Part of the original castle that long ago belonged to Squire Adelbert Schneebeli; Old Johann had seen that this room had been perfectly restored before he moved his precious Verena into the old family house. This had been their room. It opened onto its own private courtyard, where Andreas' mother had planted white roses and trained them to climb on trellises. The newlyweds could lock their door and be apart from the rest of the family. After Andreas left, Katarina rose and locked the door on her husband.

Andreas turned, abashed and deeply disappointed. He'd thought — from Katarina's eagerness to marry him — that she shared his feelings. He returned to the room he had always belonged to him and Thomann. He heard Thomann's soft snoring and was glad his brother was already asleep. He shuddered at the shame he would feel on this, his wedding night, returning to his boyhood bed.

When morning came, Katarina seemed fresh and untroubled. She let Andreas kiss her cheek and sat down beside him at the table after the family recited the psalm. "I must talk to you after breakfast, Katarina," whispered Andreas.

"Why?" she asked, looking at him with her huge brown eyes, innocent as morning.

"You know why. We must settle this."

"All right," she agreed, knowing he was right and so after the meal they went to their room.

"Don't be late for work!" called Old Johann, laughing, seeing the young couple hurrying away.

Andreas ignored him. No one expected Andreas to go to the mill the day after his wedding.

"I am your husband, Katarina. Last night — our wedding night! — I did not hold you, my beautiful bride, in my arms. You sent me away! Thank God Thomann was already sleeping. What would I have said to him?"

"You're right, Andreas. You should not have to go away. But I am afraid, afraid of all of that, of becoming a mother and old, like Heinrich's wife."

"Elsa is over thirty, Katarina! Twice your age! She has four living children! She had others, but... Thank God Heinrich is man enough not to push her down the road my mother had to take. Elsa has run this household, yes, with my mother, but for the last two years, alone. There are all of us and a dozen servants. It's a huge job. My father is not easy to live with. As for life with my brother? We've never had much to say to each other, but I know him to be good-humored and fair. He could almost be my father, and Elsa is not much younger than your mother!"

"But all those children! Everywhere! Look at her! Was she ever beautiful?"

"I don't know. I was a child when they married. For all I know, they have been like that forever."

"I'm too young to be a mother. I want to stay pretty for you," she said, "not old before my time like others. And having babies is dangerous! Many women die!"

Andreas knew that, of course he knew that, and he did not want her to die. He wanted to have her with him for always and forever young and beautiful like this, with soft cheeks and shy ways and beautiful dresses and hands untouched by any kind of work.

"We can share a bed, Andreas, but I am not ready to, ready to..."

"You are my wife, Katarina. The love between man and wife is sacred, good in God's eyes. You have taken a vow that you will honor me and obey me. The wife is a servant to her husband."

"I'm not your servant, Andreas. That's just silly."

Andreas stood up, suddenly deciding that maybe he would win her love by building her a house of her own with her own household, where she would be the mistress, away from Heinrich, Elsa and the children. "I think I'll go down to the mill today after all."

"You're leaving me here alone?"

"I will be back before dark. Maybe you can go talk to Christina about these things." As he had lain awake in the night, Andreas thought that perhaps Katarina did not know what happened between a man and a woman. Christina could talk to her frankly. Well, at least he would not have to return to his childhood room to sleep, but sleeping next to her without touching her? He shook his head. "Maybe it's often like this for a young bride, and she will come around."

***

For his part, Andreas hated living under his father's roof, under the eagle eyes of Heinrich and with his father's random, demonic rages and stupidity. He wanted money badly and thought of going off with Peter and making a fast fortune as had Conrad, but that was very risky and his religious beliefs were opposed to war. He still followed the Brethren, though he could not persuade Katarina to join him. He found her often, kneeling with her little rosary, praying for, praying for what?

For a while he tried to explain how such prayer was superstition, bargaining with God, honoring idols in the Marian Rosary. She responded by looking at him with tears in her brown eyes. "You would have me give up everything, my home, my parents and my God to live in this crowded house with you?"

"No, my darling. I will not have you give up everything." But, he wondered, had she not won something in this bargain? Had she not won his love and his protection? Had she not gained the place from which to build a home and a family of her own? But when he reached for her in the night, she continued to pull away, saying, only, "I'm not ready, Andreas. You said you would give me time."

"If you loved me, Katarina, you would want me."

"I do want you, Andreas. But I do not want to be a mother. One follows the other. You cannot deny that."

\*\*\*

Three months passed, and Andreas returned to attending secret meetings of the Brethren who'd been exiled from Zürich. They now met in the forest, holding services beneath the trees. Most nights, Katarina was not obliged to share her bed at all. If she would not join him, he would not force her, but she would pay the price of nights alone. Thomann noted Katarina's solitude, but put it up to Andreas' passionate faith. Thomann had no idea that was how she wanted it.

# Chapter 9

**Midsummer's Eve, 1526**

The family had gathered with friends and neighbors to welcome Peter, who had returned from a war in Lombardy and was on his way to see his wife and young son and to celebrate Midsummer Eve, the longest day of the year. Old Johann roused himself to a level of energy no one had seen since before Verena's death. Andreas sat at the banquet table beside his bride. He looked at her adoringly, amazed that this beauty was his wife. He took Katarina's small hand in his, and they looked to everyone as a young and happy newly married couple should look.

When the meal was over, some of the family and the friends who had been invited remained at the table with Old Johann, telling stories, listening to the musicians, drinking Old Johann's strongest cider, talking. Others decided to stroll in Old Johann's garden. Thomann was obliged to return to the mill to supervise the repair of some machinery ahead of harvest and to see that the workers were paid extra for their work on this day. Conrad and Christina stayed just long enough to be polite to Old Johann and Peter, but no longer. Andreas went with Conrad to get his horses.

When Andreas left, Katarina, too, excused herself from the banquet table. She was uncomfortable in her tightly laced bodice, bored by conversation in which she played no part and tired of the tedious attentions of her husband. Knowing Peter would be there, she had dressed in her best clothes and had her maid-servant lace her as tightly as she could to draw in her waist and push the round orbs of her breasts higher. Her beauty had stunned Andreas when he saw her, and once again he was grateful that she had honored him with her hand in marriage.

She turned toward the apple orchard. The petals of the last few fallen blossoms were scattered on the green grass. She looked behind her once to see if Peter had noticed she had left, but she could not tell and imagined he had not. In fact, he followed her.

"Wait, Katarina. Wait. Where are you going?"

"I was bored at the table. I decided to walk." She cast her eyes down. She knew they would tell this man everything.

"My little brother is very lucky to have found a beauty like you! I wish I'd seen you first!"

"You did," she said, softly.

"I did?"

"Yes, two years gone now, at my sister's house."

"Ah yes! I remember. You were a little girl."

"Not so little."

"No, perhaps not. May I walk with you, little sister?" He gallantly offered her his arm.

"You may, but do not call me sister."

He looked at her. She looked down.

"Ah," he thought.

"You are on the way to see your wife? I hear you have a son."

"Yes, but I haven't seen him. He is nearly two -- wait, yes! My marriage! It was right after meeting you at Conrad's drafty old castle!"

"That's right."

"Oh my. If I had known what I left behind, I might not have gone."

This could not be only gallant talk, flirtation, seduction. Katarina's heart nearly burst with happiness! Peter shared her feelings! She looked up at him, her eyes no longer guarded, their brown depths filled with desire. Peter might have thought the game barely worth playing at such an easy conquest, but instead he looked at her soft neck, her lips and the half-rounds of her breasts wrapped in lace.

"Would you like to rest?" he asked. "My father's apple house is just there, see? We can sit and talk and escape this heat."

"Yes," she said, hypnotized by the feeling of his arm beneath her hand.

Inside the apple house were washed and folded sacks of linen and canvas. Peter spread them on the floor and sat down. "Come," he said, reaching for her. She sat beside him.

"We have a song about you. Shall I sing it?"

Katarina nodded.

Peter began;

Daybreak in the woods.
Wake up, Katarina! Soon the hares will run.
Wake up, Katarina, sweet love!
Hy-a-ho, you are mine, thus I am thine.
Wake up, Katarina!
Daybreak in the meadow

Wake up, Katarina!
My pretty love, let's look at you,
Wake up, Katarina, sweet love!
Hy-a-ho, you are mine, thus I am thine.
Wake up, Katarina!
Daybreak in the forest.
Wake up, Katarina!
The hunters proudly carry the antlers.
Wake up, Katarina, sweet love!
Hy-a-ho, you are mine, thus I am thine,
Wake up, Katarina!

Her head rested on his lap. As he sang, he gently, absently stroked her breasts above her bodice, her neck; he traced the contour of her ear. She listened, her flesh on fire, waiting. "Did you like the song?"

"Very much," she said.

"You're laced so tightly I wonder you can breathe." He untied her bodice and opened the laces. "Better?"

Katarina nodded.

He lay down beside her and placed her head on his shoulder. "Hy-a-ho, you are mine, thus I am thine, Katarina."

"Oh, Peter," she sighed. "I have loved you forever."

"Katarina, sweet girl!" She relaxed in the warmth of love returned. She was right, then. He DID love her. He did NOT love his wife. He would carry her off. He would stay with her. They would live far away somewhere, some place where no one knew them. She would be his Katarina. He would adore her and she would adore him. She wrapped her arms around his neck. He kissed her, gently, softly, then with passion. She felt her body go hot and soft. His mouth on hers, he lifted her skirts.

Katarina's care for becoming a mother at such a young age vanished in the rush of possession. This was her man, and she was his woman. This was why she had been born. They fell asleep wrapped in each other's arms. He would stay with her forever, leaving everyone behind.

# chapter 10

## Andreas, Midsummer's Eve, 1526

"Father, have you seen Katarina?"

"She was walking toward the orchard, but don't worry, son. As you were not here, Peter followed to look after her."

"How long ago?"

"Not long. Half an hour? If you hurry, you'll catch them up."

Andreas took the hill in long strides, not wanting to look foolish, not wanting to look as if anything could be wrong.

"Katarina! Katarina! Peter! Peter!" he called out. Hearing nothing in response, his stomach tightened into a hard knot of dread. He continued silently walking through the empty orchard.

When he reached the apple shed, prickles of fear ran up the back of his neck. He walked slowly to the window beside the door. He knew already that he would see Peter's sword against the wall, his jacket and plumed hat on the floor beside it. Andreas' heart pounded. *"No, no, no!"* his heart cried. Peter's breeches were pulled down around his ankles. *"It will be some serving girl,"* thought Andreas, hoping. *"It has to be. She wouldn't, wouldn't. She's too afraid. Wait. Peter would not suffer such fear. It could be, it could be. No. She would not, she must love me. She <u>chose</u> me."*

Cold sweat broke out on Andreas' forehead when he saw them entwined on a bed of carefully placed apple sacks, their slumber lit by a single shaft of golden light. Katarina's skirts were lifted, her bodice open, her jacket on the floor.  There was bright blood on the hemp sack where she lay.

The shock took Andreas out of himself. He stared dispassionately at a scene as simple as springtime. Two healthy, lusty animals had their fill of each other, then had fallen asleep entwined in the hot memory of their pleasure.

The cold moment passed. Blood rushed to Andreas' head and the world in front of him turned red. His heart shoved against his ribs. He reached for the door handle. *"I'll kill him with his own sword here and now, where everyone can see what he has done. I'll plunge his sword into his back, through his heart, and then hers. I will have nothing to answer for. Their guilt will be painted on this floor. She'll feel his arm thrash in death. She will awaken, she will scream, she will see me. She will feel all her guilt. I will stab her through the breast, those beautiful breasts that I could never touch, that she would never let me touch. Judas. Whore."*

He slowly turned the door handle. *"I will tell her what she is, then, when she can't move and her lover is dead on top of her. She will know what she has done to me. I will have her and then I will kill her."*

The door handle felt suddenly very hot. *"Satan!"* Andreas shook in horror. He stepped back. The realization that he could actually kill them both went against everything he believed. *"This is the apple!"* He shook. *"This is the tree!"*

Did God know the hearts of men so well? *"Whoever is angry with his brother WITHOUT CAUSE."* If this was not cause what was cause? Andreas shook his head. Of course it was cause. Still, this was his own life, not theirs. What was done was done. Killing Peter would not undo anything that had happened. Killing Katarina would not bring him what he wanted. He could divorce her. The Scripture was clear on this point. *"Whoever shall put away his wife saving for fornication..."*

*"I will divorce her. That will ruin her life. A ruined life is better punishment than death. She'll return to her parents' home — if they'll have her — or Peter will have to support her. His wife will leave him. He'll lose the whole fortune of the Wyder's that he's counting on. He'll lose his son."* Then he saw he'd have to prove her sin. Peter would have to admit to it; she would have to admit to it. Would they? And if they did? Peter could shame him, say that Katarina had been a virgin, that Andreas had not done his duty as a husband. No one would know it was out of care for her; they would think he was unable. *I'm trapped*, he thought.

"Help me, Lord. Help me to clear my heart of this," he whispered.

The apple trees — familiar to him since his childhood — seemed monstrous, mocking. They KNEW; they had SEEN. A gust of wind caught the upper branches and threw some of the dried and faded petals into the air. He turned away from the shed and climbed higher through the orchard, his feet moving him to safety.

*Conrad warned me. I could have listened, but I was blinded by her beauty — and my pride.* He thought of all the nights he'd spent clinging to his side of their big bed so she could sleep peacefully, knowing she was safe — safe from HIM! He thought of the work at the mill into which he'd thrown himself, hoping to make money, to save money, to build her a house of her own near Conrad and Christina so the two sisters could be nearby. *"I cannot go back to that banquet table. I cannot go home,"* he thought. *"Where, then? And where will she go after this? Peter will not take her with him."* He shivered, thinking of how she would be left behind.

The Brothers began at the top of the orchard. Andreas turned onto the trail. His emotion-charged heart needed release. Anger might be a sin, but it was still real. He ran.

***

"How long was it, Conrad, before you and Christina..." Andreas had asked just that afternoon, as he walked with Conrad to the stable to get his horses. He and Christina endured his father as long as they had to, but never longer.

"Christina? She has never been pregnant. For a while, we were disappointed, sorely so, but now we're content living for each other. God knows I have had enough to deal with, Andreas, with you, Hannes, Thomann and the horses. And enough of pregnant women with our mother and Elsa. You are not worried, are you? You've only been married, what, three months?"

"No. Not children. How long were you married before Christina let you touch her?"

"What? Surely that little harlot does not push you away from her!"

"She is afraid of becoming a mother. She is so young."

"Ah." Conrad had other thoughts about that. It was her vanity, her way of controlling Andreas. "In truth, little brother, Christina and I had pleasure in each other before I went to war with Peter. There has never been any woman for me but Christina, nor any man for her but me."

Andreas felt cold inside.

"Katarina is your wife, Andreas. She has taken vows to honor you and obey you. Why do you give her a choice?"

"I cannot force her. She says it will just take some time for her to get used to me."

"Believe that if it makes you feel better. But there is a reason the old stories are stories of kidnap and rape. Not so long ago that was the way our men found and took their women."

"Conrad, you can't be serious."

"Those people were not fools." Conrad thought a moment of fussy mares who would not accept a mount on unfamiliar pastures. "Maybe she is uncomfortable living in that house with Father and all of Heinrich's family. Move up with us. You can have your own end of our castle, three rooms and privacy! All of this, and you can work with me and the horses. By working together we will have more time and can accomplish more. Perhaps Christina will have a good effect on Katarina's silly mind."

"There's no money in that, Conrad. Father pays."

"I pay! You would have a home, work, food and Katarina would be near her sister. That cannot be bad. It has to be better than living with Heinrich and his brood — and Father."

"It would be better, but as I said, I need money. I want to build her a house of her own, yes, nearer Christina."

"She will not appreciate what you do for her. She is used to having everything handed to her. Use her dowry to build her a house."

"She deserves a decent man who will build a house for her, as you have done for Christina."

96

Conrad snorted. "I wonder why you think Katarina *deserves* anything."

"What do you mean you wonder why I think Katarina deserves anything?"

"From what you just said, you are not even truly a couple. If she refuses you her bed, is that marriage?"

"She's still very young. She doesn't want children yet. That's sensible."

"Sensible? No, it isn't. A woman should yearn for the embraces of her husband. It's natural, normal. You are not ugly. You do not smell bad. You're a fine man from a fine family. She could have done much worse than you! But here you are, selling yourself short. You should be partners to each other, bedmates, lovers. Just take her, brother. It is your right. Young women are designed for childbirth. If you don't believe that, look at our poor old mother." Conrad crossed himself. "God grant she rest in peace."

***

This conversation was fresh in Andreas' mind as he wandered through the orchard in search of his wife. Everything had been answered by the image in front of him like a lewd painting, his wife, his brother. Well, if she went home, he would not be there. He did not want to see her, hear her. He did not want to know what she would say — if she said anything — he didn't want any part of her. Not to touch her, not to see her false face or listen to her say anything.

The sun would set, even on this long midsummer day. He resolved to let tomorrow take care of tomorrow.

He reached the castle as Conrad was leading Saladin and Prince inside for the night, preparing to brush them down, taking pleasure in their care.

"Brother."

"Andreas!"

"I must stay here some days."

"All right, but what . . . ." Conrad looked into his brother's eyes.

"It doesn't matter, but I cannot go home."

Conrad then knew the whole story, though his brother said nothing. He handed a bucket to Andreas. "Go fill this, then spread the grain evenly in these two troughs."

# chapter 11

**Katarina, Midsummer Eve, 1526**

"Katarina! Wake up, wake up. It must be late. Andreas will be looking for you." Peter gently stroked the girl's cheek, not wanting to shock her out of sleep.

Katarina fought against waking. Was that but a wonderful dream she had had?

"Peter?" she said, doubting this moment could be real.

"Yes, sweet Katarina. Wake now. You must go home."

"Home?"

"I will take you home."

"Oh my God," she said, crossing herself. She suddenly understood where she was and she saw ahead to the next stopping point in her destiny. "Do not take me back to Andreas, Peter. I beg you. Take me to my parents."

Peter could also see ahead a little ways to a moment when they would be walking together through the orchard and meeting . . . who knew whom they would meet? Or into his father's house?

"That's best, sweet girl. Wait here. I'll go down to Father's and get my horse. I'll tell them I'm going home. I'll take you to your parents and then go to my wife. You can ride in front of me on my saddle."

Katarina's blood rose. He was not staying with her? Her face flushed in anger. She clenched her teeth against saying anything. She swallowed hard, then said, "Yes, I will like that."

"What will you tell them?"

"I'll think about that on the way."

"All right. Sweet Katarina," he said, kissing her.

She forced herself not to pull away from him. How could everything she had ever wanted turn so quickly into her life's greatest loss?

As soon as he left, she dressed herself as best she could without help. Peter had left his cloak behind for her, but she decided she'd rather freeze than wear it. It would remain in the shed unnoticed until the apple harvest and then it would be a mystery.

*"Where should I go?"* She was as bewildered as a moth over a candle whose flame has gone out but whose wick is still warm. *"Christina! I will go to Christina. I will tell them Andreas and I argued, that he over drank himself, was a beast to me. Yes. Yes. That's what I'll do. I will stay there."* She knew her disheveled clothes would give credence to her story, and the fact that she was walking and alone. She would look like a runaway, desperate to escape a brutal husband.

Unaware, she followed her husband up The Brothers, hoping as he had hoped, to find a haven at the castle and comfort for a broken heart.

The long midsummer evening was only beginning to darken when she arrived. Going first to the kitchen, she expected to find her sister watching over the preparation of supper or planning tomorrow's breakfast, but Christina had gone to bed, fatigued from the banquet. Katarina found, instead, Conrad and Andreas waiting while Vreni put together a quick meal.

Andreas' back was to the door, so Conrad saw her first. Conrad quickly decided not to betray anything, not to betray Andreas' confidence or even his own knowledge. This was his brother's problem to deal with.

"Katarina! Why are you not at home, warm in your beautiful room, tucked safely into your soft bed, awaiting your loving husband?" Only Andreas would have caught the note of irony in Conrad's voice; Katarina felt only a sharp pang of something others would recognize as guilt. Andreas would not turn around. Katarina blushed.

"I wanted to see my sister."

"She's gone to bed with a headache. The banquet was too much for her, maybe for all of us. You look done in, little sister. You really should be home in your soft wedding bed."

"You're right, brother. I am very tired." Katarina wondered why Andreas didn't turn, why he didn't look at her, embrace her, and kiss her cheeks as he usually did. Surely...no, it was impossible.

Andreas' heart pounded. Tears filled his eyes.

*So,* thought Conrad, *Peter did not carry her off with him. He left her behind and went home. She's here to find comfort from Christina. I doubt she would find any there. Well, maybe now she will grow a heart.*

"Perhaps you went home and didn't find Andreas so you came here?"

"Yes."

At that, Andreas turned to look at her. She was still beautiful to him. Not even her faithlessness could change that. Here was the choice. He could choose to pretend to believe her, that she had gone in search of him, or he could choose to call it out as the lie it was. *"Ye have heard that it hath been said, 'An eye for an eye, and a tooth for a tooth'. But I say unto you that ye resist not evil: but whosoever shall smite thee upon thy right cheek, turn to him the other, also."*

"I am here, Katarina," he said softly. "Shall we go home? You can return tomorrow and see Christina. Goodnight, Conrad."

"Do you want to eat something first? No one will be awake down there when you arrive, I'm sure. I'm sure they all drank themselves into deep slumber by now. Vreni? Have you found anything?"

"Bread and cheese, sir, and some cider."

"No, Conrad. Thank you all the same. We'll go before it gets later. At least we have a moon."

***

The Brothers was silvery in the moonlight. Andreas gave Katarina his arm, and she took it as she had taken Peter's, but this time she felt no rush of desire or joy in fulfilled hope. And Andreas did not cover her little hand with his own as he had always done. They walked in silence back to Old Johann's house. The last lingering guests were staggering toward their horses or their homes as Heinrich and Old Johann bid them goodnight.

"Andreas? Is that you? Did you find your Katarina?"

"I did, Father."

"And you have been walking together in the moonlight?"

There was no denying this.

"Ah, you bring me in mind of your poor mother and me in our early married days, so much in love that time meant nothing." The old man, slightly drunk, felt tears of longing. He wiped them from his eyes with his sleeve. "Go on in to bed, children. Peter has gone already, home to his family, to his wife. No doubt he has missed her."

***

"I will leave you, Katarina," said Andreas in their room. "I have business with the Brethren."

"Must you go?"

"I should have been there before now, but..." he stopped. She knew he'd been at Conrad's. "Goodnight, Katarina." He turned and walked out the door, closing it carefully, silently, behind him. He went to his own room, knowing Thomann was asleep. His old bed felt friendly and welcoming. He found he was tired beyond measure and when he laid his head upon his pillow, he was not tortured by memories of what he'd seen, or fear that Katarina did not love him. The choices he'd made were right; his conscience was clear. What the morrow would bring he could not know, and laying his burden at Christ's feet he slept the night through, the blessed sleep of angels.

# chapter 12

## The Brethren, 1526

Thomann awoke to find Andreas sound asleep in his old bed. "'Tis no wonder," he thought. "He came in late and didn't want to wake Katarina." Having left the party early to take care of things at the mill, Thomann had no idea of any of the events later in the day.

"Wake up, Andreas."

"No, please! Let me sleep."

"Come on." No one could miss the morning psalm, not if they were in the house.

Andreas had slept in his clothes. He pulled on his boots, straightened himself and went outside. The banquet table was still there. The servants had stayed up most of the night clearing off and cleaning, but the courtyard still looked like the party had lasted too long.

"Come, my sons, come." Old Johann gathered them together. "Heinrich, where are the children? Here they are, Heinj, here, next to Andreas. You are growing fast! You are as tall as Thomann! Elsa? Little Gretchen? Where's Bernhardt? Little Hans? Ah, ah, there you are. Andreas, where is Katarina?"

"Let her sleep, Father."

"All right, all right."

They stood in a row and Old Johann surveyed what he regarded as a personal success. Yesterday all his living sons had been gathered here together, even Peter, so often gone, and Conrad, so strange and foreign though his own son. "His mother's boy, I think. More than mine. Hedinger more than Schneebeli." The others he believed he understood, though he worried about the youngest two and their fascination with the Re-baptizers. "All right, children!"

*"Bless The Lord, O my soul, O Lord my God, Who coverest Thyself with light as with a garment; who stretchest out the heavens like a curtain, who layeth the beams of his chambers in the water; who maketh the clouds his chariot, who walketh upon the wings of the wind."*

They wished each other a good day, then Elsa, Old Johann and the children sat down for breakfast, but Heinrich, Thomann and Andreas hurried to the mill to set up for the half-day labor. The workers would grind grain and sack flour all morning as people brought it to be milled in preparation for the Sabbath. Then there would be the hours of cleaning the stones and making sure the machinery was in proper order for the coming week. By mid-afternoon, everyone in the village would go home to begin preparation for the day of rest. In these days of religious upheaval, Old Johann made the rule not to inquire into anyone's beliefs, and Heinrich agreed.

"Change is coming, always coming, whether we will or will not," said Heinrich, sucking on his pipe. "I do not need to know more about the men I pay than that they give me an honest day's work."

Though the mill had the right to the free labor of the tenants of the abbey, they hired only free men. "How will those men get a crop in the ground if they are working here with us? They won't. And if they don't we have less work. It's simple," said Old Johann. Still, all had to bring their grain to Old Johann's mill and Old Johann took his share from each customer. He could sell this flour, but he did not sell it. He sent it to the abbey ovens to be baked into bread for distribution among the poor.

\*\*\*

On the eve of the Sabbath, Thomann and Andreas escaped their father's ever-watchful eye. They slept where they could, at someone's house, in a peasant's shed or in the forest, wherever the Brethren were gathering. They did not keep their beliefs a secret from their family, but they did not openly discuss their meetings, the places or the people. Later, when, in his disputation with Felix Manz, it was clear that Zwingli had compromised truth for power, the Brethren had gone from being part of a lively, open discussion about the nature of faith and God's will for His children on earth to being ridiculed, labeled criminals, exiled and jailed.

Their beliefs — belief in the separation of faith and politics, belief in non-violence, belief in individual free will, and baptism of believers — were tremendously attractive to poor people who had been, for generations, hammered down by their wealthy lords and often conscripted, kidnapped or sold into the military. Many who joined the Re-baptizers had also risen up against their lords, especially those from around Constanz. The rebellion had cost thousands of lives and led to few victories.

Without ever thinking about learning to read, these people were reading. They found themselves in small schools, sheltered by oak, fir and linden trees. Inside the pockets of their homespun clothes, or worn around their necks in small suspended pockets, were rolled papers with bits of Bible verses: "Love thy neighbor as thyself," "For God so loved the world that he gave his only begotten Son," "Men shall not live by bread alone." God's holy words were no longer the property of priests. With the advent of printing, God's words belonged to all. To these men and women, printed words that they could read were treasures.

***

On this sunny Sunday morning, Felix Manz stood before a small group that included Andreas and Thomann. Manz spoke about the nature of faith and, as had Christ, used the sweetness of nature surrounding his small flock. "I know you are poor, but if you are poor in the things of this world and rich in spirit and the awareness of God's love, then you are truly rich. God has endowed all creatures with everything they need. Here our Lord said to his disciples, just as I would say to you, 'Take no thought for the morrow, what shall you eat, what shall you drink, nor yet for your body, what shall ye put on. Is not this life more than meat, and the body more than clothing?'"

"Was our Lord never hungry, sir?"

"Yes, he knew hunger. For forty days and forty nights he fasted in the desert. He did this to test himself. He knew his privations would attract Satan, who would tempt him."

"But then?"

"Satan offered our Lord everything. Food, power and escape from the Cross that awaited him. Christ refused all that Satan offered. Only after this did Our Lord seek baptism and then he began his ministry.

Christ believed he could not minister to us until he knew the terrible temptations we suffer and what it means to be human, for our Lord was a man, though the Son of God. He knew what we suffer, the hardships of our lives. If we want something, need something, it becomes as a god to us; it pushes truth out of our vision; it becomes our religion. Food for the glutton. A beautiful woman for the man dissatisfied with his wife. Gold for the greedy man. There is no end to the enemies we must fight. Knowing God will take care of us is our protection against covetousness, dissatisfaction, and sin. Our Lord said, 'Look at the fowls of the air, for they neither toil nor do they reap, nor gather into their barns; yet your Heavenly Father feedeth them'."

"We must sow and harvest if we are to eat," said a skeptic in the crowd.

"Work is for us the same as flight is for the bird. When the bird flies, he looks everywhere for food and to guard his nest from attack," answered Felix Manz.

"There you go, Brother Hugo. So it is. Would we be men if we did not work? It is what God made us for. No one disputes that."

"My master does nothing. He would say *I* was made for work and *he* was made for sport —and to beat me!" The crowd laughed.

"Idleness is a curse of its own, Brother Otlis. Our Lord says we should 'Seek first the kingdom of Heaven.' Our Heavenly Father will see we have all that we need. You can read these things yourself, here." Manz held up a sheaf of loose pages on which had been printed some verses from the Gospel of Matthew.

Andreas took a sheet and read quickly through all that Brother Manz had read to them, and more. He was struck by the last verse: *Take therefore no thought for the morrow: for the morrow shall take thought for the things of itself. Sufficient unto the day is the evil thereof.* As Felix Manz read this, everything Andreas had held inside welled up within him and drained away as tears.

"Andreas! What is it?" asked Thomann, looking at his brother who, though he tried with the sleeve of his shirt, could not carry away the tears fast enough. Thomann wrapped his arm around his younger brother's shoulders.

"Nothing, Thomann, nothing. This is medicine for the soul."

When the brothers returned home that night, Old Johann told Andreas that Katarina had returned to her parents in Mettmenstetten for a visit. "I suppose the poor thing is homesick," he said.

"I'm sure she is," agreed Andreas.

# chapter 13

## Hannes, 1526

Hannes brought to the abbey a printed copy of Zwingli's German Bible. His fervent hope had been — and continued to be — that he could do the same work in different clothes. Brother Hannes, now Pastor Hannes, gently took the abbey under his control and transformed it from a Popish church to an Evangelical church.

The new religion had become official in all of Canton Zürich. Hannes strove to make it easy on everyone. He held meetings throughout the community and went door-to-door to talk to every family about the changes. Because it was Hannes, the people listened, thinking the changes would not matter much. Hannes explained that the saints and shrines in their houses should come down, not just put away, but destroyed. "Brothers and sisters," he said, "our Lord never said anything about us needing someone to talk to God for us. We can all talk directly to Our Heavenly Father." Hannes also told them to come to school at the abbey if they wished to learn to read.

"We knew it would come to us soon enough," said the village folk.

"'tis time," said a young farmer.

"God willing, it come peacefully," said a young mother with a baby on her hip, motioning to cross herself, then holding back. "It will not be easy for the old ones."

"Nor those who believe, missus."

"No, but I guess we can keep our beliefs to ourselves."

***

Throughout the Canton of Zürich there was an exodus of Roman Catholic priests and clerics away from their long-seated monasteries and cloisters, looking for new homes in Catholic cantons. While many monks from the Angel Mountain Abbey left for Zug and Luzern, the Prior planned to stay. He even put aside his white woolen robe for a black one.

The abbey's empty dormitory beds were given to the elderly poor where they could be watched over. Zwingli's Bible replaced the beautiful handwritten Latin/German Bible in the sanctuary. A day came when orders arrived to destroy all the trappings of the Roman church still lingering in the abbey. Zwingli would send men from Zürich to help with the process.

"Nothing makes the point more clearly than destroying the images," Leo Jud had once said to his assembled students, pastors in the new faith.

"That's true, Brother Leo, but I was shocked when I first walked into St. Peter's. An empty church creates quite a sober scene," Hannes said. He still had misgivings about the destruction of the story depicted on all church walls in the Christian world.

"It is not empty of God! God, not images, should fill the church."

\*\*\*

Deep in his heart, almost a secret from himself, but certainly not from God, the Prior hoped the change would not come. He could imagine working side-by-side with Hannes as he had for the last several years. He could even exchange roles, accepting Hannes' leadership. He believed he could adapt to the new idea of the Lord's Supper rather than Mass. With pleasure he taught in the new school and, though no one had asked, he offered his opulently decorated room to be used as an infirmary. These changes, many of them, corresponded to his own ideas for reforming the faith he loved. He was an old man and would soon step aside, anyway. He respected Hannes when, after weeks with no word, he had suddenly shown up in the black robes of the Protestant pastor. This was Hannes' way, the Prior was sure, of marrying Vreni without deception or abandoning his calling.

Was this a wrong reason, evil in the eyes of God? The Prior did not think so. Hannes had refused to lie, and the road he'd chosen might be the right one. The Prior could see the way the future was going. Other European states had suffered bloodshed during the Peasants' uprising, but, Zürich Canton had been spared. It was the Prior's fervent prayer it would remain that way. His prayers were prayers of gratitude and for strength to continue working for peace. Even if it meant he sacrificed the old dogmas, his love of God would never change.

\*\*\*

"Prior, Father..."

"Brother Hannes, what is it?"

"I've heard from Brother Leo in Zürich. I asked, you know, if for the sake of the elderly people here for whom our chapel has long been a place of inspiration and understanding, if for those old people, the paintings and hangings and statues could remain."

"He has said no?"

Hannes nodded. "Here. You can read it. You'll see I've been sternly lectured by Brother Leo, who is certainly right, that allowing our parishioners to continue in the way of superstition instead of teaching them the real words from the gospel condemns them from knowing the truth. It will keep them in darkness. He says we should not give in to their weakness. Their souls are at stake."

"Do you really believe that?" the Prior asked after reading the letter. "Do you really believe the paintings and statues lead the people to worship idols? Tell me your personal feeling, only between us."

"I understand his reasoning. If the Bible is printed and everyone can read it, what need have we of all this? And it's true. There is nothing in scripture that says we should pray to a saint asking him to talk to God for us. God doesn't need a lawyer to plead our case. He knows us already. It is WE who need to know our own sins and to go to God directly. But Brother Leo and Brother Huldrych say it is the invisible spirit of God that works in man. I think they're right, but when I see the saints all along the wall, I don't see idols. I see people just like me who did something right. If I pray to them, I am asking God to strengthen that part of them I wish to see in myself," Hannes said with a sigh.

The prior nodded. "Look at the women who go to that battered little Virgin." The Prior crossed himself. "They believe she will help them conceive a child. Some leave her money, which we collect and use for the poor.

Do these women believe they can 'buy' help from that statue? I don't know. Perhaps. Still, when they return home, their heart is lightened. They have told her their troubles and they feel less alone. Do these women worship that little broken bit of stone? Some are only acting as children who speak to their toys. Do we take dolls from our daughters or the carved horses from our boys?"

Hannes could not answer. He simply hoped no one would think of or mention the small band of broken statues who had been his friends on many hard journeys.

It would happen on a Monday. Sunday, the parishioners would have service. The people were told that if they had given statues or relics to the Order, they should take them home. Then, before the next Sabbath, the chapel sanctuary would be emptied and whitewashed. Anything of value not belonging to others would be melted and sold and the money would be used to feed, clothe and house the poor. A percentage, as always, went to Zürich for the tithe, for taxes.

*** 

Hannes found the Prior at prayer that Sunday evening at the time that would have been evensong. All the candles were lit, every remaining bit of silver, gold and brass shining. Every statue seemed alive in the flickering light, and the small shrines along the walls offered themselves to world-weary sinners. Wearing sumptuous vestments, the Prior knelt in front of the small altar to the Virgin, on which, between silver candlesticks, stood a very old painted, linden wood statue of the Holy Mother. She leaned a little forward, holding her infant son in one arm. She had kept vigil in the chapel for centuries, perhaps as long as the abbey had existed. Her one hand was raised in blessing; the other arm held the baby whose teachings would change the world.

"Our Order was dedicated to the Mother of God," said the Prior, noticing Hannes. "Long ago some Benedictines wanted to purify themselves from the corruptions that had entered the faith. They split away to start again and dedicated themselves to charity and a holy life of poverty. Perhaps we have gone wrong, too, now."

Hannes was not sure. The answer was not black or white. His whole life at the abbey had been one of prayer and service to the people in the surrounding area. That the abbey itself was wealthy was the result of local lords who sought a way to escape their sins. In this the Church had sinned. The Prior himself thought so, but the customs and endowments began long before his time. That the church taught men and women to buy their way out of hell was nothing but a kind of usury, paying gold to release their soul from debt. The abbey had given such indulgences, as had every other church.

"Tomorrow, then?"

"Yes. The commission is here already. They are sleeping in the dormitory."

"Oh, Brother Hannes. Such times. Forgive me. You know, I was asking our little Virgin to help me endure all this." Tears ran down the old man's cheeks. The Prior was trying very hard to hold firm that he could remain serving God and the people in this valley, but his heart was broken. In his mind, all of this—the statues, the paintings, the shining objects of worship, his beautiful vestments—represented mankind putting on its very best for God. These beautiful things could be found in God's house, the only place the poor, even just the ordinary people could find them.

"I'm very sorry, Father. I fear I brought them here myself, through my love for Vreni."

"No, no, son. They would have come anyway. You have made it easier for me, for the abbey. I am sad, but in my heart I think they may be right. With this printing invention, books are no longer rare treasures. These schools? People will soon no longer need me or you to tell them what Christ has said. They will read it themselves. It makes no sense to keep the Holy Word locked up. Our Lord wandered the countryside telling everyone. Still, I do not quite see why it must be this OR that. I would like that new Bible here, in this little chapel with our big one, one for everyone, and our chapel left untouched, but..."

"It is the new wine, Father. As scripture says, new wine is not to be put in old wineskins."

The prior shook his head. "It is the power of scriptures that anyone can use the words to support their argument. Even the infallible doctrines of the Holy Church were disputed constantly, no matter who set them. Blessed St. Augustine, St. Paul, Pope Gregory, even the apostles who knew our Lord, disputed. It didn't matter, really. People like to be right. They'll fight just for that. It is not so complicated to follow Christ's rule. As humans, we are fallen. We struggle against a thirst for power just as Eve defied God's order." The Prior sighed. "I very much fear that when he's finished fighting the French, the Holy Father in Rome will do what he can to squash all of this. No one gives away power. No one. More's the pity. Those in Rome should heed the warnings of Erasmus of Rotterdam — a wise man, Brother Hannes, one who knows men's hearts and the dark ways of the Church today. Mark my words. We will have bloodshed here before it's over, damage much worse than statues thrown on a bonfire."

Hannes felt a chill run up his spine. "I pray you are wrong, Father."

The Prior sighed. "The Prince of Peace could never have meant to be the reason for war, but He has been through the centuries. All the families in this valley have gone to war, year after year after year. Our land? Our land is based on war, on mercenaries like your brother Peter. Buying and selling poor farm boys. Halberd, axe, hoe, whatever tool they hold in their hand at the moment, he comes riding through, all gorgeous in red and gold and blue and white. No one wins. One day this side, the next day that side, and now? The Turks are rapidly approaching Vienna. That should tell us all that God does not favor one side of a fight over another. I do not think we should raise arms at all in defense of religion, since it goes against Christ's teachings, but it will come. You will see it, Brother Hannes, I'm sure you will, but... I ramble, Brother, I ramble."

Hannes heard echoes of his brother Andreas in the Prior's words. How strange, he thought, that the two would touch in any place, in any degree.

Looking around the chapel, Hannes' heart was full. He, too, had always loved these things, loved them for their own sakes, loved them as beautiful paintings. *Yes*, he thought, *I am guilty of worshiping images.*

As if reading his mind, the Prior gave expression to Hannes' thoughts. "I wonder why the new church does not see the power of these paintings and statues, in and of themselves. Art endures, a bridge through the lifetimes of us all, linking us one to the other. In this way, it seems to me, we should learn from the mistakes of the past, but each generation invents the world anew. The unchanging paintings are good reminders that it is we who are new; the world is old, old."

"Do you want me to stay here with you, Father? It will be for me, also, the last night to see these things in this place."

"My son, with all my heart I should like that, but you have a great deal of work to do tomorrow. Thank you for listening to me so patiently. Go to bed. God keep you, sweet boy." The Prior made the sign of the cross over Hanne's head. Not since Hannes was a child had the Prior spoken to him in this way. Filled with sorrow over the irrevocability of change, Hanne's kissed the old man's creased and spotted hand. It was wrapped around a white onyx rosary with an obsidian cross on which a small, silver Christ writhed *in extremis*.

The candles burned down; the chapel became dark. Hannes slept deeply in his little cell. At daybreak, he breakfasted with the men who would clear the chapel of its images. When be returned to the chapel, Hannes saw the linden-wood Virgin was gone. He was certain the Prior had taken her to safety at Einsiedeln or Luzern, and Hannes was glad.

# chapter 14

## Hannes and the New Faith, 1526

The following Sunday morning, the chapel sanctuary was bare. The light coming through the windows was the only decoration on the white walls. Of the Seven Sacraments, only two remained; baptism and the Lord's Supper, no longer Mass, was but a symbolic sharing of the last meal Christ shared with his apostles. It was over this that Luther and Zwingli had parted ways absolutely.

\*\*\*

In the early days of the new faith, everyone was required to attend services before beginning work each day. For Heinrich, this meant that the mill lost a full two hours every day. The men lost wages, and the amount of flour ground was reduced because the harvest was delayed. Those working in the fields started later every morning, so grain rotted in the field. The mill was pressed to meet the "tithe" of flour it still must pay the city of Zürich. There was less bread for the country towns and villages. Their share was sacrificed to fill the granaries of the city. It was difficult for Heinrich to maintain his resolution to "keep his head down." He saw that it would not "blow over" without more suffering.

"Hannes, do something," Heinrich said, finally, explaining the situation to his brother. "Zwingli is your friend, right?"

"Not friend. Teacher, I think. I could talk to Brother Leo."

"Talk to someone. This has to be the same everywhere, not just here, not just our village, not just our mill. What about the abbey? How did you manage the apple harvest?"

Hannes nodded. "We lost too many. We worked as hard and fast as we could, but a hard frost followed by a hard wind, well..."

"Yes. And if you'd been able to put all your labor and time into getting in the apples, would you have made it? You know, following the old way?"

"Probably."

"We lost almost all of our apples. There was no one to hire! With everything going more slowly than it should, no hands were free. We won't make much cider this year, and that will be a hardship for us and the men at the mill who depend on it. Never mind ale. Have you made ale this year?"

"Little," admitted Hannes. "Everyone's angry. And our services? You are there. You know."

"More like a street fair than worship, if you want to know what I think."

"I know. I cannot make myself heard above the din. Pastors from every rural parish have this problem."

"Zürich could end up with a rebellion."

"I think the same."

Finally, Hannes and other country pastors met in Zürich to make the case that the laws regarding church attendance were setting up the canton for a future famine.

"But it is the bodies of Zürich citizens that will suffer in spring because the harvest was not brought in. And why? Everyone is at church instead of in the fields!" claimed Pastor Peter from Wallisellen. "How will you keep them in the sanctuary then? With soldiers?"

"Hungry people are as likely to curse God as they are to pray," said a pastor from Wetzikon in a soft voice.

"Yes! While Zwingli disputes doctrine with Luther, your laws drive believers away. Maybe the Re-baptizers are right to say that you are not interested in God, but interested in power."

"Brother Werner! Tread lightly there! We are not here to argue doctrine with Brother Leo," said Hannes to the man standing beside him.

"You're right, Brother Hannes. We are here only to say that shopkeeper rules don't apply to growing food. Our clock is the sun, the beasts and the crops, not the clock on the tower of St. Peter's." Brother Heinj from Thalwil spoke clearly, his voice carrying the same authority as his reasoning.

Zürich ignored their pleas. Finally, many country pastors, including Hannes, simply and quietly reduced the number of required services to three each week instead of two every day. One was held mid-week after the day's toil and two on Sunday. Still, services remained raucous social events rather than moments of Christian fellowship.

Every service followed the plan Leo Jud had developed, centered on a sermon. Few pastors spoke dynamically enough to capture and hold the attention of a crowd of people who did not want to be there. Many sincere men stood helplessly in their pulpits, above sanctuaries that were no longer visibly a world apart from the other village buildings, while their congregations joked, spit, fought, gossiped, displayed their babies and complained that the pastor didn't speak loudly enough to be heard. They were silent only when the list of the newly dead was read out.

# Chapter 15

**Vreni, 1526**

Through all the changes in the world around them, Vreni served Conrad and Christina. She sometimes wondered what her future would be now that her grandfather was gone. She was sure Christina would find a husband for her, and she hoped it would be someone nearby. There were young men of marriageable age on Conrad's property, and Vreni expected any day for a roughshod boy in wooden soled shoes, a boy she'd known all her life, to arrive hat in hand to propose marriage with a beaming Conrad standing behind him. She would accept. There was nothing else to do and no better road that she could see. But a year went by and they were all well into another and still no embarrassed boy came to pay suit. Conrad never said, "Otto here is a good lad.

Christina and I will do the best by you two, Vreni. You can be sure." Conrad was waiting to see how Hannes would manage.

Vreni certainly saw him as "Brother Hannes," a function not a man. She saw him often and heard of him more, but since his return from Zürich, they had not exchanged ten words.

"The priests, called pastors, of the new church are allowed to marry, Vreni. Did you know that?" asked Conrad one afternoon, finding her stringing beans outside the kitchen door. He was finally prepared to keep his word to his brother. He had waited until the change was done and Hannes truly free of his old vows and living in the rule of new ones. "What do you think of that?"

"I suppose it was strange for them not to have families like other folk. I thought it was all right for them because they serve God and should not worry about the things the rest of us must."

Conrad was struck by the girl's naiveté, her sweet honesty. Hannes had chosen the right woman. He was every bit as naive and sweet as Vreni. "Do you know Hannes?" Conrad was suddenly nervous.

"You're joking with me, Sir. Of course I know Brother Hannes—Pastor Hannes."

"Yes. Well. Do you like him?"

"Who could not like him? He's always kind. He was good to my grandfather and to me. He sometimes talks to me when he comes up to the castle. No matter what work I'm doing, he helps, as he helped bring in the plums for jam. Everyone around likes him." She looked at Conrad, who had blushed red. "Sir, are you well? Your face is flushed."

"Oh, Vreni, when I said I'd talk to you, I thought it would be easy. It isn't easy."

"If you have something to tell me, Sir, just say it. It's the easiest and best way. Grandfather always said so and he was right."

"All right then, Vreni. Hannes loves you and wants you to be his wife. He wanted me to ask if you could love him, too."

"*Me?*"

"Yes, Vreni. You. Could you be a priest's—or rather—a pastor's, wife? Could you love my brother? Could you work beside him and have a family with him?" Suddenly Hannes was very precious, and Conrad did not want anyone to hurt him.

Now it was Vreni's turn to blush. "Sir, I'm a common girl, a servant. *You* know! How could I marry the son of a noble family?"

"How noble are we? We may have once been knights to build a castle such as this once was, but now? My father runs a mill. My other brother helps him. Noble? Not really, although I suppose these days we are better off than most. We have a name in this valley and in the canton and in the city, I know, but my father built that, Vreni. We are not rich and we are not noble."

"He could marry any girl, a rich girl, one from his own class."

"Hannes loves you. He has loved you for a long time."

Vreni wondered if this was why Hannes had not spoken to her as often as he once had. "I'll marry anyone you say," she said. "I am your servant."

"Ah, Vreni, I cannot arrange a marriage for you, not even with my brother. Think about it. I will not mention it to you again, but if you find you can love my brother, I'm sure you can find some quiet way to tell him that he will understand."

Vreni stood at the doorway, silent in her surprise, and Conrad went down the hill to the stables. If Old Johann could do anything other than explode in anger or shed sentimental tears, his sons would turn to him. As it was, they turned to Conrad, who was level-headed and had a sense of humor.

"Maybe it's because my brothers need a father that God saw to it that Christina and I have had no children. What do you think?" Conrad asked the little roan mare as he led her out to pasture.

\*\*\*

Once the changes were accomplished at the monastery, Hannes felt he could not delay his future any longer. He had to grab the moment or the moment would pass and Vreni would be lost. He set off one mid-morning, silently acknowledging the presence of the statues along the way. "I know you are there," he said. "I will keep our secret."

"Hannes! God be with you! Would you like some cider and cake?" asked Christina, finding Hannes at her door.

"No, nothing now, Christina. I've come to see Vreni." Hannes' face flushed.

"It took you long enough, Hannes," Christina said, trying not to smile.

"Too long? Has Vreni..."

"No, Hannes, no. It's just that Conrad told me nearly two years ago..."

"He was not supposed to say... Never mind. It's best you know." Hannes sighed. The day he marched off to Zürich to abandon his religion was easy compared to this.

"Go outside, Hannes, by the apple tree near the wall. I'll send Vreni."

When Christina told Vreni that Hannes was waiting to talk to her, Vreni knew everything. She wiped her hands on her apron. "Change into this one, Vreni. It's clean," said Christina taking off her own apron and handing it to the blushing girl. Vreni tied it around her waist and smoothed her hair. "Vreni, wait. Will you? We don't want Hannes to..."

"It's all right, Mistress," Vreni said, blushing, and going out the back door.

# chapter 16

## Andreas, January 1527

The long disputations had turned to exile, exile to incarceration. The incarceration had turned not to liberty, but to a street riot. Felix Manz had been taken from his cell in the Hexenturm, a prison in one of the towers on Zürich's wall, to meet Zwingli, Jud and the magistrates one more time.

"Will you now forsake your foolishness and obey the law?" asked Zwingli.

"Whose law? The law of the City of Zürich? Or God's law?" Manz asked. "When man's law conflicts with God's law, I follow God's law. I will not renounce the true Christian baptism in good conscience and confessed faith, in union with God, the rightness of which you yourself have testified, Brother Zwingli. Children who have not yet come to understand the knowledge of good and evil, and have not eaten of the tree of knowledge, they are surely saved by the suffering of Christ unless it can be proved that Christ did not suffer for children. From Scripture we have concluded that infant baptism is a senseless, blasphemous abomination contrary to all Scripture. You have not disproved that yet, Brother Zwingli. Your response has only been to imprison and exile us. That is no argument. You will not silence me by putting me to death."

Thomann whispered to Andreas, "Manz will be killed."

"I am very sorry for you, Brother Felix," said Zwingli as the guards pulled Manz forward and tied him up.

Manz was taken from the Rathaus. Crowds of Zürchers, those in support of Manz and his followers and those against him, surrounded Manz and his jailers, pressing against each other, shoving their way along the street beside the Limmat River.

Thomann saw Zwingli's men going through the crowd, seeking information. Fear could turn the faithful faithless, and so it was happening this day, this moment. Many Brethren turned informers, pointing out their brothers and sisters, hoping from this to save their own lives. The dark extreme of faith's ecstasy was dread's misery. *"What doth it booteth a man to gain his life but lose his soul?"* in this desperate moment.

"Andreas, let's get out of here," said Thomann. "This..."

"What?"

"Look around you! We will be trapped by those we thought were friends." Thomann was grateful to be on the fringes of the crowd. He grabbed his brother's arm. "Run, Andreas! RUN!"

Without thinking, Andreas ran, his feet slipping on the icy cobblestones.

"We must separate, brother. Meet me in the Ketzistürli."

Each turned into a different narrow lane, both aiming for the gate on the other side of the river, the gate that led left to The Brothers and to their home.

Away from the Grossmünster, the streets were nearly empty. Behind them, now far away, the people of Zürich stood beside the river and yelled, "Baptize him!" forcing Zürich to write history in the river with Felix Manz' life.

Andreas and Thomann reached the gate at the same time, much to Thomann's relief. "Come, brother," his breath white in the January air. "Zürich is no place to wait."

"I am not coming with you. My place is here, with the others. If I run, I have no faith. I am no better than the informers in the crowd."

"What? It is nothing like informing to get away, to save our lives, to preserve the Good News. What good are you dead or locked up in the Hexenturm? How will the truth endure if all who know it are silenced?"

"There's something in that. But how do you know you are not just saving your hide under a pretty rationale?"

"I will not even answer that, Andreas. Come. Katarina will be waiting for you, worried for you."

Andreas shook his head. "I must go back, Thomann. It is in my soul, my conscience, to join them and take whatever comes to them, to stand up for the truth."

"Andreas, you're about to be a father!"

With all his heart Andreas wanted to cry out, *"It is not my child!"* but he kept his peace. Only he knew what had happened and how that child had come to be. Katrina's single flash of spurious passion when she had returned suddenly from her father's house did not convince Andreas of anything other than her selfishness.

"I will see you later, brother," said Andreas, taking Thomann in his arms and then pushing him away to look at him. "I will see you at home." Andreas turned and ran, the nails in his hard boots scraping the icy stones. Thomann listened as his brother's footfalls were muffled by distance, then turned. Searching his heart and his conscience, he found nothing, no message from God urging him to return with Andreas. Tears streamed down his face. Snow crunched beneath his boots as he trod along The Brothers, knowing he would never see Andreas again.

*** 

Andreas ran back across the river, down the street, and pushed his way through the crowd in time to see Manz in a boat in the middle of the river. A long stick was placed between Manz' hands and legs all tied together, as farmers might carry a pig to market. Brethren stood on the shore, arms wrapped round each other, *"Yea though I walk through the valley of the shadow of death, Thou art with me..."* Even as they prayed, magistrates eyed them, waiting to gather them together and take them to the Hexenturm. Before Manz was shoved off the boat, he prayed, *"Into your hands, God, I commend my spirit!"* When Manz' head disappeared beneath the surface of the Limmat, Zwingli called to the crowd, "Who seeks baptism with Felix Manz?" A few of the Brethren in Christ stepped forward, Andreas among them.

# Chapter 17

**Kitty, March, 1527**

The little girl arrived with little commotion. The shock of Andrea's death and the strangeness of Katarina's behavior afterward gave the family no sense that the birth was a joyous occasion. She was born in the big room Katarina had shared with Andreas. Frau Beck came, delivered the infant and cared for the mother. Katarina delivered her child as if she gave birth every day, with less trauma than a heifer laboring in the spring pasture. The midwife showed Katarina the little girl, perfectly formed and very beautiful. Katarina took one look, sighed, and turned away. Two days later she asked to return to her parents' home to recover, leaving the baby behind. Thomann named the baby Katarina and immediately nicknamed her Kitty. She stayed to be nursed by a servant and raised by everyone, with Thomann standing as the father.

When Old Johann and Hannes insisted on a christening, Thomann stepped forward and said, "You disrespect this baby's father. Andreas died a martyr to his beliefs — my beliefs — that infant baptism is wrong, against God's law. When she is old enough to understand and to make that decision for herself, she can choose to be baptized as a believer and a follower of the teachings of our Lord, Jesus Christ."

The family was stunned. Thomann seldom spoke out.

"This was Andreas' wish, that we NOT christen this child?" asked Old Johann.

"He would never allow it. Never."

"But what of her soul?" asked Old Johann. "What if the tempter snatches it in the night while she is sleeping?"

"Father, that's superstition," said Hannes. "The tempter cannot snatch a baby's soul, though she should be baptized as a sign that she will be raised in the Christian faith."

"Satan cannot take a soul without the person's cooperation. We are made in God's image. We have the ability to choose right from wrong. Little Kitty will have that ability. I will teach her. I will raise her in the faith for which her father gave his life. And Hannes, it is her right to choose when she is ready, though I pray to God she chooses our Lord, Jesus Christ."

"Is it your faith, too, Thomann?" Elsa asked, softly.

"Yes."

"But you are here, and so many, we hear, are..."

"I see my faith as something to live for, not something to die for. What good is all of Andreas' faith to this little girl if there is no one here to teach her?"

Heinrich looked intently at his usually silent, good-natured younger brother. There was something here he did not expect, a depth, an intensity, a passion. "How long have you followed these Re-baptizers, brother?"

"From the beginning, Heinrich. Andreas and I followed Zwingli, but when Zwingli allied with the Zürich magistrates and not with God, we joined the Brethren. I do not speak of it. I wouldn't bring the law here, to my family or our house. As I said, I do not want to die for this. I want to live for it."

"But with Andreas?" asked Heinrich.

"Yes. Andreas and I argued this in Zürich on that awful day. He would not leave with me." Thomann's eyes filled with tears. "And I would not stay with him." Thomann missed his brother more than he could say and felt, at times, that he should have done something more to stop him so, at least, he could have seen this sweet child who was his daughter.

"Zwingli has grown very powerful," Heinrich said. "Dangerously so, I think. What good is it to break away from one power only to become subject to another? Zürich is not the same city. Sin in Zürich is now a crime against the Stadt."

"Zwingli will go too far," said Thomann, who believed Zwingli had gone too far when Manz was executed. "We do not all need to believe the same, but Zwingli seeks to control us as did the Roman church."

Heinrich nodded. "I stay out of this as well as I can. I have no strong opinions. I just want to raise my family and keep the mill running. I'll leave religion to you and Hannes." He tapped his pipe against his boot, letting the ash fall on the floor, a habit that drove his wife mad. "Sorry, my love, I forget," he said, half laughing, half contrite.

"There is no hope for you, husband. You will do that though others must clean up after you."

# Book Two

# Survival

# chapter 18

## Thomann, April 1529, the Forest

"Father, Heinrich," said Thomann, as he came out of the mill's office, "I need to go to Zürich. I know it's early, but if anything happens later this afternoon, I'll take care of it in the morning."

"Why?" asked Heinrich, even though he knew.

"I'll be back tonight. Don't worry, either of you."

"Thomann..." began Old Johann, who then threw up his hands in frustration and turned away.

Thomann left the mill. He stopped by the house and packed a meal, then walked purposefully up The Brothers to Zürich. He entered through the Rennwegturm and walked across the city as fast as he could without attracting attention by his rush. It was the first time he'd been in the city since Andreas' death more than two years earlier. Market stalls were coming down and there was a small rush to clear the lanes and streets according to the new law, which had established an early curfew, mostly to prevent the Re-baptizers from meeting in the shadows.

Thomann walked out of Zürich through New Gate, that nearest to where he had to go. The sun was setting, tinting the tops of the distant mountains with a touch of pink.

The trail over the Zürichberg was well traveled, and Thomann was able to join the small exodus of farmers on their way home after a day of hawking cheeses and produce. Reaching the burned and empty buildings of the Augustine Canons of St. Martin, Thomann turned right into the woods and, following a narrow trail, made his way across the side of the mountain.

They were meeting under a gibbous moon, risky, but as the distances many had to travel that night were long and the way unfamiliar to some, it was necessary, safer than a lantern. Thomann found the immense and ancient fallen tree that marked the turning point to the meeting place, a cave a few yards down a steep slope in a placed known as the Saw Ravine. A sawmill operated further downstream. He sat down on the tree to eat his supper, and when he had finished he made his way carefully down the hill to the cave. A narrow waterfall and a downed tree hid the cave entrance.

Thomann was soon joined by others traveling one or two at a time: a young peasant woman from Dubelstein with her baby and her father-in-law, a very old man who climbed like a goat up the hill, brothers from Fallanden, and a man and his wife who'd traveled from Zollikon with Felix Hottinger and his sister Gretchen.

When the group had gathered, and it seemed no more would arrive, Felix Hottinger spoke in a clear, but soft voice. "Brothers and sisters, the bishops and the Emperor's Regent, Ferdinand, have met in Speyer and have gone back on everything they agreed on three years ago. There is to be no freedom in the choice of religion, even for those who follow Zwingli and Luther. Luther and Zwingli have submitted a protest, and it has been signed by several nobles and the representatives of the free cities, including Strasbourg and St. Gall. This document implies that the Lutherans and the Zwinglians are prepared to take up arms to defend their churches. They have sworn oaths to this."

"We cannot do that," said Thomann.

"No," agreed Felix.

"Then what of us?" asked the young woman, holding her baby more tightly in her arms.

"We are to be hunted down and killed," said Gretchen.

Her brother nodded.

There was a sudden rush of whispers.

Felix reached into a pouch inside his jacket and pulled out several sheets on which the new mandate had been printed. "These are posted everywhere. Maybe you've seen them? When you read it," Felix continued, "you'll see that even a prince who offers us sanctuary can be killed."

Thomann took one. Yes. These were posted in Zürich. He'd seen some of them pasted onto walls and others trampled underfoot. The Zwinglians and the Lutherans were organizing protests. He and the others folded the papers as small as possible and hid them where they would not be found. There would be other meetings and the papers would be shared, read, discussed.

"There is," Brother Felix swallowed hard, "not much choice for us. Strasbourg still welcomes us, and we can go to Moravia and join Jakob Hutter. My sister and I will be going there with our father."

"So we should leave?" asked a bearded old man, leaning on his cane in the shadows.

"Leave or hide. That's how it stands now."

\*\*\*

Thomann's heart was heavy as he strode back down the mountain. Zürich's gates would be closed, but he didn't want to go the same way he had come. He turned and walked along the Zürichsee to Küsnacht. If he were lucky, no one would see him. He put his faith in God, sat down on bench near the lake. When dawn came, he took the ferry boat across. Back over the Albis, Thomann went directly to the mill.

His father looked up when he walked in, but seeing his son's sad and tired expression, he said nothing as Thomann went straight into the office and sat down in front of the books. Old Johann stood where he could see his boy and watched as Thomann dutifully entered sales and receipts into the ledger. The old man's heart was heavy. Andreas was a firebrand, but Thomann? He was a purely good and solid man.

After a while Thomann came out of the office and looked around to see if anyone were there other than his father and his brother. Finding no one, no customers or millworkers, he cleared his throat.

"Father, Heinrich, I don't know when, and when I learn I will not tell you, but at some point I will be taking Kitty away. We..."

"Thomann, why don't you just give it up?" asked Heinrich. "Day by day, how much does it matter?"

"Day by day is not what matters, Heinrich. It is what is here," Thomann put his hand over his heart, "and the Truth of God's will. That is the important thing. There is..." he pulled the tightly wrapped paper from a pocket inside his vest and began unfolding it.

"I know, Thomann. I have read it. It is posted all around. I'm surprised you had not seen it yourself."

"I did. I just didn't want it to be true. And now you, all of you, and Elsa and the children are in danger because of me. I cannot have that. I cannot stay, but I do not know how or when we will be able to go." Thomann looked around the shop again.

"If you must go, that is one thing," said Old Johann, "but Kitty?"

"She is Andreas' daughter. Our beliefs were Andreas' whole world. I..." he stopped.

"Christina and Conrad have no children. They would be very happy to raise Kitty. She is the daughter of Christina's sister, after all. Andreas was Conrad's brother as well as yours," said Heinrich.

"Father, Heinrich. If I left her to grow up with no knowledge of our faith, I would not just betray Andreas, but I would betray Kitty. She has a soul. Andreas would want her to grow up with others who have experienced what he experienced." Thomann took a deep breath. He knew what he was about to say might make no sense to his brother and father; certainly they would not see its importance. "Andreas would want Kitty to be baptized as a sign the Holy Spirit has entered her heart and she has consciously accepted Jesus as her savior."

"Oh Thomann, it cannot be such a serious matter whether Kitty is baptized now or later. Surely God understands the situation here," said Heinrich.

"Kitty's understanding of God is what matters."

"She's a child!" Old Johann shouted. "See to her safety! Go if you have to, but leave her here with Christina and Conrad."

"I'm talking about her safety, Father," answered Thomann quietly.

# chapter 19

## The Wide World, January, 1530

A dozen men, women and children shivered, huddled against a wall, sheltering from the winter wind. Snow fell in fits and starts, swirling in the corners. A closed, wooden doorway led to steps that met the Rhine. They waited for a knock that would tell them a boat had come to take them to safety. Thomann held Kitty against him, wrapped in his cloak. He pulled the blue cap Aunt Vreni had knit for her down over her ears.

"There, Kitty. Stay warm. Keep your arms around my neck."

Thomann really spoke to himself. The little girl was asleep on his strong shoulder without a care or fear in the world.

Thomann's eyes were full of tears and, holding Kitty close to him, he could not wipe them off easily. They ran down his nose and beard, making small salty icicles.

"Don't be sad, Brother," said a young woman standing nearby, holding her two children by the hand. "We will be all right."

Thomann nodded.

"It's in God's hands. We can only follow His will. It seems His will is for us to go to Strasbourg. We will be safe, anyway."

"Yes. I pray so."

"So do we all," sighed the woman. "My husband was killed at Schleitheim."

"I'm sorry, Sister. I'm very sorry."

"Thank you. God's will be done. I suppose everyone here has lost a loved one."

The problem with the faith, for Thomann, was acceptance of, even the yearning for, martyrdom. He knew he would never understand Andreas' choice. Had he run, he could still be alive, waiting on this dock with Thomann and Kitty. Maybe, Katarina, too. Maybe they would have been a family together.

"We can only have faith. There's nothing else. We can start new lives in a new place where we won't bother anyone," said an old man who'd heard the conversation.

"I hope you are right, Brother."

Thomann noticed the narrow red line of morning between the flat gray river and the flat gray sky.

He kissed the little girl's cheek. "Kitty, the sun is coming up. It won't be long now." She awakened and reached for his beard. How precious she was to him, this daughter of his brother, this unique soul. She was his whole world. "See how morning drives away the darkness?" He turned so she could see the dawn. As the little girl looked to the east, at the first glint of sunrise, Thomann leaned close to her and spoke in a soft voice, *"Bless The Lord, O my soul, O Lord my God, Who coverest Thyself with light as with a garment; who stretchest out the heavens like a curtain, who layeth the beams of his chambers in the water; who maketh the clouds his chariot, who walketh upon the wings of the wind."*

***

The refugees' first sight of Strasbourg, City of Hope, was the Heaven-reaching spire of the cathedral. The pole-men steered the boat to shore, where it was pulled up to the dock by two men with hooks. Once they'd tied up the craft, they laid a wide plank from shore to boat. The tired passengers had already collected their belongings, eager to be on land again. It had been many long and frightening days. First their flight from Conrad's house and a night spent in the forest, alone. Then their solitary journey to Schaffhausen where they met with others in darkness, waiting for a boat to carry them down the river to sanctuary offered them by the city. Any one of these moments could have been their last.

Walking across the narrow slip of the Rhine beneath the plank, Thomann held Kitty's hand.

"Thomann?" A man dressed in black tapped Thomann on the shoulder. "I'm Jakob. Come along with me. We have room in our home for you and your daughter. What's your name, little one?" he asked, turning to Kitty.

"Katarina, sir, but everyone calls me Kitty."

"All right, Kitty. So shall I. You will be with my children, Anna and Elsie. For you, Thomann, we've placed a bed at the end of a passageway and strung up a curtain so you have a little privacy."

"Thank you," said Thomann.

Kitty held Thomann's hand tightly. She'd never been in a city, not even in Zürich. Thomann's life had been primarily lived in his village and the open country between his house and the mill, the forest through which threaded The Brothers. Strasbourg seemed dark and damp, dirty, foul smelling and tired.

"Your brother," said Jakob, "was brave to join Brother Felix in a martyr's death."

Thomann nodded.

Jakob led them through a labyrinth of narrow lanes behind the cathedral to a three-story house with a window hanging over the street. "Here we are. Behind that window." Jakob pointed up one floor. He pushed open a heavy wooden door that led to a narrow flight of stairs. An old woman, caretaker of the building, came out of the doorway just to the right of the stairs. "God bless you, Frau Winkle."

"And you, Jakob! These are...?"

"Thomann and his little girl, Kitty."

Shy, Kitty kept her hand in Thomann's and snuggled close to him.

"Come in, come in. Would you like a cake, Kitty?" The little girl nodded. She was very hungry. It had been a long while since they had eaten.

Caught in the unexpected hospitality of his friendly neighbor, Jakob led Thomann and Kitty into Frau Winkle's one-room home. It was plain and tidy, with a hearth running the width of one wall. Her bed was behind a curtain in a wooden cubby. "I haven't much room, but it's enough for us all to have a bit of cake." She busied herself at a cupboard for a few moments and returned with a tray on which were a plate of ginger cakes and cups of cider. "Welcome to Strasbourg," she said. "You will find peace here."

Thomann's eyes filled with tears. If Strasbourg would give them peace, he would embrace it with all the gratitude in his soul for Kitty's sake first, and then his own.

# chapter 20

## Old Johann, Winter, 1530

It was an unseasonably warm day in late January. Old Johann sat in the sun by the south-facing courtyard wall, smoking his long pipe and thinking. All his years, where had they gone? His sons ran the business and his grandchildren were no longer babies.

"A pity only Heinrich and Elsa have children," he thought. "Maybe Hannes?" Old Johann shook his head. He had been shocked when his priestly son gave in so easily to the new religion, but when he saw Vreni's sweet beauty, he remembered his own Verena and how he had loved her.

"They say it was her father's wealth I married, but it was never that. Never. Old Hedinger? He knew how we loved each other." It was true. Seeing how his daughter's heart was set on the well-born and impoverished hired man whose father had come to Thalwil from Affoltern during the Zürich War that had expelled the Habsburgs from the Canton, Old Hedinger sat down with Johann and arranged a life for Verena.

"Come, young man," Hedinger had said. "You love my daughter?"

Johann blushed. He was barely sixteen. "I love her, sir."

"Where do you expect her to live? In those drafty castle ruins or the crumbling farmhouse?"

Johann blushed again. Old Hedinger went on. "Your family. A good family come down in the world as others. Wars," Hedinger sighed, "cost money. You're a hard worker and my Verena loves you. So, what do I do?"

Johann looked at his feet.

"Verena is my only child. She is not beautiful or intelligent, but she is good, through and through."

Johann blushed. "I find her beautiful. She is..."

Hedinger knocked the ash from his pipe, refilled it and lit it from a long twig he'd stuck into the fire. "I know you love her, Johann, or you would not be here, nervous as a goat on a glacier. More than anything, I want her to be happy, so here's what I will do. You can marry my daughter, and I will consider you my son. I will settle my mill on you and Verena at my death. In the meantime? You both will live here and you will learn to run the mill. Her dowry will remain in her possession and her control. You might wonder why."

"No, sir. It is so no one will ever say I married Verena for her dowry."

Hedinger nodded. "It would go badly for you both if that kind of talk were about, and it would be about."

They married and lived in Thalwil. Johann learned to be a miller and Hedinger's mill thrived. The couple had a son. The old man's double joy at the birth of Heinrich and the success of the mill led him to suggest to Johann that they buy the old mill in Affoltern am Albis. "If it makes a good profit, you can fix up the old house, my boy. Then, when I am gone, if you wish, you can move your family back to the home of the Schneebelis."

"So we came home," thought Old Johann to himself, "my Verena and I. We did all right, I think. My boys, none of them, are in service to anyone."

***

But it was not spring. February came bitter cold. Old Johann fell very ill, and his lungs filled with fluid.

"Get Hannes!" he rasped at Heinrich. "Please!" The old man was seized with a fit of coughing

"Get your uncle," Heinrich said to Little Hans. "Hurry!"

Ten-year-old Little Hans saddled Shorty, his own horse given him by his uncle Conrad for his birthday, and cantered along The Brothers to the abbey. Little Hans was a miniature version of his father. Solid, self-reliant, businesslike, trustworthy. He imitated Heinrich even to the way Heinrich sometimes stood back on his heels, his hands clasped behind his back, and looked across the valley in thought.

"Please! Get Uncle Hannes!" Little Hans told Magdalena, the old woman who answered the door. "My grandfather is very ill."

"Wait in the refectory where it's warm. Ask Old Barbeli for hot milk."

"Brother Hannes!" she called, finding him in the sanctuary. "Little Hans is here. It's your father."

"Tell him I'll be right there, Magdalena." Hannes finished what he was doing and hurried from the sanctuary to find Little Hans perched on the edge of the bench nearest the door, warming his hands around a bowl of hot milk. He was filled with the importance of his charge and afraid for his grandfather. Where bright angels once filled the refectory walls were now the words, "For I hungered, and ye gave me food; I thirsted, and ye gave me drink; I was harborless, and ye harbored me."

"Grandfather is dying. He wants you."

"Did you ride, Little Hans?"

"Yes." Little Hans gestured to the door. "I just tied Shorty there. You have to hurry, my father says."

"All right. Magdalena, do you know if there is a horse?" He looked at Little Hans, whose cheeks were still red from his ride.

"The horses are all working, clearing fallen branches from the road. Do you want me to send for one?"

"Take Shorty, Uncle. She can carry you even though she's small. Sometimes my father even rides her." In the eyes of Little Hans, Heinrich was immense. "You are not as fat as he is. I'll walk back, Uncle. You need to hurry," continued Little Hans.

"Find horse and sleigh for him, Magdalena, even if you have to take them from the work. The poor boy is cold enough already." Magdalena nodded and went to find the stableman to arrange a horse and sleigh that could be pressed into service for Hannes' nephew. "Little Hans, stay inside where it's warm. Magdalena won't be long."

Hannes' legs hung down over the horse's sides, but the larger burden made no difference to the little dun. She was just happy to be turned toward home.

\*\*\*

"Heinrich? Father?" Hannes pushed open the front door.

"In there, Hannes," said Elsa. "Come. I'll go in with you." Old Johann had been moved from his upstairs bedroom to the apartment he had shared long ago with Verena, the beautiful ground floor room with the big window and the rose garden in the courtyard, the room that had been given to Andreas on his marriage to Katarina. Heinrich was sitting beside the bed, his eyes wet from crying. Of all Old Johann's sons, Heinrich knew his father best and loved him most. He remembered growing up in Old Hedinger's house in what now seemed to have been a different family, a young Verena, young Johann and loving, affable grandfather. His brothers came along in due course, but as the first died almost immediately and Hannes came four years later, Heinrich's time as the only son was long enough to create a special bond between his father and himself. In the same way Little Hans idolized Heinrich, Heinrich had worshipped Old Johann.

"He wants the Last Rites, Hannes. Without them, he thinks he cannot be buried next to Mother," Heinrich said softly, expecting an argument from Hannes over the meaning of Last Rites.

"Brother, it is all right. I am prepared." Hannes opened the pouch he carried over his shoulder and withdrew a cross-shaped silver box. He'd hidden this away, knowing, perhaps better than the Zürich magistrates did or even Zwingli himself, that the offering of peace to the dying mattered more than any doctrinal argument. He never spoke about the old people to whom he had given these rites in the past years. It was, in his heart, a cruelty to deny them such peace in their last moments. The Last Rites would not bring them nearer or push them farther from Heaven, of that he was sure, but it would make the end less terrifying.

"Father," he said, "I am here with you. Heinrich and Elsa are here, also. Our Heavenly Father holds you in his hands. Through the love and sacrifice of our Savior, Jesus Christ, you will be with Our Lord in Heaven. Do you understand me, Father?"

"Hannes," Old Johann spoke hoarsely, his breathing labored, "Will I be together with my Verena in Heaven?"

"Yes, Father."

"I have not been a good man, Hannes. I have made many mistakes, been selfish and," he paused to catch his breath, "I have sinned. I..."

"We all sin, Father. Christ died for our sins. Because of His sacrifice, you are saved."

"I want to confess, Hannes. I want you to hear my confession. I cannot go to her without knowing I'm forgiven."

Hannes' heart shattered in the face of his father's deep doubts. No, Old Johann had not been a truly good man, but he had not been a bad man. In the new faith, it didn't matter anyway. Salvation did not come to a man through the man's deeds, but by the ineffable grace of God.

"Brother, Elsa, I think you'd best go so that Father can unburden his heart and I can give him the sacrament of confession. He will not die peacefully without it."

Elsa stood. "Come, Heinrich." She reached for her husband's hand. Tears still streamed down Heinrich's cheeks, but he left the room arm in arm with Elsa.

"Father, do you sincerely repent your sins?"

"I do." The old man's eyes were wet, as if he were looking at all the moments of his life in which he'd made wrong choices.

Hannes took out the small vial of holy oil and made the sign of the cross on his father's head. "Through this holy unction may the Lord pardon thee whatever sins or faults thou has committed. In the name of St. John the Evangelist, Mary the Mother of God and Our Lord Jesus Christ, Amen." From his box, he took out a tiny silver cross on which hung the suffering Christ and held it to his father's lips. Old Johann kissed it and sighed deeply, a burden lifted from his heart. "Thank you, Hannes." In Old Johann's room that snowy morning the intervening years and the great religious revolution had not happened.

It was not long before the abbey's sleigh arrived with Little Hans toasty warm, all wrapped in furs. Elsa went out into the spitting snow to get her boy.

"Martin! Come in and warm yourself!" called Heinrich.

"No, no, sir. I'd best not. Night will come and a storm with it. God be with your family, sir. Old Barbeli sent these along." He handed Elsa the bread and cider. "No doubt you'll have people arriving and enough on your minds," he added. "I have sent to the castle, too."

"That was very kind."

"Also, missus, the grave diggers have seen to things. They made space for him beside his good woman. Good day to you. God bless your family in its trouble."

"Thank you for everything, Martin. God bless you for your kindness," said Elsa, deeply touched by the man's thoughtfulness, remembering to do things she had, herself, forgotten and Heinrich was in no state to remember. "Safe travels back to the abbey."

Martin closed the door behind him, and the rush of snow that came in as he did so settled on the floor and melted. No one cared.

In the dark of that snowy night, Peter rode up to the house and banged on the kitchen door, hoping a servant was still up. Elsa answered the door. "Peter? Good Lord! Come in out of the storm."

"It's not so bad. Why are you still up?"

"Father is very ill, dying. He's had Hannes give him the Last Rites, though..."

"Hannes is no priest," said Peter.

"In Father's eyes Hannes is a priest. Peter, how did you hear?"

"I didn't. I've been in Zug, so close, I thought only to see you and Heinrich. I had no idea..." Peter's voice dropped off in the confusion of his feelings. He'd decided impulsively to visit, only to find his father dying and the family sitting up with him.

"Let me fix you something hot to drink," said Elsa, finding a helpful bridge across an awkward moment.

"Thank you."

"Give me your cloak."

Peter carefully removed his heavy woolen cloak so as not to shake snow all over the kitchen, revealing the robes of a Dominican priest beneath.

"Peter, when?"

"Not long, not long. It's why I was in Zug. Convocation."

Elsa stirred the sleeping coals into warmth and put some sticks of wood on the hearth fire. She hung the kettle over the flames, warming some cider. "That will surprise your brothers." The last they'd heard of their wild and elusive brother Peter was that he was a soldier in Glarus, sent by the Pope to control the growing religious uprising there.

Peter, clasping the welcome warmth of the mug of cider in one hand, grabbed a stool from the kitchen and joined his brothers in Old Johann's candlelit room, sitting down near the door. Heinrich, exhausted, snored in his chair. Hannes sat at the head of Old Johann's bed just in case his Father said something in his last moments. Conrad and Christina sat side-by-side, holding hands in the shadows. Conrad's changing expression reflected his confusion as he waited for his Father to die. Feelings came unbidden from the depths of his soul where his heart and mind mingled. He felt again his childhood disappointment when learning that his father didn't like him. "There is no law," Conrad thought, "saying fathers and sons must like each other. I own it. I do not like the old man, God forgive me. I do not like the way he used our mother; I do not like his grasping heart." Conrad could not know that his own closeness to Verena, who had adored him, had made Old

Johann jealous. Conrad was born while Old Johann was most consumed with building up the mill in Affoltern. The beautiful baby, who was easy to care for and always happy, filled Verena's lonely hours in that first year away from all she had grown up with. The old man resented what he perceived as an intrusion of this gentle and intelligent little boy between himself and his wife.

By morning, Old Johann was dead. The steady snowfall had blocked the front door, so Heinj and Little Hans climbed out the kitchen window and cleared the doorways, with a little help from the sun and its timid promise of spring. Elsa and Vreni washed Old Johann's body and wrapped it carefully in white linen. He was laid on a wide board atop his bed, in preparation for the time he would be carried to the abbey's cemetery.

# Chapter 21

**Brothers, 1530**

A crowd waited outside the house, ready to follow Old Johann on his last journey. Christina and Heinj brought out a barrel of cider with a gourd dipper and some wooden cups. "Thank you, everyone. We are almost ready," said Christina. "If you could move to one side of the door, we'll bring him out soon."

When Old Johann emerged, a plank with the linen-wrapped body carried on the shoulders of men from the Miller's Guild, the procession quickly formed itself according to traditions so old they seemed to have come from the time of Adam. Immediately behind the body were Old Johann's sons, Heinrich, Hannes, Peter and Conrad, followed by the rest of his family, Elsa and the children, Christina and Vreni, cousins he had barely known who still bore the old name of Lunkhofen and lived in Baden. There were Hedinger relatives from Thalwil and Christina's parents from Mettmenstetten though without Katarina. They were followed by more members of the miller's guild and men who had served with Old Johann on the Zürich council. As they passed the abbey chapel, Martin the bell ringer ignored the rules that had come down from Zürich forbidding the ringing of bells. Bells rang throughout the valley, sending the news to anyone who had not already heard.

"That miserable old man. Grasping at pennies even now," Peter thought. "No casket, no prayers for his soul? That his life should have come to this?" Peter did not know that the new law in Zürich forbade caskets except for victims of plague, pregnant women, and women who died in childbirth. Elaborate funerals and words spoken for the salvation of the soul of the dead were not necessary anymore. There was no Purgatory or Limbo, no Hel; all were saved. The corpse was the useless carapace of the soul's wandering journey on earth.

*Not so miserable*, said Peter's inner voice. *He loved your mother. He rescued the family name. He raised you and your brothers. He ran two mills and a cider press. He served his city. What more is there for a man than this? He shared with those who had less. Fully one tenth and MORE of the mill's flour went to those who had little or nothing, the local families from which you filled your army, the bodies on the hillside at Marignano, blood flowing down to the streams? You think leading those boys to death meant glory? What did they die FOR? The 'Holy Church'? What does it matter that there is no coffin? Does he know now, or care?*

Peter looked at his brothers. Hannes, presiding as pastor, had given up his beliefs because he loved Vreni who was nothing but a servant girl. She was Hannes' gentle shadow, standing now beside Christina, arm in arm. *She is a true helpmate,* thought Peter, his heart softening, thinking with a pang of the wife he seldom saw.

Heinrich was the image of the old man, though not as hard. Not as old, either. Was that it? Throughout the service, he stood with his arm around Heinj, his oldest boy. His two little ones, Gretchen and Bernhardt, clung to his coat, sucking their thumbs. Little Hans stood beside him, trying to look grownup, standing just like Heinrich, but his face was blotchy and red from crying. No, Johann had never been such a father.

Conrad's face betrayed nothing, but Peter knew how much his brother had disliked their father. *Who knows?* thought Peter, wondering. *Whatever he feels, he did his duty by the old man. Have I?*

After Johann's body was lain in the earth, the brothers stood together with their families beside Johann's grave and recited, "*Bless The Lord, O my soul, O Lord my God, Who coverest Thyself with light as with a garment; who stretchest out the heavens like a curtain, who layeth the beams of his chambers in the water; who maketh the clouds his chariot, who walketh upon the wings of the wind.*"

*** 

The night before the funeral, sitting with the family around Old Johann's body, Peter's mind had wandered through the dark alleys and damp channels he avoided in his life of action. He knew that Andreas and Katarina had a daughter. He knew, also, that when the baby was born, and its care secure, Katarina had left the baby behind and returned to her father's house.

Peter was sure the little girl was his child. Katarina had been a virgin. Some months into their marriage, and Andreas had not consummated their relationship. Had Andreas learned of that afternoon?

Had Katarina told him? Had Andreas sent her away? The questions spun round in Peter's mind, returning always to the same place. How could he have done that to his brother?

Peter had been shocked by Andreas' death. The events surrounding it had made no sense to him until he found himself no longer fighting on some Lombard battlefield, but entrenched in the religious disputes in the canton of Glarus where the Pope had sent him. After the funeral, Peter sat down at the table with Heinrich, determined to learn what he could about his younger brother, his life and family.

"Andreas remained a follower of the true faith?" Peter had asked Heinrich.

"No, Peter. He was a Re-baptizer."

"Ah," Peter thought, "the other road to execution in Zürich."

"Where is his daughter?" he asked.

Heinrich looked hard at Peter the priest. "With Thomann," he said matter-of-factly in spite of the intricate catastrophe all around him. In a strange way, it was good not to think of his father, to think of Andreas instead, to revisit a distant, old sorrow.

"Do you hear from Thomann? Of the little girl?"

Heinrich shook his head.

"What of Andreas' wife?"

"Kat-a-RI-na," said Heinrich, drawing out the word. "She went back to her father as soon as she knew Kitty, the baby, would be cared for." Heinrich shook his head. "Married now. Again."

Peter nodded. "Do you hear from her?"

"No. She no longer even visits her sister." Heinrich changed the subject. "How is Glarus, Peter?"

"Troubled. The Holy Father is making a stand against Zwingli's supporters."

"You mean that bastard Italian and his Habsburg allies," Heinrich said calmly. He had little interest, really, as long as the business of the mill was not interrupted and his own sons were not carried away. But this is what it was. There was nothing holy about the Pope and the Habsburgs. They had their own problems to keep the Turks away from the Empire even at the cost of the lives of boys bought from the Swiss Cantons. Heinrich was sure Peter was somehow involved in that trade, for all his priest's robes.

Peter sighed. "That's one way to see it."

"It's the common view here," Heinrich said. "A terrible situation. Dangerous and not good for business."

"So, Peter, after all you are a solder, though dressed as a priest," said Hannes, who'd vowed to keep his peace and now failed.

"Not unlike your Zwingli, brother. When Zwingli was head priest in Glarus, our Holy Father in Rome took care of him well enough. Zwingli kept his bargain, too, recruiting a good army and leading it, though now he sings a different song."

"I do not want my sons sold off in such a way," said Heinrich.

"Zwingli will build his own army soon enough, if he hasn't already. You realize that, don't you Heinrich? What will you do with Heinj, maybe even Little Hans? You'll be all right, though. Zwingli will just take your money. But what of the tenants on your land or the land of the abbey? More mouths than they can feed, a bad crop year, and where are they? They have one salable commodity; their sons. I recruit the son. He's eager to join! He is fed, trained, clothed, housed, paid and, yes, he may be killed, but he is a hero and he knows it. When he returns, he has a stature in the community."

"What stature, Peter? They go wild! They grab any girl they want. They steal. They ride their horses over seeded cropland." As a member of the Zürich council, Heinrich had dealt with many grievances over the behavior of soldiers on leave, between wars or simply unemployed.

"It's not the poor families who benefit, Peter. It's the nobles," Hannes interjected. "The nobles still eat, even if the peasants starve."

Elsa and Vreni came in with a small supper. Though the family felt that the crowd who'd followed Old Johann deserved to be fed, Zürich had forbidden large parties after funerals, or mourning of any kind. After all, was not the deceased on the right hand of the Lord, no longer tangled in the web of sin and temptation that was human life on Earth? Should not even the family be happy? "We'll find a way to make it up later," Heinrich had said to Elsa. "Maybe midsummer. My father loved midsummer. We can count on better weather, too." Still, it seemed a poor party with only the family gathered round the table and no good conversation.

"I don't deny what you both say is true," agreed Peter. "But, Hannes, that's one more reason our Habsburg cousins have resisted this change. Heinrich is right. They need fighting men to stand against the Turks."

"Well, Zwingli would have an end to selling our boys to fight in foreign places for strangers," said Hannes.

"It creates an army for Zwingli, is all," said Peter. "They will come out and fight, mark my words, and Zwingli, for all his talk, will lead them. They will fight as they do in Glarus, destroying holy objects, committing sacrilege."

"I don't think you care about sacrilege," said Hannes softly. Vreni reached for Hannes' hand, reminding him gently of the family rule; no argument about religion would come through their courtyard gate, let alone in the house.

"I have taken a vow to defend the true faith, Hannes, as did you, if you remember."

"So I did, Peter. The question now? Just what is that?"

"Was your concern faith, Hannes, or love?" asked Peter.

Vreni blushed.

"There is no place for this here, Peter," interjected Conrad, seeing Vreni's embarrassment. "On this day of father's burial we ought at least to respect his rule. One brother is dead. I don't doubt more of us, or Heinrich's sons, will die in this power struggle hiding under the name of God. Christina calls it a plague, and she's right. What family has escaped? Well, never mind. It's Heinrich's house now." Conrad stood to leave.

"You have not eaten!" objected Elsa, who wanted the brothers to be peacefully together on this night, of all nights. And here was Peter, so seldom with them, causing strife. She had never understood him, but she had accepted him. For good or ill, he was family.

"I appreciate your kindness, Elsa. I am just in no mood tonight. I'm going home. Will you come, my love?" Christina nodded and stood.

Ice crystals glimmered in the moonlit air as Christina and Conrad rode together along The Brothers and the breath of the horses was pale fog in the cold. In the madness surrounding them, the silence of the forest and the stones of their castle home remained a haven. The battered saints, concealed in the overgrowth, still guarded the pathway, sweet sentries from the past. Saladin and Prince nickered as they approached home, and, in that sound, Conrad's world was righted.

\*\*\*

Hannes slept badly. He had judged his brother and allowed himself to fall into anger in his father's house over the question of faith.

"Vreni, I must go talk to Peter before he returns to Glarus," he said before they even left their room the next morning. "Where's my cloak?"

"Eat first, Hannes. It's cold, and I'm sure you will not ride." Vreni knew her husband would want the time to think.

"Breakfast?" asked Old Barbeli, seeing Vreni and Hannes come into the kitchen. "The porridge isn't ready."

"Just bread and butter. I'm going out right away."

"Sit down, sit down. I'll bring it. Sister?" she said, turning to Vreni.

"I'll wait and eat with all of you," said Vreni.

Hannes watched the hunched old woman hurry to the kitchen. "Barbeli. Little Barbara," said Hannes to Vreni. "Perhaps my father knew her then."

"It was a long time ago," Vreni answered, smiling.

Old Barbeli returned with a plate of bread, butter and a piece of cheese. She set a heavy, white earthenware mug in front of him filled with steaming milk. "That will hold you."

Vreni wrapped Hannes' black woolen cloak around his shoulders. The love she'd felt first for him was gratitude mixed with wonderment at his love for her, but in the few years of their marriage she had grown to love him for himself. "Are you sure you will not ride?"

"No. No. The sun is out. The snow is melting. It might be messy, but a walk will do me good. I'll be home before dinner. Any messages for Elsa?"

"Thank her again for supper last night and her patience with all of us. All of those children and your quarrelsome brothers! Oh, here, take this to Elsa." Vreni handed him a corked gourd containing cloves. "She will need these for the applesauce."

Hannes slipped the little gourd into his pocket and pulled out the mittens his wife had knit him for Christmas. Whenever he slid his hands into them, he felt Vreni's gentle love.

"Goodbye, my sweet girl," he said, kissing her tenderly.

*** 

"We keep peace in this house, Peter. In this I agree with Father, God save him," Heinrich said. "We've lost one brother to this 'religion plague' already. We must care for the family and the business, whatever the times."

In Heinrich's wise counsel, Peter heard a businessman speaking. "You're right, brother."

"You were not here when Andreas and Thomann came back home in the early hours as intoxicated as two drunks. 'Filled with the spirit' they called it. Andreas preached to the household every morning after the psalm. He would have converted us all! Father told him to hurry up because work was waiting. Meanwhile, our poor mother worried for his soul. As for me? Father and I told Andreas to keep his peace at the mill, not that he was there often. Thomann had better sense and kept his beliefs to himself, but Andreas was ruthless. Hannes forbade little Rudolf from lying beside Mother in consecrated ground. That broke Father's heart."

"Why?"

"Andreas was the only one home when Rudolf was born and, because of his beliefs, Andreas did not baptize him."

"Good Lord," replied Peter, crossing himself.

"Many are the prayers sent up in the meantime, I'll tell you, to bring our small brother together with our angel mother," said Heinrich. "Though the new faith insists that there is no Limbo."

"It is all too much for me," admitted Peter.

"Then Hannes converted, and Andreas was drowned. Father made his rule."

"God rest his soul." Peter crossed himself.

"You need to make peace with Hannes, Peter."

Peter nodded. "I will go to the abbey. I was wrong to say what I did to Hannes. The fact is, I don't blame him at all for marrying Vreni, for leaving the church. It was an honorable decision. In any case, who am I to judge anyone?"

"Peter, you surprise me."

"Why? I know what I do. I understand soldiering. It brought me out of the barley fields. It made me rich, but no man wants to look at headless corpses or bodies with their guts spilling onto the ground. Your Zwingli lost his stomach for it quickly at Marignano."

Heinrich nodded. "You'd best go find Hannes before he starts on his daily rounds to the sick and poor."

"You're right. I'm off." Peter pulled his monk's cloak around his shoulders and lifted the cowl over his fur hat to keep the wind from his neck.

\*\*\*

The brothers met at the T-crossing — Hannes about to turn onto the Brothers Path, right, Peter about to turn left. The hut that had sheltered the battered Virgin remained, but the Madonna? Where was she?

"Brother," each said at once, reaching out his hand.

"Come back to the abbey with me? Vreni will fix you a hot drink."

"All right, brother. I imagine I'm safer walking with you in this hostile place anyway." Peter was joking. He felt no danger anywhere. The cross hanging from his belt was but a different sword.

"We always hope all that is behind us, then it comes back. Three were killed last week, a father and his son and daughter, all from Zollikon. Re-baptizers. The father and son burned, the daughter drowned."

"Where?"

"Zollikon. We keep thinking they have all left, fled to a friendlier place, Strasbourg or to Moravia, but the movement only grows, especially with the peasants, and the Zürich leaders become more angry."

"So even the powerful Zwingli has enemies?"

"Enemies?" Hannes shook his head. "Hardly enemies. They are pacifists; they don't fight back. It is that they challenge the authority of the Zürich government. The enemy is the Roman church..." Hannes stopped. "Tell me honestly, Peter, now that you're a priest yourself. What do you think of all these arguments about faith that end in bloodshed? Does it make sense to you? It does not make sense to the Re-baptizers."

"For this they are called radicals, brother." Peter laughed inwardly at his gentle brother's contradictions.

As they neared the abbey, Hannes reached for Peter's arm to hold him back. "Peter, please forgive me for accusing you last night. It was wrong, wrong in principle, not just wrong in that place."

"Forgive me, too, Hannes. I..." Peter didn't finish. The two brothers embraced, and all bad feeling fell away. They entered the abbey arm in arm, pastor and priest.

"Vreni, I've found Peter coming to us!"

Vreni curtsied to the tall priest.

"No need for that, little sister." Peter reached for her and lifted her. "We are family."

Vreni blushed and curtsied again quickly and hurried to the kitchen.

"Sit down, sit down." He motioned to a bench at one end of a long table. At the other end, old women worked knitting socks, hats, mittens and scarves they would sell in the market or give to the poor. One woman read aloud from scripture as they worked, all trying not to stare at the priest sitting with Hannes.

"Sit down with us, Vreni?" asked Peter when Vreni returned with hot cider and gingerbread.

"They need me in the kitchen. There is dinner to prepare for all these people." She looked around the room. "And baskets for the shut-ins."

"My life has not changed much," said Hannes. "I miss the old prior, but the poor are now inside where once we lived with our ritual, routine and vows. Living here, these poor old folks are safe, and the things they make are part of our evangelical work."

Peter laughed loudly. "You convert souls by making them knit mittens, Hannes?" The women stopped working; the reader stopped reading. "Forgive me, forgive me," Peter called out. "My brother has said something funny." The Evangelicals' driven, earnest seriousness amused Peter.

"Don't mock them, Peter. They have put their hearts and their faith into this."

"So it will bring them closer to Heaven."

Hannes shook his head. "No, we believe man is saved by grace, not by doing good deeds. These poor people do not need to buy their way into Heaven. Salvation is Christ's gift to us."

Peter shook his head. "That's not what led you here. You wanted to marry Vreni."

"Yes, I did want to marry Vreni. It was a big problem of conscience for me because I did not want to leave my work. I did not want Vreni to be my concubine, though, well . . ." Hannes stopped. He did not want to embarrass Peter, who was married long before he became a priest. "I did not want to live without her. I could not lie to the Church. It had given me a life, a good life, one I believed in. From there, I... I talked with the Prior and then went to Zürich. I met Leo Jud that day. I came back, well, I thought to come back. I went to Conrad."

"Conrad? That seems odd..."

"Vreni was a servant in his house, you know that, Peter. But maybe you do not know Conrad very well. He has his own kind of wisdom. He said something to me that helped me think. He said that we use our vows to control fate, but fate may have different plans for us. Mother and Father sent me here. Good, it suited me. No one could know that God had placed Vreni in the pathway of my destiny. When I encountered her, it was with a conscience developed here, with the lessons taught by the good Prior who raised me. The Re-baptizers refuse to make vows, swear oaths of any kind. They believe the future is in God's hands, not man's. I see the wisdom in that; it is — more or less — what Conrad said."

Peter thought of all the oaths he'd sworn in his life. How seriously had he taken them? They were but necessary words to accomplish what lay in front of him to accomplish, the gateway to deeds. Peter nodded. "What did you do with that advice, Hannes?"

"I couldn't immediately come back to the abbey. I went back to Zürich and attended the Prophezei, the school led by Zwingli and Pastor Leo. It was the first time I heard discussion, real discussion, about the Bible."

"It seems that it's all a lot disagreement over matters no one understands. What do you think? Do you believe that the bread becomes our Lord's body, Hannes?"

"Between us, brother, it was nothing for me to be persuaded that bread it begins and bread it remains. That was not the important question for me. I..."

"You would not kill for that belief?"

"No."

"You would not bear arms against another? Are you like the Re-baptizers?"

"I don't know, Peter. Scripture tells us, 'Put away your sword: for all they that take the sword shall perish with the sword.' I pray Zwingli remembers this." Hannes sighed. "But, I do not want to predict the future. Too much has happened that I could never have imagined. Anyway, it nearly came to that near here, just there." Hannes pointed down the hill toward the village of Kappel, a village on the border of the Catholic Canton of Zug. "I do not want to find you my enemy, Peter. Can you imagine? What if the anger is stirred up again by some Habsburg duke on the other side of the mountains who wants our sons to help him fight the Turks? You and the others, with them, the Pope's army, will come down from your mountain strongholds. And we will stand there, perhaps facing each other on a battlefield. Left alone we would not fight, but?"

"Zwingli needs to curb his ambition."

"Perhaps it is ambition. Thomann believed so. So did Andreas. But perhaps it is his belief that followers of the Roman faith and the Re-baptizers are lost in sin and damned to eternal fires. That makes it Zwingli's duty to fight to the death for the salvation of your soul."

"Do you believe that?"

Hannes shook his head. "I can only pray it does not happen."

"You may believe Zwingli would lift his sword for the good of my soul, but Zürich wants to expand its territory. That's common knowledge outside this canton."

"I cannot say what Zwingli thinks. Zürich has always..." All of Hannes' life, and before, the city of Zürich had controlled the farmlands surrounding it, often leaving the men and women who grew the grain hungry while the grain stores of Zürich were filled against famine. "Andreas and Thomann believed Zwingli had changed his mind about important things just to get the Zürich magistrates on his side because he wanted power."

"Very likely. Zwingli is no fool, and every move he's made has led to more power. It's a natural alliance, a way for the magistrates to take power and wealth from the Holy Church." Peter spoke and thought like a military man. "But, Hannes, don't *you* follow this man?"

"I hope I do not follow Zwingli. I hope I follow God." Hannes sighed. "Peter, I believe no man can stand in judgment over another in these things. Only God knows our hearts and what is in our souls."

Peter looked into his brother's eyes. Here was no charlatan monk, no pious hypocrite. Hannes acted from a faith as innocent as the smile on Vreni's face. Chills ran up Peter's arms; the small hairs on the back of his neck stood on end. "A shadow over your grave," the old people always said. "An omen of sorrow to come."

# chapter 22

## Conrad, Spring, 1530

The walk up the trail in the cold night had cleared Conrad's mind of the confusion he felt at the death of Old Johann. What a mystery his father had been to him! He was sure he had been equally a mystery to his father but doubted his father thought much about it.

"It's the end of an era, Christina. There will be no times like those in which my father lived. They are over. With each death of that generation, the times vanish further from us. I feel we're in a, in a..."

"Oh my love, such times as these have never happened in anyone's memory. Once there was one church and we all went. We all prayed in the same way, the way our fathers did, and their fathers and their fathers back and back through time. Now?"

"The church has long been corrupt. Look at Peter!"

"I know, but for us? It was a tie that held us all together. Without it? The only good I see to come from it is Hannes has married Vreni!" Christina smiled. "And they are happy."

"As are we." He wrapped his arms around his wife and held her to him. "We're living in the past, Christina. I know we are, in this old castle."

"You are wise to stay away from the arguments, Conrad. What can you do? Do you know the answers to all those questions?"

"No, I don't, Christina. I don't think Hannes knows either. Andreas believed he knew, but..."

Christina's heart filled at the thought of Andreas. Such a shining young man! Almost the equal of her Conrad! Gone, and his little girl gone now, too. Christina admitted to herself she even missed Katarina, selfish though she was. In one sad motion, her family was gone. Beloved brother-in-law, sister, niece. She could not understand how Katarina could have left behind her own daughter to be raised by anyone who would take the job. And it had been Thomann! Her heart ached for the little girl. Christina would have loved her and given Kitty a home here at the castle as her own daughter. Thomann knew this. Why?

"We hear nothing of Kitty. I no longer ever see my own sister."

Conrad looked at his wife. "Do you want to visit Katarina? We can go to  Mettmenstetten and visit your family. It would be a change for us."

Christina shook her head. "No, I don't, Conrad. But something is wrong there. I feel it in my bones. Something happened between the two of them, between Andreas and Katarina. I don't know what, but... I think my sister had something to do with Andreas' death."

"How? Was she in Zürich? Did she stand beside Zwingli and push Andreas into the river?" Conrad attempted an exaggeration, hoping Christina would take it as a ridiculous comment. He'd never told her of his talk with Andreas at the Midsummer feast that now seemed so long ago.

"No, silly, of course that isn't what happened. Andreas acted from his conscience, but something was wrong there, just the same. Why else would Katarina abandon Kitty? Do you think Andreas...?" Christina could not even form a question that made any sense. Her dark fears were beyond words.

"No. Absolutely not, Christina. And, Kitty was hardly 'abandoned.' She had — has — a whole family to care for her and love her."

"That's not the point, Conrad. What mother leaves behind her child? And, for that matter, Kitty is not here. She's God knows where with Thomann! Conrad, that..."

"You know how much Andreas' faith meant to him. It was everything. Thomann believes, rightly, I'm sure, that Andreas would want his daughter to be raised with those beliefs, too." Conrad put his arms around his wife, "I know you wanted the little girl, Christina. I'm sorry I never gave you children. I..."

"I thought that was why, Conrad. God wanted us to give a home to Kitty." Christina began to cry in her husband's arms.

"Oh, my precious love. What can I do? Should I write Thomann? I'm sure Heinrich knows how to find him. If you want me to, I'll go look for them. Anything."

A hard knot of sorrow Christina had held within so long broke open. "No, Conrad, no. I would not put them in danger — or you in danger! I am sure Thomann loves our Kitty and is a good father to her. I don't want them hurt just because of my silliness."

"Are you sure, my love? The little girl has no mother."

"I wonder. If she were nearer, would Katarina stay away from her?"

"Katarina? I do not want to speak ill of your sister, but..." Prudence silenced Conrad.

"She's selfish, Conrad. I know that. She has always been my father's pampered pet, from the moment she was born. If she felt responsibility, even normal motherly affection, for Kitty, she..."

"A child in tow would have hurt her chances for remarriage, maybe?"

"The child is there, whether with Katarina or not. She was no longer a fresh young girl. I don't think it would have made any difference. Maybe she was afraid another husband would not want to raise the child of another man."

# chapter 23

**Easter, 1530**

Spring snow, heavy with water, clumped and fell, filling the valley, muffling even the noise of the mill. The moisture eased the journey of crocuses and daffodils from their winter sleep, and when the storm ended, the people rejoiced to see the flowers. Easter was late that year and winter had been long.

The new church did not hold with Lent. Of the weeks leading to the celebration of Christ's resurrection only the Sunday before, Palm Sunday, and Good Friday were observed. How many of his parishioners fasted in the old style, Hannes did not know.

On this snowy Saturday, the sanctuary of the Abbey was cleaned from top to bottom, but there was no polishing of silver and gold vessels. The Lord's Supper was served from rough wooden plates, wine — part of the sacrament in the new religion — drunk from a simple, pewter cup.

A new white linen cloth was spread over the altar. The flax had been spun and woven by the women living in the Abbey. A line of simple crosses embroidered in the same white marched along the edges. No more ornamentation than the women would do with the cloth for the Lord's Table or their own.

"It'll do us good, this snow," said Martin, as he swept the floors clean.

"Good for the rhubarb, they say," Barbeli added. "It will stop soon, I'm thinking. We'll have a fine Easter."

The heavy door opened and a tall man wearing a black cloak entered.

"Take off your boots please, sir," said Martin. "We are cleaning the church for tomorrow. It'll be dirty enough after service, but we can start well."

"I'd be happy to," said the man. "Martin, is it?" He slid his cape and cowl from his shoulders. "I am here to help, brother."

"Peter!" said Hannes, turning to see his tall brother no longer dressed in the robes of a Dominican. Hannes set down the plates and cups and went to greet Peter. "What brings you here? Let's go where we can sit down. Barbeli, could you bring us some hot drink in the refectory? My brother has ridden all the way from Glarus, no?"

Peter nodded. "I came straight here. I will go to Heinrich later, when his day is finished at that infernal mill." Peter gave a false shudder and grinned.

"Martin, are you all right to finish in here without my help?"

The old man nodded. "We're nearly finished. Don't worry."

The two walked arm in arm down the long passage to the refectory where Barbeli had already set out a lunch for Peter. "I have had a change of heart, Hannes. I have joined Zwingli and his followers."

"Has the Pope stopped paying you?" Hannes was only half joking. The situation was so strange, so surprising.

Peter shook his head.

"What? How?"

"I've been thinking often of Andreas and Thomann. And of you. They, and you, followed your conscience, no? I thought about it all the way back to Glarus after father's funeral, the hypocrisy of..."

"Your marriage and your vows?"

"Yes, that, certainly. My wife and family are with me now. I am no longer a false priest and a false husband at once." He took a long drink of the cider. "That is good," he said, wiping his mouth on his sleeve. "Hannes, there will be war. I am sure of it. I'm...well, you know what I am. I also had to think about that. Could I fight with the Habsburgs and the Pope against my own brother, against the people in my home village? A paid fighter in a faraway land is one thing. To accept money to fight against friends, the people I grew up with? No. I cannot do that."

"What about God, Peter? Is God in any of this?"

"I cannot say. I only know that it is wrong for me to take up arms against my brothers. As for the rest? I can't begin to know if this bread," he held up the chunk he had wrapped around a piece of cheese, "is the flesh of anything or anyone. It is bread from beginning to end and I'm grateful for it and that it is so."

Peter was Peter, joining the new church so he would not have to kill his friends when, as he expected it would, a real war broke out. "Welcome, then, brother. How long will you be staying?"

"I came to hear you preach. I have to preach my own sermons, damn me. I don't know what to say."

Hannes had to smile at his brother the soldier. "Pastor Jud has put out instructions that set that out clearly. Just follow them."

"Fine, but the sermon? What have I to say about God's will and the right doctrine or any of those things? My parishioners KNOW I was a priest. Because of that, I fear, they do not listen."

"No, Peter. Most of us were once priests. Zwingli himself was, as you know. Disorder is a problem in all our churches. Our parishioners do not see the difference between a service and a meeting at the town hall. I would have," Hannes hesitated, then took a deep breath, "I would, perhaps, have waited before I stripped bare the churches, or made that change more slowly."

"Surely you still have the beautiful things I remember here as a child?"

"Oh no. All melted down and used to buy clothing and food for the poor, to set up schools, some sent to Zürich, too. Well, it is God's will in any case."

"How do you know?"

"Nothing happens without God willing it."

"I have used the 'God's will' argument myself. It puts great ugliness on God's front step." Peter shook his head. "I am no mystic, Hannes. I am not you or Andreas or Thomann. I'm a soldier. I want only to know the right thing and to do it. That has not been made easier by your Zwingli."

"We are in agreement there, Peter."

"I want to stay with you for a while, Hannes. I want you to teach me. As a priest, I simply served the abbot and made the rounds of Glarus. I tried to keep the peace. I was a soldier, Hannes. No priest, no real priest."

"Go to Zürich. Attend the Prophezei, Zwingli's school. I did that. It taught me."

"Not for me, Hannes. Long days in Zürich listening to them expound on the Bible are not for me. I want only to know how to reach the men and women who come to my church."

"How long will you stay?" Hannes asked, finding himself in sympathy with what his brother said. In truth, what was more important? His inner and outer conflicts with Pastor Zwingli all revolved around how the spiritual needs of farmers and peasants differed from the needs of men and women in the city. "I'll tell you what, Peter. You can help me with the service tomorrow. Easter Sunday, we have the Lord's Supper. Have you...?"

"Not yet. I have a general sense of it, of course. I have attended one or two."

"It's all set out in Pastor Jud's pamphlet, but if we do it together tomorrow, you'll understand better."

"How does the service go on Easter? Different from other Sundays, I imagine?"

"It is longer. The sermon is focused on the Risen Savior and his triumph over death. I'll go over it with you now, unless you want to rest. You had a long ride."

"No, no, Hannes, let's do this. Tell me how it will be tomorrow."

"Then let's go to my study where I have my materials. You can see how I work on the service and maybe some of the books and pamphlets I've collected will help you, too. Consider my study your study, Peter."

Hannes had appropriated the Prior's old study for himself, not so much because he felt he needed such an elaborate room, but out of respect for the man who'd raised him. He'd given up the Prior's beautiful relics and statues that had been part of the Abbey for centuries, but the Prior's old books remained beside Zwingli's Bible and other printed works from Zürich. Among them were all the writings of St. Bernard of Clairvaux, who had worked hard to build the Cistercian order and to reform the Church. Like Pastor Zwingli, the Prior had been an admirer of Erasmus of Rotterdam, and Erasmus' Latin Bible and *Handbook of the Christian Soldier* sat beside the works of St. Augustine.

Peter looked around the wood paneled room with its clay stove and south windows, the large desk spread with Hannes' papers. "All your books are new?"

"No, no. Only the covers. We had to turn over the silver, gold and jeweled covers to Zürich, but not the books. I removed the covers myself and had those made in town, by the saddle-maker."

"Is this the whole library?"

"This isn't St. Gallen. We are — the Order was — dedicated to prayer and serving the poor, not to scholarship, not to copying books. If we needed to copy a book, a monk or even the Prior retreated to that little closet there and worked on it until it was finished. Here we go, Peter. Here's Pastor Zwingli's Bible, and here are the rules for the Lord's Supper. Which gospel do you think we should use tomorrow?"

Hannes had already chosen the account in the book of John because it emphasized not only the miracle of the resurrection, but it clearly showed that belief in the Lord is a choice people must make if they are to experience salvation. Hannes liked the passage because it also showed the humanity of the disciples and how unbelievable it was to them to see the risen Christ.

"God forgive me, Hannes. I can't tell them apart."

"Peter, you might want to read them." Hannes smiled at his brother, but suddenly wondered, "Can you read, Peter? Mother did teach you, didn't she?"

"She did, but I take no pleasure in it. I sit down with the text and soon I'm sleeping in my chair."

Hannes knew that many of the pastors, especially in the countryside, were not learned men. The Roman church provided every secular priest with a Sacramentary for a year of services, and while the Evangelicals had set forth basic rules for conducting services, for many pastors, such as Peter, the sermon was a great difficulty.

"I've chosen for the scripture tomorrow John's account of the resurrection of our Lord. It tells about how the disciples found Christ after the stone had been moved from the tomb. The organization of every service is laid out here." Hannes handed Peter the booklet that explained how to conduct a service. "You have this, don't you? The pamphlet Pastor Jud has published? I've turned it to the page that instructs us on the Lord's Supper."

Peter took the book and looked over the pages and said, "First is the sermon. All the rest? I can do it, but the sermon?"

"Yes, even Pastor Jud has said it is the most difficult part. But every sermon is based on the scripture, and I begin with that. Tomorrow you will serve as my Deacon. You don't have to worry about the sermon. Here is the scripture I will use." He opened the big Bible to the place he'd marked for his own use on Easter Sunday. "I'm going to go back and help Martin and Old Barbeli. You look at these things and when I come back, I'll answer your questions."

\*\*\*

Hannes found everything was ready. The table had been set in the center of the front of the chapel as it was supposed to be, and the plates were set on top, ready for the morning when they would be filled with bread. There was nothing left to do. Hannes went in search of Vreni and found her in the kitchen helping make the unleavened bread for the morning.

"Vreni, Peter has come. He is in my study, preparing for tomorrow."

"Tomorrow? What is he preparing?"

"He's become a pastor, Vreni." Hannes sighed in half-amusement, half-irritation. "He's become a pastor so he will not have to kill me if this all comes to war."

"I think that is a good reason, Hannes. What kind of man would be willing to kill his brother?"

"I feel the same, but this involves faith, and it involves God."

"Does, it, Hannes? Peter is not like you. He's an active man. His life has been war. He's lived in hard places and fought against enemies he never even knew and others who were but the sons and brothers of families in the next Canton. Not to want to kill you — or Heinj, or anyone here — that speaks well of him, to me. How many pastors are pastors only to save their own lives? At least Peter wants to save yours!"

"How can he lead the flock in Glarus when he..."

"Why is he here?"

"To learn."

"That shows he knows well his faults." Vreni had always found Peter somewhat frightening. He was always so assured, so handsome and so different. He'd killed people for money and had become rich.

Vreni's grandfather said that as a boy Peter had been wild, that Old Johann could not control him and had thrown him out when he was still young. "He worked in the barley fields until he got the idea of selling himself to one of their Habsburg cousins. Then he made his fortune. I can't imagine he will live long," sighed Old Stefan, crossing himself. "But only the good Lord knows that and I wish him no ill, poor boy."

Hannes returned to the study to find Peter deep in the pamphlet. "I need this, brother," he said, looking up. "May I take it back with me to Heinrich's house to study more later?"

"You can have it, Peter. I don't know how you will manage in Glarus without it. The Prophezei might help you more."

"I'll be ready to help you tomorrow, Hannes. If I'm to do this, I will do it well. Well, I'd better be off. Heinrich will be home soon and I don't want to surprise them during supper."

"Give them greetings. I'll see all of you tomorrow!"

\*\*\*

The Easter service lasted a full two hours. Except when called upon to kneel, Hannes' flock stood, dressed in their best and glad of spring, on the stone floor of the abbey chapel. Hannes did all in his power to excite them with the story of the doubt and wonder felt by the Apostles on seeing Christ's risen form. Hannes led his congregation to the moment when they would share in the Lord's Supper. This one ritual was the most radical departure made by the Evangelical reformers. There was no miracle, no mystery.

Hannes read from Zwingli's formulary, "We now desire, dear brethren, in accordance with the custom instituted by our Lord Jesus Christ, to eat this bread and drink this cup, as He commanded should be done in commemoration, praise, and thanksgiving, because He suffered death for us and poured out His blood to wash away our sins. Therefore, as Paul suggests, let every man examine and question himself as to how sure a trust he puts in our Lord Jesus Christ. Let no one behave like a believer who has no faith, and sin against the Body of Christ which is the whole Church by showing contempt for it. Let us pray as our Lord taught us to pray."

The congregation knelt and joined in the Lord's Prayer after which Hannes prayed, directly from Leo Jud's book, "Lord, God Almighty, who by Your spirit has united us into Your one body in the unity of the faith, grant that we may live purely as is right for Your sons and Your family, that even the unbelieving may learn to recognize Your name and Your glory lest Your name and glory come into ill repute through the depravity of our lives. We always pray, 'Lord, increase our faith, that is, our trust in You, who lives and reigns God's world without end.'"

"Amen," said the congregation, standing.

"The Lord Jesus the same night in which He was betrayed to death took bread," Hannes took the bread in his hands; "and when he had given thanks, he broke it, and said, 'Take, eat: this is my body, which is broken for you; do this in remembrance of me'."

Hannes handed a plate to Peter and one to Martin who passed the bread among the people standing in the chapel who shared it with each other.

"In the same manner he took the cup." Hannes lifted one of the pewter cup and lifted it so everyone could see, "and gave thanks and said, 'Drink ye all of it. This cup is the new testament in my blood; do this as often as ye drink it, in remembrance of me'." Peter carried the cup and shared it among the people.

"Be mindful, dearly beloved brethren," read Hannes, "of what we have now done together by Christ's command. We have borne witness by this giving of thanks, which we have done in faith, that we are indeed miserable sinners who have been purified by the body and the blood of Christ, which He delivered up and poured out for us, and have been redeemed from everlasting death. We have borne witness that we are brethren. Let us, therefore, confirm this by love, faith, and mutual service. Let us, therefore, pray to the Lord that we may keep His bitter death deep in our hearts so that though we daily die for our sins we may be so sustained and increased in all virtues by the grace and bounty of His Spirit that the name of the Lord shall be sanctified in us, and our neighbor be loved and helped. The Lord have mercy upon us and bless us! The Lord cause His face to shine upon us and be gracious unto us! We give thanks unto Thee, O Lord, for all Thy gifts and benefits, who lives and reigns this world without end. Amen. Go in peace."

# chapter 24

## Thomann, 1530

Jakob found Thomann sitting on the edge of Kitty's bed, holding her small, hot hand between his own. Tears streamed down his cheeks.

"Is she better, brother?"

"She doesn't know me."

"The doctor says that half the children in Strasbourg have been stricken with this."

"Oh God! All the poor families." Thomann began to sob. He was without work, living on the charity of the community. Still, he was lucky. Kitty was lying in bed, though ill. The streets of Strasbourg were filled with brethren, families with children, who had nowhere to live. "Hope," Thomann thought, "is a complicated gift. It is much, but it is not all."

"Brother, let me sit with her a while. You are exhausted. You need to eat. How long has it been?"

"I don't know. Frau Winkle brought..." He gestured at a plate sitting on a table behind him, on which sat his uneaten breakfast.

"You will become ill, Thomann. Where will Kitty be then?"

"I know, I know, but, Jakob, God forgive me, she is my world."

"We all feel so about our children, just as our Heavenly Father cares for us. Is she very much like your wife?"

Thomann looked up in surprise, thinking to correct Jakob, then decided not to. He was the only father Kitty knew. It seemed an age ago that his father had offered him to Katarina's father as a husband for his daughter, only to be turned down for Andreas.

"It's this city," Jakob said, quietly. "It's dark, dirty, cold, crowded. You and Kitty are used to the countryside."

Thomann agreed. Strasbourg, city of hope, was packed with people. The lanes were dark. There was filth everywhere, and no way to breathe. Kitty was homesick. She missed her little bed, her cousins and her aunts. Thomann often wondered at what price he'd bought their safety. Even here, in the City of Hope, hope was not always easy to find.

***

Strasbourg's community of Re-baptizers was so large that it controlled the city, but it was not in agreement with itself. It was fractured into schisms, divided over everything from tolerance for "the weak," those who could not easily give up the Old Church, to the meaning of inner and outward faith, to the importance of following the law vs. following the spirit, to the imminence of the Last Days. Only a man called Pilgram Marpeck held to anything Thomann recognized.

Marpeck's own spiritual search had begun in his hometown of Rattenberg, near Innsbruck, where he was a mining engineer and a councilman. Because of his friendship with a convicted evangelizing Re-baptizer, he was branded a heretic. The penalty? Death.

Marpeck and his wife fled to Moravia. There he was baptized and fully joined the close community of Re-baptizers led by Jakob Hutter. After a few months, Marpeck found he could not accept the complete communalism or the rejection of society required by Hutter's philosophy. He left for Strasbourg where he soon became not only a leader in the community of brethren, but an engineer for the city.

The first Sunday after his arrival, Thomann went with Jakob to the meeting at Pilgram Marpeck's house. Thomann's heart opened as he listened to Marpeck's sermon and to Marpeck's responses to questions that came from the community afterward. His message was a simple one. Love was the first commandment and the essential one. All other things in human life needed to be measured against that, against, "Love your neighbor."

"We do not need to live separately from the life of the city of Strasbourg," said Marpeck that Sunday morning to a small collection of Re-baptizers from all over the region, from St. Gallen to Moravia to the local group of well-to-do women who had been convinced early on by Balthasar Hubmaier. "Our Lord is clear on this point throughout the scriptures. The purity and cleanliness of the saved soul is part of his covenant with us. Our teaching will shine through our lives, through our adherence to the new law given by Our Lord to his disciples at the Last Supper as we read in the Gospel of John, '*A new commandment I give unto you, That ye love one another; as I have loved you, that ye also love one another. By this shall all men know that you are my disciples, if you have love for one another.*' This is how all men will know us, not by the way we separate ourselves from them, or the way we search for martyrdom or persecution for our faith, but by the love we bear toward our fellow man thanks to the Holy Spirit working in us. In fact, in Matthew, Our Lord tells us that our faith should be a secret thing, between ourselves and God, '...when you pray, you should not do as the hypocrites do: for they love to pray standing in the synagogues and in the corners of the streets, that they may be seen by others.' When we talk to Our Heavenly Father, no one need know what we say or how. It is between us and God. What good are we," said Marpeck, "if we separate ourselves, remove ourselves and our abilities, from the world we live in?"

"But what of the rules, brother?" asked a young man who'd recently arrived from a community of the Swiss Brethren. "Cannot we tell our friends and foes by how well they follow the rules of our faith?"

"What do you mean, brother?"

"If one of us strays from the path, shouldn't that person be separated from the community? Wouldn't that protect the Godly from the ungodly?"

"God is the only judge, brother. It's clear in scripture what God wants us to do, here in Matthew, our Savior says clearly, *"Judge not...for with what judgment you judge, you shall be judged.'* Has it not happened to many of us that we judge our neighbor, then we see we have done something ourselves against Christ's teachings? Christ talks of this, too. *'And why study the fleck of dust that is in thy brother's eye, but do not consider the beam that is in your own eye?'* How often are the faults we judge in others nothing but the faults we refuse to see in ourselves?"

"But if our brothers and sisters break the commandments, shouldn't they be called to account and separated from the community as sinners?"

"Christ has said many times that we all come short of the glory of God. We are human beings. If we were perfect, our Lord's sacrifice would have no meaning. We are tasked to make something of this life, though our world is so far from Heaven and our hearts so far from goodness. This is why He gave us two new commandments so that we would have a chance of reaching Heaven. *'You shall love the Lord your God with all your heart, and with all your soul, and with all your mind. This is the first and great commandment. And the second is like unto it, you shall love your neighbor as yourself.'* Tell me, Brother, is it loving God or loving our neighbor to judge and shun our brothers and sisters because of their human failings? Our Lord says clearly, *'On these two commandments hang all the laws and the prophets'*."

The young man from St. Gallen fell silent. He now had much to think about. He was in Strasbourg having been shunned by his community. He had looked at a girl, simply looked at her, and had been criticized and shunned for "lusting after her in his heart." In shame and secret he'd made his way up the Rhine to the city that offered sanctuary. In his heart, he had felt the shunning was unfair, but the community had judged him. What could he do?

"Only by knowing God's word and the spirit of our Lord inwardly can we understand the scripture. This inner knowledge leads us to act in harmony with God's will. We will not break rules because we are impelled not compelled to obey. Through the presence of the Holy Spirit, God's will becomes our will. I will leave you with that thought, brothers and sisters. The Lord bless you and keep you; The Lord make His face shine upon you, and be gracious to you; The Lord lift up His countenance upon you, And give you peace."

In his first weeks in Strasbourg Thomann's heart had swelled and opened with all he heard, with the freedom to come and go, to worship almost without hiding.

But when Kitty became ill, Thomann's world fell away in the cold dread that he'd made a terrible mistake.

"Maybe God is testing you," Frau Winkle had said, "to know the measure of your faith."

Thomann shook his head. "God knows that." Still he had felt his faith waver watching the feverish and delirious little girl, and it frightened him.

***

"Have the spots come?" asked the doctor, taking the steps two at a time. "If the spots have come, then she is likely to recover." Reaching the small room where Kitty lay alone, Jakob's children having been sent away to avoid the illness, the doctor set down his bag and went to the little girl. He first looked at her neck and chest, hoping to see the red rash that would reveal the progress of the illness. "Good," he said. "As I hoped. It will be a few days more. You must see she drinks soup, broth, cider, whatever you can get down her. If she does not drink, her brain will inflame and she could die."

Thomann shook his head. "She doesn't know me, doctor. I cannot get her to take anything. She's..."

"How long?"

"Two..."

"The spots have come. She may come back to herself any time now, Thomann. The Good Lord holds her in his hand, keeping her from suffering. Pray. Wait. See to Kitty's comfort. There is nothing else."

"Will she...?" Thomann's voice shook and he could not finish his question.

"She may, Thomann. I will not lie to you. If she does, take heart in two things. She will be with our Heavenly Father, and she will slip into death with no pain or suffering."

"Do you think she will? Tell me the truth, doctor, so I can prepare my heart, with God's help."

"The spots are a good sign. That she is delirious is a bad sign. She stands between this world and the next. God will decide. We can only wait and see. Send for me if there is a change. I must go. There are many such children in Strasbourg today."

"Thank you, Brother."

"Pray, Thomann — and eat something."

"Thank you, Brother."

"I have told him," sighed Jakob.

"Listen to your friend." The doctor laid his hand on Thomann's shoulder. "I'll call tomorrow."

"Some of the women are coming to sit with Kitty so Thomann can rest."

"Good," said the doctor. "Let them carry your burden for a little while, or when Kitty recovers, you will be ill," said Jakob.

Thomann, comforted by the doctor's kind honesty, stood up from the stool on which he'd spent most of the last day and night. "All right, Jakob. It is in God's hands."

"Better hands than ours, Thomann. Frau Winkle has something for you to eat downstairs."

Thomann went into the hallway where a basin and towel waited. He scrubbed his face with soap made from tallow and ashes, careful not to use too much. It was expensive and must last a while. Candles were more necessary than soap, so soap was taxed to preserve the tallow for candle making. That was life in the city. Such small things made Thomann yearn for home.

He walked downstairs and poked his head into Frau Winkle's room. She was sitting by the fire knitting a scarf of soft blue yarn. "Frau Winkle?"

"Is our little girl better? The doctor has been here?"

"The spots have come out. The doctor said that is a good sign, but, he said — and he is right — Kitty is in God's hands." Thomann struggled to keep his features steady, to hold back tears rising from his heart. Was it a lack of faith that made him worry now? Or just the nature of man? He shook his head. "I'm sorry. I am very worried."

"We all are, Thomann. In this dark season she is a little bit of sunlight." She stood and set her knitting on the chair. "Come, my boy. I have a bit of supper here for you."

Winter days in Strasbourg were short and dark, darker still in the canyons formed by the three and four story buildings, with their windows and often whole floors overhanging the street. There was no green anywhere. The beautiful cathedral spires could not break apart the clouds, or drain the damp, or move the wood-smoke out of the way. Only a fresh breeze could manage that, not winter's cold wind that held everything down in its frigid weight. No amount of faith could change the effects of winter on the hearts of the people, especially those who had suffered so much, leaving everything behind them, losing husbands, wives and children to the fight over religion.

\*\*\*

The women of the community took the watch in shifts of two, each staying three hours. Thomann, in his exhaustion, was asleep as soon as he lay down on his cot. When he awoke, lost for a moment, he did not know where he was, thinking he should hurry to the mill before his father missed him. "Thomann, come," he heard in his half-waking state, followed by, "She's awake!" It was not his father calling him. It was Jakob.

Thomann sprang up and rushed into the little room where Kitty lay. Sister Emma, a plump, cheerful woman with white hair, sat beside Kitty on the bed, one wrinkled and spotted old hand on Kitty's forehead, the other holding Kitty's hand. "Her fever has broken. She is awake."

Sister Emma moved to get up but Kitty held tightly to her hand. The woman laughed, "'Tis no matter. I can stay."

"Kitty?" said Thomann.

"Father," Kitty answered. "I am so thirsty."

"Here you are, my sweet girl." He handed her the cup of cider that waited beside her bed.

"Good morning Kitty!" said Jakob, looking into the room. "Thomann! Do you want the doctor?"

"Please, Jakob. I need to know that she is really better."

"I had nine of my own," said Sister Emma. "I have seen this many times. She will get well now. It will take time for her to get her strength back, but she will be well."

"I think Sister Emma knows. I'll just ask the doctor to stop by on his rounds."

Thomann nodded.

"Father, is it morning?"

"It is, little one. It is morning."

"Father? Shouldn't we?"

"Oh, my love. God will know even if we don't speak it. He knows it's in our hearts."

"What does Kitty want?" asked the old woman.

"For many generations, I don't know how many, our family has recited a psalm before beginning the day's work. I don't know how it started."

"Bless me," she said, smiling, "I would join you on this glorious morning." She gave Kitty's hand a gentle squeeze.

"It begins, 'Bless the Lord, who coverest'..." said Kitty.

The old woman smiled. "I know it." She began and Thomann and Kitty joined her.

"*Bless The Lord, O my soul, O Lord my God, Who coverest Thyself with light as with a garment; who stretchest out the heavens like a curtain, who layeth the beams of his chambers in the water; who maketh the clouds his chariot, who walketh upon the wings of the wind."*

# chapter 25

## Thomann and Kitty, 1530

Kitty was very weak and remained in bed two weeks more. Spring was still more than a month away. Thomann resolved that the moment Kitty was well enough, they would go home. But one drizzly Sunday afternoon, after meeting, Brother Marpeck reached for his arm.

"Brother Thomann, have you a minute? I hear you were a miller before coming here. Is that so?"

"I worked in my father's mill from the time I was a boy."

"What kind of mill?"

"Flour. We had the license to mill for the Abbey and the town, tithing to Zürich of course."

"A good business, then."

"Very good. My father built it, almost from nothing. He worked in my grandfather's mill in Thalwil. That did well, so my grandfather decided to buy and expand an old mill in Affoltern. My father rebuilt the old Schneebeli home, our old family home, in the village, and when my grandfather died my father moved the family there."

"Affoltern? There is a village with that name around every bend in the road." Marpeck smiled. "Near Zürich, you said?"

"On the southeast side of the lake, over the mountain."

"Have you run a sawmill?"

Thomann shook his head. "Grain and cider. I have no experience with lumber. Why, Brother Marpeck?"

"You know how crowded the city is. Building materials are in short supply. The council has hired me to solve that problem, so I'm working up the Rhine, finding lumber and building easy ways to bring it down the river. Villages all around stand to make money from this. They are places where we could build communities. I'm looking for brethren who could work with me."

"I know nothing about sawmills, brother."

"A mill is a mill is a mill, no? Managing men, inventorying stock and keeping books could not be so different, be it apples, grain or wood. And the mechanics? Perhaps only the saw. It is still water running over a wheel, turning gears."

"You are right, Brother Marpeck. It could not be very different. Saw or millstones."

"I'm going up river to Illenkirchen next week. Come with me. It's a village on the edge of the wood and beside the Ill River that flows into the Rhine. It looks promising. The villagers suffered many losses during the recent war and now the population is mostly women, children and old people. They are trying to rebuild, but it's difficult with no leadership and little manpower. They won some victories, regained their hunting rights and their right to cut wood, but the village needs skilled and godly men and women. Many of these villages are in sympathy with us anyway."

"Work!" Thomann's heart leapt. Was this the answer to his prayer? His heart ached for home, but the bigger problem was safety from both persecution and disease. A village up the river might be the answer.

"Yes, I'll go with you to look at the mill and the village, but I don't want to say yes to something that is beyond my ability or in such poor condition that..." He hesitated. "Or to a village where I would be an unwelcome outsider."

"The sawmill itself is working, so I don't think the condition is too bad. It belongs to a man named Hans Beckerle. He lost both his boys in the uprising against the lords. He himself took a pike through his thigh and lost a leg. He's kept the mill running, but now he fears he will have to sell it. You would be helping this man keep his business, so you would certainly NOT be an unwelcome outsider."

Thomann tried to imagine a one-legged man running a mill short-handed. "He cannot do it, if, as you say, the village..."

"I've offered him a deal so he can keep his mill if he hires some of us. Brethren. He knows the risk, but he wants to keep the mill for his grandson, a little boy about the same age as Kitty. They live in a house in town, he, his daughter-in-law and his grandson. The mill-house is empty."

The risk to the miller, Hans Beckerle, was real. The mandate from the Emperor that had sent Thomann and Marpeck into exile also promised severe punishment to anyone who sheltered, or even knew about, a Re-baptizer.

The uprising in which Beckerle lost his leg had occurred five years earlier. For years, through much of northern Europe, winters had been longer and colder than usual, resulting in one poor harvest after the other. Bad harvests or no, many of the lords demanded the same amount of grain as their due, the same amounts, "tithes," of vegetables, fruits, animals, and all the other goods for which they relied on their serfs. This left the serfs hungry and with nothing to sell for their own income. On top of this, the serfs were restricted, often forbidden, from hunting or fishing, while the lords had the right to hunt across the serf's allotments, destroying crops and depleting wild game.

In many forest areas, serfs were forbidden to cut downed trees or collect fallen branches. This left them with no way to repair damage to their houses or collect fuel to warm their homes or cook through the harsh winters. Money they might have made from making charcoal was lost to them as well. As many of the lords were abbeys, bishoprics, convents and other church properties, the peasant's anger converged with the religious protests begun by Zwingli and by Thomas Müntzer, who offered the common people a vision of a new world order under God's Law. Luther, on the other hand, had been opposed to the rebellion, calling it "the Devil's work."

Like many other men with businesses dependent on peasant labor and natural resources to survive, Beckerle and his sons had joined the war on the side of the peasants. Their livelihoods had also suffered under the abuses of the lords. In the end, hundreds of thousands of working men died, leaving villages struggling for survival and land lying fallow. Marpeck's quiet hope was that the empty homes of Illenkirchen, and villages like it, could be filled with refugee families such as Thomann and his little girl, skilled and educated men who now struggled to make a life on charity.

\*\*\*

Like the flour mill in Affoltern am Albis, the sawmill at Illenkirchen sat on a channel diverted from a river. The channel ran just enough water to keep the mill wheel turning evenly. "Not so different," said Thomann to Beckerle at the end of his tour. "Only the saw."

"That is the truth," Beckerle replied. "That great saw is a bit different from great stones." He smiled at Thomann.

"How is that blade kept sharpened?"

"A dull saw blade is not just useless but dangerous, so we keep two blades. That way one is sharpened at all times. Thanks be to God the man who keeps the blades in order here in Illenkirchen stayed out of that unholy business." Beckerle crossed himself. "He has always been on my payroll. Twice in a month he comes. We shut down. We take down the saw blade and replace it with the other. Then he sharpens the one not in use. Sometimes it needs fixing, teeth repaired, replaced. The important thing is to keep a spare ready and in working condition. I will teach you about all of that, Thomann."

Thomann looked up at the high end of the immense saw blade. The mechanism driven by the mill wheel lifted the blade then dropped regularly and evenly as the log was pulled along through the work of gears moved by the water wheel and guided by workmen. "I won't deny it's frightening, sir."

"It is. Accidents can happen and have happened. The important thing is to keep everything in good order. That has been almost beyond me for these last years. I cannot climb up there to see that all is well. I...my...well. The mill needs managing by some careful soul who cares for the well-being of others. Marpeck here tells me you are such a man."

"God-willing."

Hans Beckerle, in reflex and reverence, made the sign of the cross. "Would you take on the job? I can teach you as my father taught me. I hear your father is also a miller. I guess he taught you?"

"From a child I worked in my father's flour mill," said Thomann, smiling. "My father is old now. Heinrich, my oldest brother, runs the mill. My job was keeping the workers happy, productive. I kept the books and helped my brother and father oversee the milling and maintain the workings."

Beckerle nodded. "The mill house is empty. You have a daughter, Marpeck tells me?"

"In truth, she is my brother's daughter. He died before she was born. Her mother . . ." Thomann stopped. "I adopted her as mine."

"Your daughter, then," said Beckerle. "If she hasn't known any parents but you, who would you be to her but her father? You need not tell the story, son. I see it is hard telling and all too common these days."

"I will take your kind advice, sir," answered Thomann, and from that day forth, he never again sought to explain to anyone. Thomann liked this man. Old religion or not, it didn't matter. Thomann would follow his own father's rule and let Beckerle find his own road as he had found his.

"I cannot pay you in cash, yet. Not until the mill begins to run at a profit again, but the mill house will be yours and your daughter's to live in. Lisbeth, my daughter-in-law, can look after your daughter — what's her name?"

"Kitty."

"We live just across there." Beckerle gestured toward the bridge and a large, white-washed, half-timber house standing between two ancient linden trees. "My grandson will like having a playmate. I'll find someone to clean and cook for you. You'll have a share in the mill profits, when they begin. What do you think? The mill-house and board? Fuel for the winter?"

Thomann thought of his hallway cot, of the bed Kitty shared with Jakob's children. Of the dark street, the smells and sodden smoky air of Strasbourg. Jakob would have his home again.

"I should sleep on the decision, but..."

"Come see the mill house."

The building that housed the sawmill was the largest in the village and sat on a corner; the mill faced the high street with a lumberyard behind it. It was made of stone and half-timber with a steeply pitched roof. Divided into three sections, that closest to the river was the mill. The middle was storage and a shop for repairs. At the far end, facing a side street, was a small family home with two rooms downstairs, two above and an attic. An enormous hearth ran the length of the two downstairs rooms open to both. There were windows on three sides upstairs and down. It was bright and airy. It would be warm and the upstairs rooms had clay stoves.

"I was born in the front bedroom. So were my boys." Beckerle stopped. He took a deep breath. He had resolved not to dwell on his loss but to look to the future of his grandson. "Would it do you, then, Thomann?"

\*\*\*

The Sunday meeting started early. Church bells throughout Strasbourg rang, calling people to worship, and the narrow streets and wider lanes opened to a different clamor than they knew on weekdays. The cathedral followed the ideas of Martin Bucer, as did the Strasbourg magistrates. Their beliefs were related to those of Zwingli's followers. Other groups held meetings in homes. Pilgram Marpeck and his wife opened their home to the group of Re-baptizers who did not follow the spiritualistic views of Caspar Schwenkenfeld or the legalistic perspective of the Swiss Brethren. Marpeck's prayer was to find a way to bring everyone together in one brotherhood, even the followers of Zwingli, Bucer and Luther.

"Heavenly Father," he began, "we thank you for your care of us. Thank you for bringing us all safely through a long winter and for the gift of salvation in the person of your son, Jesus Christ, who came to show us the way, through the presence of the Holy Spirit. We ask your blessing on Brother Thomann and his little girl, Kitty, as they leave us for Illenkirchen. Keep them safe from harm as they do your work. Even though they will be apart from the brotherhood, keep their hearts and minds safe in the light of your grace and love, knowing that we are here and will keep them in our prayers. In Jesus' name, Amen."

As the meeting broke up, everyone shook Thomann's hand. "Come back, brother, and tell us about it."

"I'll pray for your safety, Brother Thomann," said one of the women who'd looked after Kitty.

"Our little girl will have a bloom in her cheeks again," said Sister Emma, "once she's out of this dark and dirty city. Won't you, little one?" Still pale and easily tired, Kitty really didn't understand what Sister Emma had said, but she knew it must be good. Nothing bad could come from her guardian angel. Sister Emma bent down, and Kitty wrapped her arms around the woman's neck.

***

"Come and visit us, Jakob," said Thomann the next morning, as he gathered his and Kitty's few belongings. "It is a large house and there is room for all of you. Come, truly, brother," he said.

"We will, Thomann. We will miss you. I know Frau Winkle will miss Kitty very much."

"Frau Winkle should..." Thomann hesitated.

"I know. She should go with you."

"I think so. She could keep house for Kitty and me. She would be very welcome. It would leave Lisbeth,

201

Beckerle's daughter-in-law, free to work in the shop as she has been, and I think she would like to continue."

"Have you asked her?"

"No, no. Perhaps Frau Winkle is needed more here."

"We will find others to live in her rooms, Thomann. God knows there are so many without homes."

"That is true."

"You should ask her."

"I will. I'll go down now."

"Send Kitty."

Late that afternoon, Thomann, Kitty, Frau Winkle and Pilgram Marpeck arrived in Illenkirchen in a wagon that carried their possessions. More prosperous Brethren, of which there were many in Strasbourg, had donated furniture and other things to help them set up housekeeping. Beckerle was waiting for them when they arrived. He had built a fire and the house was both warm and light. Kitty ran inside and looked around the large front room with its windows looking out at the river and at the setting sun.

"It's beautiful, father!" Kitty exclaimed. "Come in and see!"

"Go, Thomann," laughed Marpeck. "This moment will not happen twice. We'll start unloading."

***

Lisbeth was in the kitchen making a supper for the travelers when she heard Kitty's joyous voice. Wiping her hands on her apron, she came out in time to see Kitty dragging a laughing Thomann by the hand.

"Thomann?" she said, stepping forward and dropping into a little curtsey. "I'm Lisbeth."

Thomann saw a round, pleasant looking woman with a wide smile. Her brown hair was neatly pushed under the sides of her cap, her apron covered with flour and cherry juice.

"Welcome to your home," she said. "This," she motioned to a little boy to join her, "is Georg, named for his father."

Georg looked to be about a year older than Kitty, with dark hair and playful eyes.

"Welcome, sir," he said to Thomann.

"This is Kitty, Georg," said Thomann.

"I hope you two will be friends," said Lisbeth, as the two children stared at each other, Kitty with her fingers in her mouth.

"This is Frau Winkle," said Thomann, seeing her come into the room carrying two bundles of clothing. "Frau Winkle will be keeping house for me and watching Kitty. I was thinking, also, that if you wish, she can watch Georg, if you..." Thomann stopped. "The thing is, she and Kitty have become very attached to each other and I, I..."

"Didn't want to leave her alone in the city and you didn't want Kitty to be alone in a completely strange place?" Lisbeth smiled.

"That's right." Thomann was relieved.

"That's good," Lisbeth said, looking over the neat person of the old woman. "I can help father in the shop. The children can spend the day here, nearer me. Frau Winkle? I'm very happy you have come. Well," she said, looking toward the kitchen, "I've made a pie."

"Can I help, missus?" asked Frau Winkle, with tears in her eyes. Never had she dreamed of living in a home such as this one. It was an answer to her prayers. A home, a family, warmth, none of which she'd had since her husband and children died in the ravages of the plague's last visit.

"Yes, yes, of course. Thank you!" said Lisbeth. "It is a very simple supper, I'm afraid, because we did not know when you would get here, but it's something for us to share tonight."

Beckerle took care of the horse while Marpeck and Thomann unloaded the wagon. The table, benches and chairs donated by the brethren were set up in the front room. The beds they'd brought were taken upstairs. Frau Winkle and Kitty would share the quiet room in back. Thomann took the front room, it being noisier and not as warm.

By the time the wagon was unloaded, the supper was ready. They sat around the elegant carved table with its one short leg propped up by bits of kindling, and passed a tureen of steaming soup made of bacon, dried peas, onions and carrots, followed by a plate of bread.

Pilgram Marpeck, his mind always in the track leading to Christ, thought, as he listened to the conversations all around him, that though nothing would be said, when they broke bread together it would be a true communion. "When two or more are gathered in my name," the Lord had said.

"Let us thank God," he said, before anyone dipped a spoon into the soup. Reaching out, he took the hands of the people nearest him, Georg and Thomann.

Beckerle looked around in surprise when Kitty reached for his hand.

The awkward silent moment was filled by Marpeck's gentle voice. "Thank you, Lord, for bringing us safely here, for the work we have to do, for the meal we are about to share. Bless our hosts for their kindness. In Jesus name, Amen."

Beckerle, Lisbeth and Georg crossed themselves. "I have to say," began Beckerle, "'tis no matter to us, your faith. God knows better'n we. For me it's enough that you are honest, Thomann, and can run my mill. 'Tis difficult in these days, even following the old faith. We, too, have enemies everywhere. Bless me," he crossed himself, "as I do not see how that's God's will."

Marpeck nodded. "These arguments have ever only ended in death and torture. I do not believe that could ever have been God's will when the two commandments our Lord gave us are to love our Lord God with all our heart and to love our neighbor as ourselves."

# Book Three

# War

# Chapter 26

**Conrad, November 1530**

Conrad's stable boy was up early, mucking out the stalls.
"Have you fed them, Ueli?"

"Not yet, sir."

"I will, then."

"Do you want to turn them out to grass? It's going
to be a fine day." The late autumn morning had dawned
with the whisper of summer, a break after a week of
storms.

"Yes, let's do that," Conrad answered, anticipating
his joy at watching his horses run free in a green
meadow after being cooped up in the barn. It would also
make it easier for them to clean out the stalls, a job that
had been waiting too long. He sold the manure to the

abbey and they would be putting in their winter barley crop soon.

Two by two they led the horses out until eight were happily running and bucking and jumping and eating the meadow grass.

Meanwhile, two men came on horseback, their horses kicking up the fallen leaves on the shaded road to the castle. Then there was the blast of a horn.

"Who could that be?" Conrad asked Ueli, who was heading toward the open meadow leading two of the geldings Conrad was training. He could see across the field up to the house.

"Bailiffs, sir. Two of them. From Zürich."

"Conrad Schneebeli!" one called out.

Conrad sighed. "Ueli, take the horses back. And these." He handed Ueli the reins of the two horses he'd just bridled. "Can you handle all four?" The boy nodded. "Get Saladin and Prince. Take them to the meadow, as far out as you can, as fast as you can. Don't ride them! Stay low. Then take the little roan mare and her colt. Run!" Conrad ran up the small hill to the back door of his home, grateful that the castle, its wall and the house blocked the men's view of the stable.

Christina was in the kitchen. "Conrad?"

"Bailiffs from Zürich. I don't know what they want, but I suspect it is the horses. Bring cake and beer to the hall. Maybe we can hold them a moment."

Christina nodded, her heart pounding. Conrad went through the house and out the front door.

"Good morning, gentlemen! What brings you here?"

"Conrad Schneebeli?"

"Yes. Would you gentlemen like some refreshment?"

"We have a warrant to requisition your horses." He handed Conrad a folded paper with the wax seal of Zürich.

"My horses?"

"We know you sell horses. But now? Your horses belong to Zürich."

Conrad looked calmly at the men's faces. "How is that, sir? I bought them, raised them, trained them. Some were bred here of my own mare and stallion, both of which I bought as colts and trained myself. How is it they belong to Zürich?"

"You live on the land belonging to Canton Zürich. You benefit from the laws and protection of the city and its government."

Conrad looked thoughtfully at the men, then at his feet. He was buying time for Ueli. "Excuse me, sir, but I don't understand. This land has been the freehold of my family for at least eight generations. Men of my family, including my father and now my brother, Heinrich, have sat on the Zürich council. Several have been Zürich mayors. None of them ever told me this land belonged to Zürich, and they would certainly have known. And how does your telling me my horses belong to Zürich go along with my benefiting from the laws and protection of the Zürich government? Isn't there a law against horse theft?"

One of the men bristled and put his hand on his sword. The other man reached over and stopped him, shaking his head.

"Under the law, we can take your horses for the city's defense. It is better for everyone if you just give them to us."

"I haven't got many," said Conrad. "Hard times. Feed is expensive. I've already sold what I could." This way he explained the nearly empty stable and why there would be more evidence of horse than there would be horses to make it.

"To the Habsburgs, no doubt," muttered the man who'd reached for his sword. The Habsburgs had allied with the Catholic cantons against Zürich.

"Where's the stable?" asked the other, the older and calmer of the two, yet, in Conrad's perception, the more dangerous.

"Follow me." Conrad led the men out of the gate, around the castle tower, and down the hill to the stables where Ueli was shaking oats into the feed troughs of the four horses standing there.

"I'm short handed," explained Conrad. "I let most of my men go when I sold the horses. This is the time of year when... Well, never mind. You know you are taking my livelihood and that of my family?"

"Your family has a mill. Go work there," said the man who'd gone for his sword.

"These are truly all your horses, sir?" asked the other man, looking doubtfully around the stables. "The manure..."

"Belongs to the abbey," explained Conrad, shrugging. "They said they'd come for it weeks ago, but they haven't. They need it for the barley fields."

The short-tempered man got off his horse and went outside the stable to look around. He was sure Conrad was lying, that there were more horses, but nothing Conrad had said was contradicted by anything the man saw. Conrad knew that if the man went far enough on foot, he'd see the small herd in the meadow. He hoped that the large spurs the bailiff was wearing would impede his walking as much as they probably hurt his horse. The man came back. "Nothing, sir," he said to his companion.

"We got four good horses. Perhaps another day we'll have better luck here." He eyed Conrad narrowly

Conrad shrugged. "You are always welcome, sirs."

"We'll take them now. Bridle them, would you? Have they saddles? We'll take those, too."

\*\*\*

That afternoon, Conrad and Ueli put up a makeshift shelter for the remaining horses. "They'll have to stay here until I figure out what to do," said Conrad. "I need to sell them quick. Those men will be back. Maybe tomorrow. They know I was lying. Can you stay with the horses, Ueli, for the time being? We'll bring down your cot and make you a canvas shelter against the wind." Ueli nodded. He loved Conrad almost as much as he loved the horses. "Keep your dog close by, boy, you know." Ueli's brown, black and while little dog with its tightly curled tail was not just Ueli's loyal friend. He helped keep the horses where they were supposed to be and barked a passionate warning when needed.

When they finished, Conrad headed down The Brothers on foot to talk the situation over with Heinrich. He arrived as the family was sitting down to supper. "Join us, Conrad," said Elsa. "There's plenty."

"I need to talk to you, Heinrich..."

"I know, I know. After. Just sit down and have something to eat." Heinrich led the family in prayer and they shared a supper of mutton stewed with carrots, barley and onions. There was fresh bread and butter, followed by cheese. "Come then," said Heinrich when they were finished. "What is it?"

"Bailiffs from Zürich took four of my horses this morning."

"Only four? How in Heaven's name did you manage that?" said Heinrich, sucking on his pipe. "There is talk of war with the Catholic cantons and the Habsburgs. Zürich wants to be ready."

"War?"

"Some rabble-rousers in Thurgau killed a priest last year, remember? Well, now a pastor has been killed by Catholics in Schwyz. They're spoiling for a fight in Zürich."

"How does that allow them to steal my horses?"

"You can't stay out of it, Conrad. You've seen now how it will come to you. So what did you do?"

"Luckily, we were taking them out to pasture that morning and most of them of them were already in the meadow. Ueli and I were able to hide them. They got four. I need to sell eight of them. I don't think they'll want old Prince, or Saladin, the mare or her colt that's still on the tit. If Zürich is going to take my horses without paying, I will find other buyers. But I need to find them fast. Do you..."

"I know some men in Zürich who will buy them. Like I said. They're building an army. You have seen yourself they want horses."

"How soon, Heinrich, can we go to Zürich and arrange this?"

"You can't go, Conrad. How soon do you want them gone?"

"A day or two at the most. They're..." Conrad decided not to tell Heinrich where the horses were. The less he knew the safer it would be for him to make the deal.

"Move them here," said Heinrich. "We can bring them down The Brothers tonight. I'll part them out between the mill and here; maybe take a couple to the mill in Thalwil. I'll sell them from there. Will that work? I can take four of them to Zürich from Thalwil tomorrow, leave a couple here and a couple at the mill and maybe sell the rest off slowly. Let's go," said Heinrich, reaching for his coat. "Heinj, you and Little Hans come too."

They worked through the night. When morning came all that remained of Conrad's herd were the Arab stallion, Saladin, the young, unbroken colt and his mother. There was Prince, Christina's own riding horse, an elderly and peaceful gray gelding. Heinrich sold six of the horses to Zürich businessmen in anticipation of war. He bought two himself, to work on the farm and the mill, but mostly to keep his brother's heart from breaking.

\*\*\*

The bailiffs returned three days later. Finding the uncut stallion, a brood mare and her colt, and the old gelding beyond much use, they looked at Conrad and demanded, "Where were these when we were here earlier?"

"Saladin, here, was out at stud. The mare and her colt were over there, in that pasture," Conrad gestured to a small pasture behind the stables. "I thought you saw them. We had just started taking all the horses back there when you rode up. My wife was riding old Prince here." He patted the gray on the rump. "She went down to the abbey to visit my brother Hannes' wife. There you have it."

# chapter 27

## Conrad, Spring 1531

"Sir! Sir!" Ueli stood behind the house, yelling as loud as he could, trying to wake Conrad. Christina awakened first and smelled smoke. Sitting up in bed, she looked out the window.

"Conrad!" She shook her husband. "Wake up! The stables are on fire!"

Conrad roused himself from a dream of old times, of a man knocked unconscious by robbers as he was running across a green field toward a burning barn. "Oh God, no!" he said.

Ueli was already trying to get water onto the fire, but even after the others in the household were roused and ran outside to help, it was hopeless.

"Ueli, did you save the horses?"

"They're gone, sir. Whoever started the fire must've taken them."

"Saladin?" Conrad asked under his breath as they worked with shovels to put out small fires around the stables started by bits of burning roof dropping to the ground.

"Gone, sir, and the mare and colt."

"But not Prince."

"No sir. He's over there." Ueli pointed at the side of the house where Prince stood tied to a tree.

When the fire was out, Conrad was grateful that the spring had been wet. Bad as it was, it could have been worse. There had not been much feed in the stables, either.

"That's the end of it, my love," he said to Christina, who stood beside him, holding an empty pail in one hand, soot on her face and clothing, smelling of smoke. "They must have learned somehow that I got rid of the horses."

"You knew that was dangerous," sighed Christina.

"Still, I never imagined this. This is spite."

"How are we going to live now, with Saladin gone, the others, gone? Should we move back to the village? Your father is dead. It would not be..."

"I don't know, my love. I don't know what we should do."

***

"They have spies everywhere, Conrad. Any number of people could have told them, or seen one of your horses on the street in Zürich and asked its owner how he came by it," said Heinrich the next morning, looking in dismay at the burned rubble of Conrad's stables.

Conrad nodded. "They have no use for those horses. Saladin?" Conrad shuddered. "I can ride him. Ueli has ridden him, but he's not dependable. Just beautiful. He's just a good stud. Well, they'll find out.

And the mare? They can use her, but they'll have to get rid of that colt first. She won't leave him, and he's useless as he is."

"What are you going to live on?"

"Savings, from the horses you sold for me, I guess. The produce of the farm; fruit from the apple trees. I can sell the grain I no longer need for my horses, hay, but..."

Heinrich sighed. "All because of that silly business two years ago in Kappel. I don't think that's the end of it, brother. Hannes believes it is a fair treaty and everyone will abide by it. But, why should they?"

"Hannes, the pure of heart. If you read those old stories, you'd find Hannes marching off to find the True Cross and lifting long-lost sacred swords from mystic forest pools."

Heinrich laughed. "That is Hannes. The inner cantons have no reason to honor the treaty. Peter is sure there will be war."

"Peter is probably right, but that doesn't explain the desperation over three useless horses. Why steal my horses, burn my stable?"

"If you sell horses to anyone but them, you are aiding the enemies of Zürich. It was either steal your horses or try you for treason. Their best chance was theft. They might not have gotten a conviction, and if they did? They'd have to kill you." Heinrich sighed. "How would that serve? It would make enemies."

"Did they take the horses you bought from me?"

"No."

"It's personal, Heinrich."

"Yes, I know. You lied to the bailiffs and sold your horses. They see you as a traitor."

"What would you have done, Heinrich? Would you have done differently?"

"In your situation? I might have done the same. Come, Conrad. There's no point looking back or talking about what if this and what if that. I came to see if you'd come to work in the mill again."

"Again? I've never worked in the mill. You know that. What can I do there, Heinrich?"

"Work with our horses. They may not be beautiful like Saladin, but they are horses. You can make deliveries, Conrad, as you used to do."

Conrad thought of the working horses kept by his family when he was a boy. He had seen them as wondrous creatures, magnificent, strong. Docile and calm, the big horses pulled the wagons and the plows. As a boy, Conrad had driven the pony and donkey carts belonging to the mill to the farms to pick up sacks of grain. When he was older, he had driven the big wagons to deliver sacks of flour to the abbey and to Zürich. He could not even say if he was born loving horses or if his love of horses came from working with his father's patient beasts. His favorite moment was the end of the day when the horses were set free in the field. Big though they were, they leapt and ran in joy at their liberty, yet they still followed him contentedly into the barn and submitted happily to the yoke the next day. From those horses Conrad developed his philosophy and his temperament.

"Do you really need my help, Heinrich, or is this pity?"

"I need your help, Conrad. My workload has doubled and more, now that father's dead. The horses are extra work for me, and my boys are not old enough."

Conrad laughed. "At young Heinj's age I was in charge of the horses."

"Heinj has his head is in the clouds, or, I don't know. I fear... Well, never mind. You could teach little Hans. He cares well for his own horse."

"I have to talk to Christina, Heinrich."

"I know, I know. You want me and the boys to help you pull down that mess?" Heinrich nodded toward the burned stables.

Conrad nodded. It was a heartbreaking ruin of burned wood and shattered dreams.

"There will be other times, Conrad, other horses. I know you miss Saladin."

Conrad nodded. He made light of the bond he'd had with his little stallion, but man and horse were friends, and now the horse was God knew where.

***

"Christina? Where are you?" Heinrich had gone home, leaving Conrad to talk things over with his wife. Working in the mill would mean moving to the family house in Affoltern.

"Out here!"

Christina was in the kitchen garden with Anna, preparing the soil for summer vegetables.

"My love," said Conrad, a deep sigh behind his voice.

"What is it?"

"Heinrich has asked if I would work in the mill with him."

"And do what? You don't know anything about operating the mill."

"Deliveries. Care of the horses."

"Oh, Conrad." Christina looked at her husband, knowing that while Heinrich had offered them a rope out of hole that would grow deeper through the winter, it was not what either of them wanted. "Will it mean moving down into the village?"

"Yes. We have to do that. There's no way to manage living here and working there. Anna and Ueli could stay here and care for the castle, but we can't pay them much."

Anna heard everything and resolved, then and there, that she and her son would care for the castle as well as they could. With only the chickens, geese and the kitchen garden to care for, it would be manageable for the two of them. When the apples were ready to harvest, she was sure Conrad would return with his family to do that. "Sir?" she called out. "This is your home, and you'll be back soon, God willing." She crossed herself. "Ueli and I will stay. We can work out for extra money. They always need help at the abbey."

Christina and Conrad looked at each other, their eyes brimming with the feelings they had held back since the bailiff's first visit. "Are you sure, Anna?" asked Christina, the first to find her voice.

"Where would we go, Missus? This is our home, too."

And so it was left. Their move to the village would be temporary. Anna and Ueli would stay at the old castle, all of them hoping for the future moment when these sores could be healed and the stable rebuilt.

***

The next morning, as expected, Heinrich and his two older sons, Heinj and Little Hans, came up The Brothers to help Conrad tear down the burned out stables. Conrad was surprised to look down the linden-shaded lane to see Peter, Hannes and Vreni following behind.

"Christina!" Conrad called out to his wife. "Hannes and Vreni have come too. And Peter!"

Christina ran out from the kitchen where she and Anna had begun preparing dinner. "Oh Conrad," she said, turning to her husband, who put his arm around her shoulder. Seeing the family all on the way to help them, Christina felt much less alone.

"I'm so sorry, uncle," said Heinj. In the last year, Heinj, now sixteen, had grown tall and manly. He reminded Conrad of Andreas.

"Thank you, my boy. Thank you for coming to help," Conrad replied.

"I don't understand it," said Hannes. "This should not be the way of a new faith. This is not new wine; this is the old wine, the old ways."

"Human nature is not wine, Hannes. It cannot change so quickly. We were not born into this world the moment Zwingli had his revelation. Nor was Zwingli. We have been at this, in just this way, for a long time." Conrad sighed.

Heinrich nodded in agreement.

"I had hoped...prayed..."

"I know, Hannes," said Conrad to his gentle brother whose eyes had filled with tears when he saw the ruined stable. Conrad knew that Hannes blamed himself for what had happened, as if he were one of Zürich's henchmen.

Christina and Vreni embraced, Vreni feeling that what was happening at the castle was happening to her own home; she had been born there, had grown up there.

"Come on. We have work to do!" said the ever-practical Heinrich.

The brothers and Heinrich's sons worked into the early afternoon, pulling down the stables that once held Conrad's dreams. He had built up his stable of horses slowly. His reputation as a breeder and a trainer had begun to be known, and his stallion Saladin to be sought after.

"When will you be ready to move down to us, brother?" Heinrich asked as they piled burned wood and broken lumber into a bonfire pile.

"Friday next, Heinrich? I have to put things in order here and we have to finish putting in the garden."

"Saturday is a half day at the mill. We'll come up that afternoon with the cart to bring your things to the house."

"All right," said Conrad in a low voice. "Christina and I will be ready. Go ahead, Ueli. Light it. Let's get this behind us." The dry and half-burned timbers, aided by an old broom and scraps of fabric and old clothes, straw, fallen branches and bits of rope from the stable quickly caught fire.

Watching the flames, Conrad felt a surprising sense of relief. At least he had a livelihood until, until what? He didn't know. The future was uncertain. He knew only that, for now, he had to let go of the castle and his dreams. Conrad's heart ached for Saladin, and he hoped the little stallion fared well, was cared for, understood, but? *Nothing I can do,* he thought. *Maybe there will be other horses. Maybe I'll find him, even if I have to buy him back.*

The next day they raked the ground where the stable had been, and, after mixing the stable's rich earth with ashes, and shoveling it into the wheelbarrow, they dumped the mixture into the kitchen garden.

Vreni stayed to help Christina sort through their belongings to take what they would need in Affoltern. Over the week, they carefully packed other things to store in apple boxes until the day they would return to the castle. Conrad and Ueli sealed off the rooms Anna and Ueli would not need. When Heinrich came with the cart and horses Conrad and Christina were ready. Their belongings were soon loaded and they were on their way down the shaded roadway, under the linden blossoms.

# chapter 28

## Heinj, Call to Arms, Summer 1531

"Are you sure, son? This is what you must do?" asked Heinrich, swallowing his fear after hearing Heinj's plans. Elsa stood beside the basin, pretending to wash up, hiding her tears.

"I cannot take up arms against anyone, or swear an oath of any kind. I've tried to follow a middle road, but now it is impossible."

Peter's prophesy was coming true and Zürich was building the city's army in preparation for war against the Catholic cantons that had allied with the Habsburgs. But, until that afternoon, Heinrich and Elsa had not known that their oldest son had joined the Re-baptizers.

"Do you know where Uncle Thomann is, father? I would join him."

"Do you have any idea what this means, how dangerous it is?"

"Don't I, father? How often have I heard the story of Uncle Andreas? How often have you bewailed in whispers the absence of Uncle Thomann? In my meetings with the Brethren, I've heard more stories, and seen..." Heinj stopped.

"All right, son. You're telling me that with your eyes open, you've taken a road that has led to the death of many, many people, burned, drowned, hung, tortured, starved in the Hexenturm or the Kratzturm or some other tower prison in Zürich. The Emperor's mandate is clear and absolute, and he has not backed off from it."

"I know, Father. Such deaths are..." Heinj had no interest in martyrdom and sensed the hypocrisy in using it as an argument for his faith. "Uncle Peter is right about war. If I don't leave here now I will be conscripted. When I'm conscripted I must refuse to fight. If I refuse to fight, I will be tasked to explain why. That will be the end, Father. There are places I could go..."

Heinj was right. It would likely be death for him whether he agreed to fight or not. Heinrich sighed. He did not want his sons going to war, and only this one was old enough for Zwingli's growing army. Heinrich walked over to a tall cabinet beside the back door and opened the bottom drawer. He carefully put aside some old ledger books until he found the one he wanted. From it he took out a folded paper with a broken wax seal.

"Here." He handed Heinj the paper.

Believing, correctly, that it was from his Uncle Thomann, Heinj opened it eagerly and scanned the words written in his uncle's neat hand. "Dear Heinrich, Elsa and children, I hope this finds you well. The plague has passed over us, praise be to God. Yours, Thomann." Any family member in these times might write such a message; many did.

Heinj turned the letter over looking for some sign of where it had come from, then looked at his father. "And?"

"Your uncle, at any rate, knows the danger. Give it here." Heinrich took the letter and held one side of it above the flame of the candle sitting on the middle of the table. "Can you read it now?"

Heinj nodded. "Did you know this, Father?"

"We agreed that he would send only one message to tell us he and Kitty were safe. There you have it." He motioned to the milk-writing, now and forever brown from the heat of the candle. "In these days not knowing where they are is the safest knowledge." He took the letter from Heinj's hands and threw it in the hearth fire. "Do not speak of this to anyone, not even those you believe share your faith. I will not have him put in any danger because of you. He's in enough danger on his own account."

Heinrich spoke with a ferocity Heinj had never heard. He felt that he had as much to fear at the moment from his own father as he had from any Zürich soldier who came looking for recruits.

*** 

The question then was how to get Heinj out of the canton safely. The family decided that Heinj should stop meeting with other Re-baptizers immediately, and Heinj agreed. He doubled his efforts at the mill to give the appearance that he was just one more ambitious and hard-working Schneebeli, the coming generation, eager to learn, to step into his father's footsteps when the time came. Because Heinj's best chance lay in his being hard to find, he often went with Conrad on deliveries. Their routes became labyrinthine, with stops in random directions rather than in a neat circuit ending at the mill, often keeping them away for the whole day. The villagers and farmers soon expected him to be with Conrad, but they never knew when.

As they had all expected, in full summer, a recruiter from Zürich came to the house looking for Heinj. The housemaid let him in and told him to follow her. He found Elsa, Christina and Gretchen in the kitchen, where they were busy making bread, darning socks and washing up. Bernhardt, a little boy of six, was leading around a wooden horse on wheels Heinrich had made long ago for Heinj, still fun, but the worse for wear. Little Hans was in the barn cleaning out the stalls.

"Sit down, sir. Let me get you some refreshment." Elsa hung a small cider-filled kettle on the tripod over the hearth fire and began to fuss about the cupboards, looking for something. "I'm sorry I had no idea you were coming, and I have nothing ready, but it will take only a few minutes to warm the cider."

"Can I help you, sister?" asked Christina, standing. Gretchen kept her head down, looking at her darning. The family had prepared themselves for this moment, but she did not trust her eyes.

"Yes, Christina. Thank you. I believe there is some pie in the cupboard."

"Don't trouble yourselves, please," said the recruiter. "I've been sent to talk to your oldest son."

Elsa gave him a puzzled look, "You mean Heinj?"

The agreed upon plan was that if recruiters showed up at the house, Elsa would get word to the mill. That would best be accomplished by Little Hans on his pony.

"Heinj may still be in the barn. He planned to help his father and uncle with deliveries today, but I don't know if he's left yet. I haven't seen him this morning. Gretchen," the girl looked up, "go see if your brother has gone to the mill yet." Gretchen, glad to be sent out of the room, knew this meant she must go tell Little Hans to saddle his pony and get down to the mill as quickly as he could.

But Little Hans had heard the recruiter ride up and had seen his horse in the courtyard wearing the blue and white livery of Zürich. When Gretchen got to the barn, Little Hans was already leading the little dun out of the back barn door. "Hurry, Little Hans," she said, running up to him. Little Hans nodded with justified self-importance, and, in minutes he had led his horse through the orchard at the back of the house. Then, once out of sight, he mounted and ran as fast as his horse could carry him to the mill.

Gretchen walked slowly back to the house. "Well?" asked Elsa when the girl opened the back door.

"I looked everywhere, but Heinj is not in the barn or in the orchard, Mother. He must have gone down to the mill early with Father and Uncle Conrad."

The officer sensed that Elsa was stalling, but he could not see why or how. She would tell them, he knew that. Not to would be treason punishable by torture and death. *I should have gone to look for him myself,* he thought. But this was a good family, an old family. Heinrich sat on the Zürich council.

"I'm so sorry, sir. You'll have to go to the mill and ask my husband. Very often I don't see Heinj until supper time when he comes home with Heinrich."

"You're saying he's at the mill?"

"I don't know that, sir. He may be out making deliveries. In any case, Heinrich will know where he is." Elsa spoke calmly and evenly. There was no lie in what she said. This was the truth of every morning.

"Thank you, Frau Schneebeli." The officer bowed low in front of her and nodded to Christina and Gretchen, then left. Elsa did not know if she'd been believed or not. When she knew the recruiter was well on his way, she went out to the barn and saw that Shorty was gone. "Dear Lord," she said, crossing herself, "let Little Hans get there in time!"

***

"Father!" called Little Hans, riding up to the front of the mill.

Heinrich stood at the counter, facing the door. He put his index finger in front of his mouth, motioning Little Hans to silence. Little Hans' sudden arrival told Heinrich everything.

"Let's put you to work, son," said Heinrich.

Little Hans nodded.

"Here, sit up on this stool and let me show you how to enter these orders into the ledger. The sooner you learn the better, right?" He set a slate in front of Little Hans on which were written all the receipts and orders for the day. "All right, these are orders that have been paid. They go in this column. Write the name of the customer, and next to it, here, write the amount he's paid. You got that?"

"Yes, Father."

"Here, if the order shows that he still owes us money, write that in this column, all right? If we still have to fill the order, don't write anything. Those are these." Heinrich showed Little Hans the entries with only the name of a customer. "Be very, very careful. Don't get them confused or we could be cheated, miss a delivery, or, worse, cheat someone. If you make a blot, use this." He put a blotting page beside the ledger book. "Go slowly and carefully. You will be here alone. You know what to do?"

Little Hans nodded. He knew exactly what to do. Little Hans understood that Heinj's life — all their lives — depended on what happened now.

"Yes, Father."

"If anyone comes in with grain to mill, get their name. Tell them we're behind on deliveries today, so we are not milling until morning. They can leave their grain. Can you do that, son? If someone comes in for flour we have milled, check the book. I am leaving you with a great deal of responsibility, but I think you are man enough to take care of it. I must go. Tell everyone that I am on deliveries and will be back later. Invite them to wait."

Heinrich knew Little Hans would do his very best to write the numbers without blots or mistakes. He wouldn't get far, but he would not move until his father returned and the workday ended.

By the time the recruiter appeared, Heinrich was long gone and grateful he'd bought one of Conrad's well-trained horses. "Walk steady, boy. We must find your master, but we must not appear to hurry." As if he understood the words, the sorrel palfrey took off at a rapid but steady walk that looked to passersby as if Heinrich was off to meet a customer, but in no big rush. Once Heinrich knew he was out of sight of the mill and nowhere near the way the recruiter would take from the house, he nudged the horse to a canter. He caught up with Conrad and Heinj as they were leaving the Blickensdorfer farm.

Heinrich jumped down from the horse. "Heinj, get down. Take the horse." Heinrich handed his son the reins. "Do not stop to see or speak to anyone. Follow the road to Baden, then go west. Leave the horse in Basel and take a boat. Here's money for that." He took off the leather purse he wore around his neck, inside his shirt. "Go. I pray to God no one stops you."

Heinj said nothing. He simply looked into his father's eyes, knowing it could be the last time they ever saw each other. "Go, son. Go." Heinrich climbed on the wagon with Conrad and took the reins. "Walk on boys, walk." They went down the road with the load of flour sacks to make the next delivery. Heinrich rubbed his eyes on the shoulder of his jacket.

Heinj soon found the trade road to Baden. Once he might have stopped to visit cousins in the town of Lunkhofen; today he did not tarry and did not look back.

\*\*\*

"Where is your father? Your mother said he would be here." The recruiter was not surprised to see a boy in charge of the shop, but he'd believed Elsa.

"My father will be back soon. He had to make an emergency delivery today."

"How long ago did he leave?"

"This morning, so he should be back soon. Please sit down, sir. I'll get you some cider." Little Hans hopped down from the stool, went to a cupboard in the back and returned with a pitcher of cider and a cup. "This is our cider," Little Hans said with pride. "We make it in our cider press, there." He pointed out the window to a small mill slightly upstream from the flour mill. "We use our own apples, too."

"Your brother, Heinj? Is he about?"

"I don't know where Heinj is. Maybe making deliveries, too. I haven't seen him today."

"Did you see him yesterday?"

"Yes, I did. But he often gets up and comes to the mill very early, and sometimes I'm not awake when he leaves the house. We are very behind. That's why he and my father are not here and I am. I can't make the deliveries yet."

After waiting the better part of an hour, the recruiter saw that if he did not start back to Zürich, the gates would be locked. It had been a useless mission, and he didn't know if he'd simply had bad luck or had been tricked. He stood and set the cup on the counter. "Tell your father I will be back soon," he said as he stormed out. His spurs jangled and banged on the wooden floor, leaving their mark.

*** 

Elsa sat in the sunny side of the courtyard shelling peas with Gretchen and Christina. The best ones they would cook with potatoes and cream for the evening meal.

Most of them would be dried and bagged for winter. Elsa nearly wept in her uncertainty. God willing, Heinj had managed to get away. Finally they heard the mill wagon on the road leading to the house. Gretchen prepared to stand, but Elsa motioned her to sit down. How could they know who was in the wagon, whether it was Heinrich and Conrad, whether they were alone or not?

When the wagon reached the courtyard gate. Heinrich jumped down, leaving Conrad to take the horses round to the pasture and turn them out. Elsa heard them talking, but she didn't catch their words. No matter, Heinrich was soon beside her. He kissed the top of her head.

"Well?" she whispered.

"Little Hans might make a good bookkeeper like his uncle Thomann."

And so Elsa knew everything she needed. While no news in the situation was all good, at least Heinj was not in the hands of the Zürich recruiter, but on his way, they prayed, to Thomann. God willing, Thomann was safe and able to offer a haven to their boy.

***

The recruiter returned within a few days, going straight to the mill. He found Little Hans perched again on the stool, but this time Heinrich was there.

"Where is Heinj, your oldest son?" the recruiter demanded.

It was not difficult for Heinrich to look stricken by grief. He was afraid for his son and had no idea where he was. At least now he knew that Zürich had not found Heinj and picked him up.

"We..." Heinrich's voice caught in his throat. He swallowed hard and regained some composure. "When my wife and little boy here told me of your visit. I told Heinj he must go to Zürich. We had some strong words. He walked out. He did not come to you, then? He was so

angry at me that...but I thought he would surely..."
Heinrich's voice trailed off.

The recruiter set his lips in a thin line. This story could be true. Such things often happened. He had no way to know. The Schneebelis were reputable citizens of Zürich with everything to lose if they broke the law. Heinrich sat on the council. The recruiter sighed. "If he returns, or you simply hear from him and learn his whereabouts, you must report to us. Failure to do this will lead to punishment for treason by the Zürich magisterial court. Is this understood? This is no time for shirkers."

Heinrich nodded. "So there will be war, then?" he asked. "Between Zürich and the Catholic cantons?"

The recruiter nodded. "They have broken the treaty. We have no choice. Remember what I've told you." His spurs and boots clanked and thundered on his way out.

# chapter 29

## Heinj, August 1531

Curled against the side of a riverboat, Heinj could do little but shiver and pray. This boat was his third. He'd made his way north from Basle by climbing on boats and hiding, getting off in morning's darkest hour and losing himself in groups of passengers. He had been lucky, but he did not expect his luck would last forever. He yearned to reach Strasbourg, to have the freedom of his own existence once more. Life as a shadow was dangerous, and he had been a shadow now for more than three weeks. He carried no possessions and traveled on foot. In towns, he was just another workman; in the countryside, he was someone going home.

The boatman poled the boat to shore, nearing the pier of a large village. Heinj sat up slowly. He watched the dark shapes of tired passengers stir and rise. Not so many, but, Heinj had learned that the appearance of confidence was itself a cloak. He stood and joined them, walking down the plank as if he knew where he was going.

The passengers went their separate ways; Heinj followed one large family across the bridge into the village heart. The village was itself beginning to awaken. Church bells rang against the rising sun and street criers called out the time. Heinj sat on a bench beside the village well and took a drink. He still had money in the leather pouch his father had given him and when he saw the door of the baker's shop open, he went across the square and bought some bread. He was very hungry. It had been a day or more since he had eaten.

*"If ye have faith as a grain of mustard seed, ye shall say unto this mountain, remove hence to yonder place; and it shall remove; and nothing shall be impossible unto you."* The verse from Matthew had kept him company through everything. "All I need is faith. With faith I will find my uncle. And if I am caught and killed? I will find the Kingdom of Heaven. I don't have anything to fear." This he had told himself over and over.

"Heinj? God be praised!"

Heinj looked up. Standing there with the sun behind his red hair stood his Uncle Thomann. "Uncle?" Heinj dropped his bread and embraced his uncle.

"My boy, how in Heaven's name did you find me?"

"I was on my way to Strasbourg to find you, Uncle. I didn't know you were here. What is this village, anyway?"

"This is Illenkirchen. Oh Heinj! Let me look at you!" Thomann held Heinj at arm's length. "Yes, taller, more of a man, but still Heinj. I am so happy to see you! How is everyone? Heinrich? Elsa? The little ones? Conrad and Christina? How are they? And Hannes and Vreni, how are they? Do you hear anything of Peter?

How is father?" Thomann's words spilled from his mouth, each one, for him, the image of someone in his family.

Heinj looked at Thomann in confusion for a moment, then realized he could not have known about Old Johann. "Grandfather? Uncle Thomann, grandfather died last winter. In February."

Thomann nodded. "How, Heinj?"

"He became ill; his lungs filled with fluid. It was a cold February."

"It was," agreed Thomann, not feeling shock or sorrow at the news of his father. He even wondered what there was to feel. The old man had lived a good life, a long life, and Thomann's choices had propelled him far from Affoltern, his father and his own youth. "What of the others?"

"Everyone is well. Conrad and Christina are living with us now. Zürich bailiffs burned Conrad's stable and took his horses. Uncle Peter is a pastor. He even studied with Uncle Hannes."

Thomann shook his head. "Peter? A man of God?"

"Something like that."

Thomann smiled, imagining his brother Peter delivering a sermon in an Evangelical church. "In Glarus?"

"Yes. Now his family can be together."

"Heinj, Heinj." Thomann slapped the boy on the back in affectionate happiness. "I am so glad to see you! Come on. Come home with me. We'll get you a proper breakfast. You look tired, too. How...?"

"It's a long story, Uncle."

After Thomann bought a basket full of soft rolls, they walked arm in arm back to the mill house where Frau Winkle was putting breakfast on the table for Hans Beckerle, Kitty and Georg. Lisbeth had just put on her apron and was about to sit down next to her son. Frau Winkle spooned the porridge into the bowls. A plate of cheese lay in the center of the table beside a bowl of berries, the treasure of late summer. Thomann looked in, then pushed Heinj ahead of him.

"Go on, Heinj. See if Kitty recognizes you! Here take this." He handed Heinj the basket of bread he'd bought for breakfast.

Thomann stood just outside the door as Heinj went in.

"Anyone want some bread?" Heinj asked. Kitty looked up, hearing the accents of home. Seeing her grown cousin, she squealed in joy and nearly knocked over her porridge in her rush to go to him.

"How's my Kitty?" asked Heinj, lifting her in his arms and kissing her.

"Are you going to stay with us?" Kitty asked. "Because I think you should."

"Lisbeth, Frau Winkle, Brother Beckerle, this is my nephew, the oldest son of my oldest brother, come to stay?" Thomann looked at Heinj, who nodded. "Heinj, this is the mill owner, Hans Beckerle, his daughter, Lisbeth and her son, Georg. The good woman who's gone to get a bowl for you is Frau Winkle."

"You are most welcome, young Heinj," said Berckerle, "most welcome."

# chapter 30

## Kappel am Albis, October 1531

The grass, that morning green, sprinkled with dew and bright autumn leaves, lay flattened and glistening red by late afternoon. Arms, legs, heads, feet and hands were strewn across the hillside. Intestines and livers languished on the ragged edges of pike-opened bellies. Small fires, used to light cannons, smoked beside the wheel-torn earth. The arquebuses had done their worst. Pikes and halberds lay on the field beside the men who'd held them. Though a banner of Zürich stuck in the ground, leaning at a crazy angle, the warriors who had carried it were long gone, back to Zürich to save their own lives. Two thousand poorly trained and exhausted Zürich troops had been ineptly led against seven thousand troops of the Catholic Forest Cantons and the

Habsburg armies, professional soldiers, all. At the end of the day, five hundred lay dead, among them Huldrych Zwingli. Zwingli was so hated by the Catholic cantons (which he had attempted to convert through starvation, an embargo on food) that his corpse was tried and convicted of heresy, then cut in quarters and burned— a usual punishment for heretics.

Peter rallied his few soldiers and retreated to Affoltern. Glarus was too far and in a dangerous direction. Some of his men had already ridden home. Peter hoped to find a haven with his brother, perhaps room in Heinrich's barn or maybe in Conrad's nearly empty house for his weary and disheartened men to spend the night. He arrived to find Vreni sitting with Christina and Elsa at the kitchen table, her face white with fear, her eyes red from crying.

"My God," said Peter, crossing himself. "What hellish idea was that? What a stupid, blundering, ill-thought-out mess. What waste. The fight was what, five minutes? We were completely routed. Taken by surprise! An informer, I think, betrayed us, crossed the lines and told them where we were. Our army, no, Zwingli's army, more than half ran away. I don't blame them. What were they doing there? No training, poorly armed, unpaid? An army of churchmen to do what? Pray for victory?"

"Peter," said Heinrich, nodding toward Vreni.

Peter stopped.

"Hannes?" said Elsa, looking up at Peter.

Peter's face paled. "My God. No. Hannes wasn't there, was he?"

"Yes, he was there."

"He should not have been there."

"What would he do? Zwingli called the pastors to Zürich and sent them back with a call to arms."

"Vreni," he said, taking a deep breath, "I did not see Hannes, not before, during or after. But Zwingli?" Elsa gave Peter a hard look, and Peter stopped. Life had its own horrors, all inevitable. Perhaps one was on its way to this house, to these frightened women, to this loving wife. "Can my men stay in the barn, Heinrich?"

Heinrich nodded.

"I'll get something for them to eat and have it taken to them," said Elsa.

Except for Peter, who was exhausted and slept with his men in the barn, the family stayed up all night waiting, in case Hannes should come home.

*** 

Night's heavy mist and the smoke of smoldering fires lingered in the valleys as dawn broke the horizon. Conrad and Peter tied their horses on the edge of the battlefield and walked in silence among the dead, moving efficiently through the carnage, using the tips of their swords to turn over the bodies they found face down. Among them were several of Zwingli's evangelical pastors, some wearing plate armor over their pastoral robes. Most not.

Between two trees, Conrad saw a pastor's body with golden hair like that of Hannes. His hand shook as he reached down and gently turned over the fallen man. Conrad retched, then wiped his mouth with the back of his hand. "Peter?" he called out in a loud whisper. "He is here. I have found him."

"Is he in one piece?" Peter first thought of Vreni, how it would be for her to see Hannes mutilated.

"He has a gash to the back of his head. Clubbed, maybe, with the hilt of a sword. Maybe he fell to cannon fire. I don't know."

"Let's get him out of here. I saw what they did to Zwingli. For all I know they will give all these corpses such trials for heresy."

They wrapped Hannes in Peter's long cloak, then lifted the body onto Peter's charger in front of the saddle. The brothers mounted their horses and turned toward home. Conrad could not help but think how under everything the gentle Hannes had been a crusading knight. He'd given up everything for his lady love, then fought valiantly to the death for the cause he had adopted.

The family knew everything when Conrad and Peter rode up. There was something in the sound of the horses' hooves on the stone courtyard that rang with the din of a hero's death knell. Before anyone could stop her, Vreni was at the door. She gasped seeing Hanne's body draped so expediently over the front of Peter's saddle, his head covered by the woolen cloak.

"Little sister," said Conrad, jumping down from his horse, tears streaming down his cheeks. "Little sister." He opened his arms to Vreni, who fell into them. No one in the world knew Hannes' and her story as did Conrad. He'd shared it since the beginning. "No man ever loved a woman more, Vreni. Maybe you will find some comfort in that. No one."

He felt her nod against his shoulder. Hannes' love had been a great gift to her. No day of her life had passed since their marriage that she had not thanked God for her husband. She had long wondered if her grandfather had somehow been her good angel, and, as he lay dying, had given her to Hannes. She resolved then to be as brave as Hannes had been in facing the changes rushing through their world.

\*\*\*

They buried Hannes beside his mother and brothers in the Lunkhofen/Schneebeli section of the abbey cemetery. The rules of the Evangelical church meant nothing to anyone in the valley, and the cemetery was filled. People of the village, the abbey, the farms and cottages all around had come to honor the gentle soul who had gone inexplicably to war.

"My brother, Hannes," said Peter, ignoring the injunction against speaking over the grave, "and the brother of Heinrich, here and Conrad. The husband of Vreni and the friend and confidante of all of you. Hannes was the heart of this valley. I've been a warrior, a priest and now a pastor." He gestured at his pastoral garb. "In truth, I am simply Peter Schneebeli, not a very good man but no worse than most. Hannes, however, was good through and through. I am sure there is not one man or woman here, including me, who has not taken their troubles to Hannes and come away with their burden lightened and their way a little clearer. My brother Hannes, our brother Hannes, was God's true servant."

Vreni stood sorrowful but calm between Christina and Heinrich's daughter, Gretchen, who was in that moment sweetly poised between girlhood and womanhood. Each had wrapped an arm around Vreni, as if to hold her up.

Conrad realized that he would miss his brother forever. Every day of his life he would feel that absence. His mind puzzled over the man, Zwingli. The story was that seeing his men dead on the field at Marignano and witnessing the suffering and death during the plague in Zürich, Zwingli had been inspired to find a new path to God. Yet, Zwingli's path had not led to peace, but to the deaths of hundreds in a futile, poorly planned war. "How are those bodies, those deaths, those lives, more tragic than my brothers' deaths?" Conrad murmured. "Peaceful hearts, both. Andreas drowned in the river, Hannes face down on a battlefield." Christina knew what was in Conrad's heart and slid her hand into his. He grasped it tightly, almost to the point of pain, as if he needed something to hold onto. He was angry and broken-hearted both, at once.

That afternoon and evening, there was food and drink in the Schneebeli courtyard for everyone. The party lasted until morning. Vreni served those who came to honor her husband, though her heart was torn and filled with sorrow.

As the sun rose over the distant mountains, the family gathered with those friends who had stayed the night, and recited, *"Bless The Lord, O my soul, O Lord my God, Who coverest Thyself with light as with a garment; who stretchest out the heavens like a curtain, who layeth the beams of his chambers in the water; who maketh the clouds his chariot, who walketh upon the wings of the wind."*

# chapter 31

## Conrad, November 1531

Affoltern am Albis returned to agriculture's timeless rhythms, even though the harvest had been hindered by war, labor was short, and families mourned the loss of sons, fathers and brothers.

"Like a storm that floods the rivers so high that towns are washed away and everyone must start over. Like fire," thought Conrad, as he backed the horses into the wagon hitch. "Whoa, sorry, boys. I'll pay better attention." He patted both horses on the rump. "At least you missed out on the fighting." He put two fingers up to his mouth and whistled loudly. Little Hans came running out the back gate, cap in hand.

"I'm sorry, Uncle. Mother said I must wash."

"Get up here. I don't know what we have today beyond taking flour to the abbey. Here, take the reins. Time you learned to drive."

"Really, Uncle?"

"What did I say?"

The horses ambled down to the mill. Little Hans concentrated intensely on not making any mistakes. He'd never been allowed to drive the wagon, and he felt like a man beside his uncle, holding the reins though the horses knew where they were going.

Fall leaves, dried and brown, spun up and away in front of them. The more tenacious and frost-blackened clung to the trees, refusing to accept the shorter days and angled light of November. The wind now carried the breath of snow, the advance of time. Conrad hoped the winter would be mild for all the poor people and their uncountable losses. Today they would be taking the tithe of flour to the abbey. It would not be much. It would be a frugal winter for all. He sighed.

They reached the mill and had to back the wagon up to the loading dock.

"Can you do this, Little Hans?"

"I want to try."

"All-right, boy. Just take your time. The horses know what to do. Go straight forward first."

Little Hans, with manly seriousness, clicked his tongue and snapped the reins over the horses' backs. They lurched forward.

"What did I tell you?" Conrad grinned. "Let them work. They'll teach you how to do this better than I can. Now slow down."

Little Hans tried once more, more gently urging the horses forward. "Is that far enough, Uncle?"

"That's fine, Little Hans. Now back them up. Keep those lines straight. You can talk to them."

Little Hans clicked his tongue. "Back, boys," he said, as he'd heard his Uncle Conrad say many times. "Back, boys."

"Slow now, Little Hans. There's no rush."

The horses paused, for the moment testing the conviction of their driver, then they began backing. Slowly, slowly the horses brought the wagon up to the dock.

"Good. Always remember; don't rush the horses and don't be afraid. Trust them to do what they've been trained to do. They are only two parts of a team of three."

"Do you think I'll ever be as good as you with the horses, Uncle?"

"Why not?" Conrad rubbed the top of Little Hans' head affectionately. "Hold them there while I load the wagon." Conrad got up from the seat, turned and walked across the wagon bed. "Heinrich! Heinrich! We're here!"

Heinrich came rushing to the storeroom. "Who's your driver there?" he asked.

"Little Hans."

"Good for him."

"Anyone show up for work?"

"Old 'Dolf and his boy, Markus, have been helping me in the warehouse. I'm on my own in the mill until you come back." Markus was bringing sacks of flour to the front for Conrad to load onto the wagon. "I think this will be the first winter I will be glad for bad weather when it comes."

Three of Heinrich's workers had been killed in the battle, along with Hannes. The two others, Old 'Dolf and his sweet, simple-minded son, Markus, who could calm any animal and often helped Conrad with the horses, were the only ones left. Keeping the mill running was not going to be easy.

"If that boy learns to drive, we just might make it," Conrad said, taking the sack of flour from Markus and setting it on the wagon bed.

"Can you unload this yourselves? I can't come along. I can't send Markus, either."

"God-willing there will be someone at the abbey to give me a hand."

"See if there is anyone there who might like a job," said Heinrich. "He doesn't have to be young or all that fit to help out here. It's not a bad living."

"I'll ask," said Conrad.

After the wagon was loaded, Conrad and Little Hans headed to the abbey. It would be Conrad's first visit since Hannes' death.

Martin was waiting, and he opened the big gates to the abbey yard. The barn was on the north side.

"You have to back the horses again, Little Hans. But that barn is less familiar to them than our dock at the mill. Are you ready to try? You have to bring them around first."

"Let me get the doors open all the way for you, sir," Martin called out. "It will be easier for Little Hans, if the doors are out of the way." Martin swung the doors against the barn walls and hooked them to the barn wall to keep them from swinging.

"I think I can do it, Uncle. Anyway, I want to try."

"All right. Remember, the horses know how to do this. You just have to guide them. Can you?"

Little Hans nodded, but he really wasn't sure. He took a deep breath, clicked his tongue and pulled straight back on the reins.

"Slowly, slowly." Conrad looked over his right shoulder. "Now tell the horses they need to go a little right. Can you do that? Keep the lines taut or the horses will be confused. They must work together."

In his nervousness, Little Hans had let one of the reins loosen. The horse looked back at him as if he were saying, "Come on, boy. You must help me do this right."

"He's telling you to tighten that line, Little Hans. He is the guide horse here. He needs your help."

Little Hans quickly figured how to communicate more clearly to the horse and tightened the line just enough. The horses began to back and turn at the same time. It felt like hours, but in just a few minutes, the horses had backed into the barn.

"Stop, Little Hans. We're where we need to be." Conrad stepped over the wagon seat and got into the wagon bed. "Martin! Can you help? Can I hand down these flour sacks to you?"

Martin came running. "Yes, sir. Happy to help. Short-handed now at the mill, are you?"

Conrad sighed. "Terribly. It's me, Heinrich, Old 'Dolf, Markus and Little Hans here right now."

"How can Heinrich run a mill on a crew like that?"

"I don't know that we can. And there is the cider. We haven't begun with the cider. We had to let most of the harvest go."

"Aye. We are pushed to finish pressing the cider here, too."

"Have you finished?"

"Not nearly."

"I was hoping to find men in need of work here."

"After, maybe, when we get the cider put up. Maybe there will be some who want work. I will ask. The valley will be short of flour if your mill..."

"We won't shut down, Martin."

"Have you heard anything from young Heinj?"

"No." Conrad looked down. He did not want to talk about this.

"Zürich never found him?"

"I don't know."

He shrugged. "Many a family these days..."

"Yes."

"That about does it, then."

"Ask, would you? Once you get the apples pressed, ask if anyone wants to work at the mill in Affoltern. Two men would be a big help."

"I will, sir. Thank you and send thanks to Heinrich."

"All right, Little Hans. Forward. See how easy that was?"

Little Hans nodded and urged the horses forward. "Slowly, now."

"Yes, Uncle."

"Conrad! Conrad! Wait!" Seeing Vreni running into the yard, Little Hans stopped the horses.

"Sister!" He jumped down from the wagon. "Hold them, Little Hans." He embraced his sister-in-law and felt the pang he'd hoped to avoid, the absence of Hannes. "How are you? Are you all right?"

"I'm fine, fine, we've been busy with the cider and all, but we're nearly done. What about you? What about your apples? Will you be bringing them down soon?"

"I don't know, Vreni. Honestly, I haven't had the time to think about them." His voice drifted off. Last year — and for years previous — Conrad's apple harvest had been a family party, with Hannes and Vreni and all the mill workers joining in, followed by a feast in the castle courtyard celebrating summer's end.

"Ueli has been helping us. I hope that is all right."

Conrad suddenly remembered. Ueli was too young to have been conscripted by Zürich, but not too young to work in the mill. "Ueli," he said.

"Yes. He was asking if I knew what you were going to do, if you wanted him to bring down your apples."

Conrad decided at that moment to go home with Christina for a few days and sort out his own business. He hadn't been at the castle since the harvest. Then there was the war, the funeral, the emptiness in the countryside, the problems at the mill. He yearned for his own home.

"I'll go up tomorrow or the next day and look things over. I don't doubt we'll be back sometime next week with a load for the abbey mill. I'm looking for men to work in our mill in Affoltern, too. It's just Heinrich, me, Little Hans here, Old 'Dolf and his son."

Vreni nodded. "I'll ask around after we finish, Conrad. You can tell Heinrich."

"Thank you, little sister." Conrad embraced Vreni gently. Once Zürich was able to regain its balance and sort through the debris of the Evangelic faith, a new pastor would come to the abbey, but for the time being it clung to the image of Hannes and his ways.

*** 

Saturday was a half day at the mill. By then Conrad had told Heinrich his plans to return to the castle for a while. "My apples need to go down to the abbey. I don't know what shape everything is in. Ueli's been working at the abbey mill, and I want to see if he wants to come down here and work for you, for us."

Heinrich had heard, "For you," even though his brother had quickly back-tracked. "Do you want to take a wagon and team up there, Conrad? You could use them to carry the apples. I won't need it. There's the cart. Little Hans can drive and just make more trips if we need to make any."

"I'd be very grateful, Heinrich."

The team was hitched to the wagon and he and Christina went home, the long way, not along The Brothers, but through the village, past the abbey and up the linden shaded road to the front courtyard of the castle.

"Anna! We're here!" Christina called out, glad to be home.

"Mistress! Sir!" Anna came running from the house. "Thank the Lord!" She crossed herself. "Are you home to stay?"

"I don't know, Anna. My brother needs me at the mill more than ever. There is still no livelihood here. No horses."

Anna looked at Conrad strangely and shrugged. "Come in, come in. I'll fix you something to drink. Shall I open the house, too?"

"Yes," said Christina emphatically. "I'll help you." Conrad uncoupled the horses and led them behind the house where he and Ueli had built a simple lean-to shed after the fire.

"Sir?" Ueli came up to Conrad, grinning.

"Ueli! So you've been helping at the abbey with the cider?"

"I have. They're short-handed and the money is helpful."

"Do you want to work in the mill in Affoltern? My brother has only Little Hans, Old 'Dolf and Markus right now. And me, but..."

"Yes," answered Ueli, "I do. That is, until, unless..."

"I don't know when I will have horses again, Ueli. By then? Maybe the situation will be different, better. But now? Workers are scarce and the village needs a mill and you need a better living, you and your mother. It would be money. You could board with Heinrich."

Ueli nodded. He had been thinking often of learning a skill he could use anywhere. He loved Conrad and the castle, but without the horses, he wasn't so sure of his future, and he knew he would, someday, want to marry.

"I brought the horses and the wagon for us to take the apples down to the abbey Monday. Let's see how much we have to worry about."

They had stored the apples in the great hall of the castle. It was cool and damp and undisturbed these days. In the current market, the apples would bring in good money. Not enough to replace the horses, but maybe enough to work as a hedge against winter.

"What of the garden?"

"We did all right. Mother has pickles and onions for the winter. We killed a pig and made ham and bacon.

The beans were good. We've dried some, and peas, too. Over there." Ueli gestured toward the other side of the great hall where he and his mother had stacked bags and barrels against winter and wet.

"When you go down with me to work in the mill, let's take a ham and some beans and peas with us, you know, for the family." It would be Ueli's board. "You and your mother have done very well and I'm grateful. Candles?"

"Oh yes, ask my mother. We rendered the pig fat. We've been busy, but now?"

Anna came to the back door and called her son to help her move a heavy trunk. "Go on, boy. I'll see to the horses."

Conrad tied the horses to the back wall of the house, sheltered by the lean-to. He brushed them down, savoring the silence of the castle and the hillside. "Here boys, eat up." The sun dipped below the horizon and the chilly day gave way to what would be a cold night, still, Conrad did not want to go inside. He patted their rumps affectionately and decided to walk down the small incline to the empty ground where the stables had been. He heard a horse nicker on the other side of a break of alder trees that had once separated a pasture from the stables.

Fastening his jacket and turning up the collar, he walked around the alder hedge and down the slope to the small pasture. The moon had risen. He heard Christina calling him in the distance. He walked along the forested edge of the pasture slowly, waiting, thinking. He stopped. The sky was clear; the moon was bright. The mist that would build later still clung to the valleys. Conrad loved his family and was grateful to his brother for his help and support these past months, but he had missed his life, the solitude, and most of all, the horses. He sat down on a stump and inhaled deeply, gratefully.

*I'm staying,* he thought. *We can get through the winter. Ueli can take my place at the mill. If Heinrich needs me, I'll go down and help him. Maybe Christina will be lonely but maybe Vreni will come back.* Conrad was captivated by possibilities for the first time since the bailiffs had come after his horses.

He heard a horse nicker again, this time closer. "All right," he thought, "where are you?" He was sure horses had wandered off the battlefield where Hannes had died, and from all the battlefields since then. "I'd be surprised if the woods are not full of horses." He felt something warm on his bare head. He heard a nicker again, this time right above him. He felt a gentle push on his shoulder. His heart beat suddenly faster; he struggled to suppress hope, and failed. Hope rose anyway.

He reached behind himself slowly, without turning around to feel the soft lips of a horse brush against his open palm, looking for something, a slice of apple, a carrot, or maybe? Maybe the horse was looking for him. Conrad stood and turned.

Saladin pawed the ground and nickered.

In disbelief, Conrad stroked his horse's nose. Saladin put his chin over Conrad's shoulder. Wrapping his arms around his horse's neck, Conrad unexpectedly and suddenly broke into lurching sobs for the death of Hannes and the return of Saladin. When his emotions were spent, his heart was lightened. Taking a deep breath, he stepped back and looked at his horse carefully in the moonlight. "Well, you seem no worse for your adventures, Saladin. I bet you gave some noble soldier a wild ride." As if in agreement, the little stallion tossed his head. "Let's go home, boy."

Saladin followed Conrad back to the house, nudging him in the middle of the back with every step. With each nudge, Conrad's heart soared a little higher. Never in his wildest dreams had he imagined he would see his horse again. The wasteland of loss faded into the garden of hope and love in which Conrad had long ago chosen to live.

"Christina!" he called when he reached the courtyard. "Come out here! Ueli! Anna! Come out and see! Bring a lantern."

Christina heard a timbre in Conrad's voice she had not heard in a long time. "Come on, Ueli, Anna, supper can wait. Hurry!"

Ueli took down the lantern from its hook beside the front door and lit it. Holding it high, he could not believe what he saw. Beside Conrad, who smiled so wide it seemed his face might break, stood the little black stallion.

"Saladin, sir?"

"It is," said Conrad.

"Oh!" exclaimed Christina, wrapping her arms around the horse's neck. "You have come home."

"It seems he was in that battle and ran away."

"Has he been hurt?"

"Ueli, bring over the lantern. Let's see what we can see."

Conrad carefully examined Saladin. He'd taken a hit to the left thigh, but it seemed nearly healed over. "I can't see everything now," said Conrad. "Tomorrow I'll look again."

"Where will we put him?" Ueli didn't want to put Saladin in the lean-to that was open on three sides and could only hold two horses. He wanted to keep the horse safe, hidden, even. "Do you think anyone will come looking for him?"

"No. I think they have bigger problems in Zürich now than a runaway stallion they probably couldn't ride. I could be wrong, but he's been on his own, what? Three weeks now?"

"Do you think he'll eat grain at all after grass, apples and acorns?" laughed Christina.

"We'll find out soon enough," laughed Conrad. "Oh, Saladin, my boy." The horse nudged Conrad's shoulder in answer. "Where shall we put you?"

"Old Stefan's rooms are empty, remember? We cleared them out."

"Sir! You can't put a horse in a bedroom!" said Anna, horrified.

"What's the difference between a stall in a barn and the back room of this tower? Who knows? Maybe it sheltered a horse or two in its time. The tower was a place to go for safety. I wager there were horses waiting patiently for the danger to pass."

"Is it really empty, Ueli?" asked Christina.

"It is, missus. Don't you remember? We packed everything that was worth keeping," said Anna. "And we put away Old Stefan's furniture when Vreni married, whatever she didn't want to keep for herself and Hannes, God rest his blessed soul."

"We don't need the room. Saladin does," said Conrad, wondering why they were debating this at all. "For the night, anyway, until I can build a proper barn for him to live in. Ueli, is there any tack? Did it all vanish in the fire?"

"There's not much left, no. We have what was on Prince and a halter I was braiding. Almost finished."

Conrad saw that he would be starting over, rebuilding not only his barn but all the equipment he would need for his horses. Everything.

"I thought I saw him in the forest," said Anna, "a week or more past, but I wasn't sure. I sent Ueli out to call him, but... I decided it was shadows between the trees."

"I tried more than once, sir. I took him grain and called him, but I never saw him. Only my mother saw him."

"I was thinking that if it was Saladin, he would not come home until you came home, too, sir," said Anna.

"The cannons alone could frighten him. He wasn't raised to them or to warfare."

"No. He's been your spoiled pet, my love," said Christina, chiding her husband.

"Yes, yes, that he has, but is there another like him anywhere?"

They all agreed that not only was there no other horse like him, but there was also never likely to be one.

"Put him away, if you can bear a little separation, so we can have supper," said Christina, kissing her husband on the cheek.

Saladin followed Conrad to Old Stefan's room where Ueli had spread straw on the floor. "Here you go, boy. Now you're safe at home."

He set a pail of water where Saladin could find it and hung a bucket of oats on a peg on the inside wall. "Don't kick over your water, boy, or you'll be sorry." Saladin nickered and nodded his head.

# chapter 32

**Thomann, Spring, 1532**

When he was younger, Thomann assumed his father would arrange a marriage for him, probably something that would benefit the mill, maybe with a distant cousin, someone who had some money to bring along with them. He knew that, compared to his brothers, he was an unimpressive figure. He wasn't very tall. His hair was red. He was not charming like Peter, or intelligent like Conrad, or passionate as Andreas had been. He was no businessman like Heinrich. As for Hannes? Thomann had been as surprised as anyone when Hannes left the old church for the new and married Vreni.

Until he heard the preaching of Felix Manz and Conrad Grebel he had never known he was capable at all of passion. Though his faith and his ideas were deeply held, he respected himself and others enough to keep his own peace. That was a cornerstone of the Re-baptizers, and Thomann believed in it heart and soul. Thomann admired Conrad and Christina for their dedication to each other and for their romantic attachment, just as he had admired the love his parents bore each other, but he believed such things were rare.

The words of Felix Manz and Conrad Grebel had struck a flame in Thomann's heart that brought out his courage and his strength. There was something true in life, not simply practical or expedient, but something good beyond the day-to-day business of running a mill. It was a goodness man could reach through the grace of God.

After he had worked for Beckerle for nearly a year and saw how quickly Kitty had taken to Lisbeth, Thomann began to think that maybe he was not enough for the little girl. She would need a mother to help her learn all the household arts and guide her into womanhood.

Late one Sunday afternoon, Thomann attended a meeting held in the mill house for the few Re-baptizers who had joined them, a handful of men and women, a few children. Brother Marpeck's plan was slowly gaining ground in Illenkirchen and other villages, but the Emperor's mandate had not changed and there was great risk, still, to anyone who knew a Re-baptizer.

After the meeting, Thomann asked Frau Winkle, "What do you think of Lisbeth?"

Frau Winkle looked up from her knitting. "You could do worse. She's hard-working and kind. Why are you looking at me that way?"

"Sometimes I wonder if you read my mind."

"I have been on God's green earth a long time. Will she change her faith from Papism to ours? That is important to you, to Kitty, and to your future lives."

"I have to talk to her about that when, after…"

"I'm sure my parents would never have imagined such a conversation. Nor my man and me, time was."

"I'm sure my father would rather life had gone on the same way. Andreas and I? First we went one way, then another, bringing the new ideas straight to the old man's doorstep. Then Hannes! I'm sure the old man never imagined Hannes would want to marry anyone, but he did. My brother fell right into the changes when he fell in love with Vreni. What if he hadn't? Would he have stayed at the abbey when it was converted or would he have joined so many others and gone to Einsiedeln or Luzern? I don't think he would have considered any of this at all."

"But what about you and your brother Andreas?"

"I'll tell you from the beginning. We were in Zürich one Sunday on an errand for my father. We naturally went to church, and Zwingli preached. He spoke about God in a way we'd never heard before. Everyone standing in the congregation was captivated. God loved us. Christ's sacrifice was the salvation for all of us. More. Andreas and I spent a lot of time in Zürich after that, listening. Pages of the Bible were passed to everyone. It was exciting to read the words ourselves. The discussions were exciting, but things gradually fell apart. Well, you know how that is."

Frau Winkle nodded. "When will you talk to Lisbeth? Let me know when and I will help you. I can take the children to the river to play."

"I was thinking Saturday, on the half day, I would ask her to take a walk with me. Can you keep the children here?"

"Lisbeth makes bread on Saturday. I'll start it before she comes home. You deserve happiness and so does Lisbeth. Have you talked to Beckerle?"

"I will talk to him today."

"Good luck, Thomann," Frau Winkle said, wiping her eyes with her apron.

***

"I'm troubled by this religion thing, Thomann. You understand that, surely."

"I do, sir. I know that you take a risk having me working here for you, with my little girl and Frau Winkle living in your mill house. I..." Thomann stopped.

"I have no objection to your faith itself, Thomann. It's..."

"What, sir?"

"Were it not for the danger, I could see myself joining you. As it is, I have so much to lose."

Thomann thought of the soul of this man and wondered what more there was to lose. "It's on the line already, sir, forgive me saying so, with me managing your mill, my nephew working for you, my child and Frau Winkle living in your house."

"You're saying I might as well be hung for a sheep as a lamb?" Beckerle smiled.

"I guess that is what I'm saying."

"Have you spoken with Lisbeth?"

"No. I wanted to talk to you first."

"Thomann, I like you. You've saved my mill and my livelihood, and, God willing," he crossed himself, "my grandson's inheritance, at least as far as I can know. If the future is anything like the past, well. We do the best we can, don't we, Thomann? That's all we can do."

"With God's help, yes."

"Will you expect Lisbeth to change? I don't know if, I don't know how she..." Beckerle suddenly thought that though he'd known Lisbeth since she was a girl and had lived in the same house with her since her marriage to his son, he really didn't know her.

Thomann shook his head. "I don't know. We will have to talk about it, Lisbeth and I, if she will have me. Maybe she won't. Maybe my faith is a problem."

"Such problems did not exist in my time." Beckerle shrugged. "Thomann, you have my blessing to ask Lisbeth, but, I'm — you won't be going away? You won't take Georg away from me, will you?" Beckerle's heart froze.

"No, sir. Why? Kitty and I have made our home here. As long as we can stay, we..."

"I fear that, Thomann. I don't deny it."

Thomann nodded. How could he pretend he did not fear it as well? "The future is in God's hands. *'Sufficient unto the day is the evil thereof.'* Today is enough."

***

"Heinj, can you take over here? There isn't much left to do. I want to clean up, you know, before..."

"Yes, Uncle, I can." Heinj knew Thomann's plans. He felt grown up and manly being in his uncle's confidence. So Thomann hurried over to the mill house while Lisbeth was still minding the store. He went in the kitchen door, hoping to wash in the basin by the back door, but the children caught his attention. Kitty and Georg were playing with blocks on the floor. Each block had a carved and painted number. A little older and more advanced than Kitty, Georg was trying to explain how to stack the blocks to make sums.

"I'm building a house for my dollies." Kitty had a small family of clay figures along with their animals, a horse, cow, sheep and a dog.

"How are you going to do that?"

"I can. Watch." Kitty began stacking the blocks so they formed two walls facing each other, but when she wanted to put a roof on the house, she didn't know what to do. Georg watched in curiosity, then had the idea that his handkerchief could stretch from wall to wall for a roof. The idea wasn't bad, but the cloth fell in. Thomann watched them, fascinated, then went out and found a small flat board to add to their blocks.

"Here, Georg, see if this will work for a roof on Kitty's house."

"Uncle, it has no number."

Thomann laughed. The little boy was nothing if not systematic about things. "Here." Thomann took a chunk of cold charcoal from the hearth. "What is the biggest number you have, Georg?"

"Fifty."

"All right. What should the next number be?"

Georg looked at his blocks. He couldn't see all the numbers the way the blocks were stacked. "Sixty!"

Thomann wrote "60" on the board with the charcoal. "When Kitty is done playing, see if you can find blocks to add together to make one hundred. I'll help you if you get stuck."

Lisbeth stood in the doorway watching Thomann solve the problem of the roof and the block. "Father sent me. You wanted to talk to me about something?"

Thomann jumped at the sound of her voice. He'd lost his chance to clean up, to make a good impression. "Lisbeth," he said, blushing.

He wiped his charcoaled fingers on his already dirty trousers, then took off his cap and got charcoal on his face. "Would you go for a walk with me? Along the canal, maybe? It's a pretty day, that is, unless you have something else to do," he said, after taking a deep breath. "Frau Winkle is making bread so you don't have to."

"You work so hard, Lisbeth," answered Frau Winkle. "I have to watch these two, anyway, so I may as well get the bread done."

Lisbeth was struck with a flash of insight. It was her turn to blush.

With a roof on the little block house, Kitty was happily playing with her painted clay family and their animals. Georg had a new top, carved by Heinj, and he was trying hard to get it to spin the way Heinj had shown him.

"Thomann," said Frau Winkle, "you might want to wash your face. You have charcoal on your forehead."

Thomann blushed again. "I will be right back." He dashed out to the porch behind the kitchen to the washbasin and gave his face a good scrub.

Frau Winkle came out. "Then she's going to walk out with you?"

"Yes."

"God bless you, Thomann. I'll say a little prayer."

\*\*\*

During the time — nearly a year — they had known each other, Thomann and Lisbeth had unconsciously blended their lives in the running of the mill and the mill store and the children's lives. In daytime, the mill house was filled with the sounds of children playing and all the other sweet qualities of life. In the evenings, when Lisbeth took Georg home to Beckerle's big house across the river, Thomann had, more and more often, noticed her absence. The house fell silent and a certain heart was gone.

Below the mill was a canal used to send lumber and other things downstream to the river and on to Strasbourg. Shaded by old linden trees, the pathway beside the canal was the perfect place to stroll on a warm early summer afternoon. As they walked, blossoms dropped on the pathway in front of them.

"My brother, Conrad, has a song about this tree," said Thomann. "It's an old, old song, from the days of knights."

"Do you know it?"

"No. I don't have Conrad's cleverness. He plays the lute and sings sometimes, beautiful old tunes, some he learned from our mother and others from our Grandfather Johann. Conrad is . . . " Thomann was at a loss for words.

"Where is he?"

"Still at home, I believe. I cannot write to them. It's..." The conversation was veering in a direction away from what Thomann wanted. "It's a love song. It's about..." Thomann blushed. How in the world, he wondered, would he get this conversation where he wanted it to go?

"I may know it," she said. "Two lovers met under a linden tree."

"That's the one. Well, maybe there is more than one. I don't know."

"My mother sang it to me as a lullaby," said Lisbeth. She began gently clapping her hands to keep time. "Under the linden by the heather, where our bed was, there you can find, beautifully broken, the flowers and the grass. Before the forest in a valley--Tandaradei--Beautifully sang the nightingale." She blushed.

"Yes," said Thomann, a feeling of homesickness passing through him. "My brother had a big tapestry made of that song to hang in the hall of the old castle."

"Your brother lives in a castle?"

"Yes and no. He lives in a house much like your father-in-law's. He and his wife built it when they married, but it shares a wall with an old castle tower that belonged to our ancestors hundreds of years ago. Conrad raises horses and grows some apples and crops for his stock. He calls himself a farmer with a stone tower. Long ago, a knight lived in the castle, which is more like a fort, I think. It sits on a hillside looking down on the valley. It's been burned and attacked and rebuilt over the centuries. It's not much more now than a ruined tower and some walls beside a stone courtyard."

"Such as we see all up and down the river, small heaps of stone, too small to rebuild, barely a home for anyone. Stables, maybe."

"Yes. Like that." Thomann paused, taking a deep breath. "Lisbeth, I, uh, I didn't want to walk with you to talk about my brother, I..." Sweat broke out on Thomann's forehead. His mouth was suddenly dry.

Lisbeth slipped her hand into his hand. She knew well enough what he was feeling. He squeezed her hand gently.

"Well, then," he said.

"Yes, Thomann."

They walked hand-in-hand under the linden trees until the sun began to drop.

# chapter 33

## The Orchard, 1532

"What does it say?"

"What, Gretchen? What 'it' do you mean?" Heinrich teased his daughter.

"The letter, Father. What does it say? Is it from Heinj?"

Elsa smiled to herself as she pulled the perl stitch over the needle. Socks, endlessly, socks, darning or knitting. That was a family.

"Yes, Gretchen. Heinj's letter is with one from Thomann. But don't go telling the news about. There is no reason to believe Heinj is safe, though now he is with Thomann. It seems..."

"Seems what, Father?"

"Thomann has married. A widow-woman with a little boy just a bit older than Kitty."

"Married? Uncle Thomann?" Gretchen could not believe it. Uncle Thomann was short. His hair was red. He was uglier, even, than her father.

"He's working in a sawmill. His wife is the daughter of the owner. This is happy news!"

"Where? Does he say?"

"No. It's better not to know. Come. We have work in the orchard. Conrad and Christina will be here soon. Boys!" Heinrich called to Little Hans and Bernhardt. "Elsa?"

"As soon as I get the top on this sock, Heinrich. I'll bring Gretchen."

\*\*\*

"Conrad? Are you ready?" Christina called out the back door.

"Almost, my love. I need to put Saladin inside." Conrad still worried that someone would come and take the horse.

"Ride him to your brother's." Christina hated to imagine a moment when Conrad might have to choose between her and the stallion.

"What about you?" Prince had surrendered to time, and Christina was now without a horse.

"No matter, Conrad. I'm no great help clearing out an orchard. I'll walk and get there in my own time."

"Are you sure, Christina? Ride in front of my saddle, you know, like when we were young. Come on. He won't mind."

"I don't know, Conrad. I don't think Saladin thinks anyone but you should have the privilege of his back. I'll walk down. You're not ready and I am. You can catch up to me."

"I'll walk with you. I'll lead him. How about that?"

"You spoil that horse, Conrad."

They walked down The Brothers, hand in hand, Saladin plodding slowly and happily behind them. As unwilling as Conrad was to let Saladin out of his sight, Saladin was equally reluctant to be anywhere without Conrad. They arrived at the Heinrich's white, half-timbered house and Conrad put Saladin in a stall in Heinrich's barn.

"All right, boy. You're no help in the orchard today. Maybe tomorrow."

The upheavals of the past years had meant that too many apples had rotted on the ground, branches had gone straggly and unpruned, parts of old trees had died, their dead wood drying and waiting for a strong wind to do the work that man had had no chance to do. Heinrich and Conrad shared their labors and their time, doing what they could to tend each other's trees in the year since the war, hoping to regain some mastery over their orchards. The Schneebeli family of Affoltern wasn't itself without apples.

Conrad and Heinrich set up ladders to reach to the tops of the older trees. The boys raked fallen leaves and debris below.

"Some of these trees are dead," said Conrad. "We'll have to cut them down."

"Times like these, I wish Heinj was here to help," sighed Heinrich.

"We're fine as we are," said Conrad. "The boys are growing up. It just takes time."

"Father! There's something here!"

"What is it, Little Hans?"

"I don't know. My rake got stuck on something. There's a stick here, deep in the ground. I can't pull it out."

"Oh my," said Elsa, catching her breath, crossing herself. "Could it be?"

Heinrich hurried over to where Little Hans had raked his way through a heavy pile of leaves, rotten apples and broken branches between two old trees near the top of the orchard, not far from The Brothers.

"Conrad!" he called out to his brother. "Did Thomann or Andreas ever say where?"

"No. All they ever said was that they buried him in the orchard."

"It's a lovely spot," said Christina, looking around. The oldest trees were in the upper orchard, near the forest trail. She looked down the slope at the sunlight filling the valley below. If it were Rudolf's grave, they'd put him near The Brothers Path to be noticed, to be remembered. How could they have known all that would happen to drive that sad event from everyone's memories?

"What should we do, Conrad? What would be right? Leave him or...?"

"We dig, Heinrich. If we find him, we dig him out and give him a proper funeral and bury him with Mother and Father."

Elsa felt as if she would suffocate. She could see Verena lying on her bed, her eyes closed, the apple box beside her. "Conrad, his little coffin is an apple box."

"Elsa, are you all right?" Heinrich looked at his wife who stood, pale as death. "Maybe you should take the children back to the house."

But Elsa was fixed to the ground, trapped in time.

"Come, Elsa," said Christina, putting her arm around Elsa's shoulder; Elsa began to cry. "Let's get the children. Little Hans, find Bernhardt and take him home. Come on, Gretchen. Let's prepare some supper for them when they finish."

"What did they find, Auntie? Mother is very upset."

"She is," Christina agreed. "Come on, boys." She reached out to take Bernhardt's hand, but he wriggled free. "You're growing up," said Christina. "I keep forgetting you're not a little boy now."

"I think we can get it out of there," said Conrad, "without disturbing..."

"I hope so."

Conrad got the back of his shovel under the box and they gently lifted it out of the hole.

"It seems firm enough, but..."

"I'll go in the shed and get an apple sack. We can slip the box inside."

"Good idea."

Conrad walked down the slope in long steps. The day had carried them far from where the morning had begun. He pushed open the door of the apple shed. As always, the apple sacks were folded and put away on the shelf according to size. He pulled one off a loose pile and shook it open, hoping it would prove large enough to hold the box. "This'll do," he murmured to himself, and he took the bag up to Heinrich.

They put the box in the bag, filled the hole and tamped the soil down over it. Heinrich raked some leaves and debris over the bare dirt to hide the scar.

"I think," said Conrad, "we'd best take him home with us and see if we can arrange a funeral for him, soon if possible. Poor little thing."

They set the box in the wheelbarrow and trudged down the hill to the house, a day's work lost in the discovery of their little brother.

"I'll ride over to the abbey and see if there's any chance we can take care of this tomorrow," said Conrad, the box safely stored on a shelf in the barn where no one would bother it.

***

Heinrich came into the kitchen and went immediately to his wife, whispering in her ear, "We found him."

"Is he..."

"The box is still closed. It's in good shape. It's in the barn, safely put away. Conrad rode his pet pony to the abbey to see if he could arrange a funeral tomorrow." Heinrich smiled at Conrad's love for Saladin. "Then, I hope, we can get back to the orchard. After we finish here, there is Conrad's grove, and then I said we would help down at the abbey. What are you cooking there, Gretchen?" He turned to the others.

Spring, early summer, the lean season. The winter stores were stretched to their limits, so Heinrich didn't expect much.

"We killed a chicken, father," she said. "Christina is making dumplings." Sure enough, in the kettle hanging over the fire a chicken simmered in its final bath of broth, carrots and onions.

"I've made a pie, Heinrich," said Elsa. "Dried apples I put to soak last night. Supper will be..."

Conrad appeared at the door. "All set. They're working already. I brought Vreni. I thought we should all be together since there's no more chance of work today, and in the morning we'll have the... Little Hans, would you like to take Saladin and Aunt Vreni's pony and see them safely put away for the night?"

"Can I take the pony?" asked Bernhardt.

"Can he, Uncle?" asked Little Hans.

"Yes, you can. Little Hans, be sure your little brother properly cares for Aunt Vreni's noble steed."

"Noble steed? Goodness, Conrad," Vreni laughed, "that's as much a noble steed as I am a princess."

"Will we have a funeral tomorrow then, Conrad?" asked Christina when the boys were safely out of earshot.

"Yes. They're digging a grave for the little one now, next to Mother."

"As it should always have been," said Elsa, wiping her eyes with the hem of her apron.

"Who, Mother?" asked Gretchen.

"You were still a little girl. Younger than Bernhardt is now," said Elsa, "so you probably can't remember the day your grandma died. Your Uncle Rudolf was born that day and died soon after. Your uncles, Andreas and Thomann, buried his little body in the orchard."

"But why, Mother? Why not in the cemetery with Grandma?"

"Daughter," said Heinrich, "in your short life, the world has changed."

"How?"

"Oh my little girl," sighed Heinrich. "You were, what, six years old?"

Gretchen nodded.

"Your grandmother was too old to have a baby, so the baby came early and died. Your uncle Andreas... Do you remember Andreas?"

"Not well, Father. Only from your stories."

"Your uncle Andreas was the only one home. He had already accepted the new religion, so he did not baptize the baby. When your uncle Hannes came to give the Last Rites to your grandmother, he told us that the baby could not be buried with her because the baby had not been baptized and could not go to Heaven."

"Uncle Rudolf would be eight years old! Like Bernhardt!" said Gretchen in wonder."

"That's right," said Elsa.

Heinrich emptied his pipe and refilled it, tamping down the tobacco with his thumb, and lit it. "In those times, your uncle Hannes was a monk, a Catholic. Most of us were. Only a few, your uncles Thomann and Andreas among them, were then following Zwingli, though that changed."

"Uncle Hannes was a priest?" Gretchen looked at her father in amazement.

Tears streamed down Vreni's cheeks.

"Aunt Vreni?" Gretchen laid her hand on her aunt's arm.

"It's all right, Gretchen. I'm all right." Vreni collected herself, dried her eyes and put her arm around Gretchen, who was now the age Vreni had been when Hannes had first noticed her.

"I don't imagine it matters to anyone anymore if this tiny baby born before his time is buried beside his mother in sanctified ground. Do you think it does, Conrad?"

"Only to us, Heinrich."

The room grew silent, for in that moment, they all sensed the presence of Old Johann and Verena, sitting by the kitchen hearth fire, where now the chicken simmered. Andreas, who had just come in the door, drunk on the Holy Spirit, was telling them of the new ideas in Zürich, while Hannes, his face pale, grasped his rosary tightly in his hand, worried for the safety of his brother's soul.

# Epilogue

While most Americans are familiar with the stories of the British Pilgrims and the Quakers, we are less aware of the number of Swiss who emigrated to the US during the 17th and 18th century. It's difficult to determine precisely how many because many Anabaptist Swiss, like Thomann and Kitty, migrated to the Upper Rhine area during times of persecution in Switzerland, and then migrated back. We do know that some 300,000 Swiss — many of whom were included in lists of German speaking people from the Palatinate — came to America in the eighteenth century. Most arrived in Philadelphia and settled in Pennsylvania, but many also came to Maryland and Virginia, where they had been invited to settle. You can see this in the names of towns such as New Bern. They were predominantly farmers and village craftsmen, and many were Amish, Hutterite and Mennonite, faiths derived from Anabaptism.

One fundamental Anabaptist belief is that the powers of church and state should remain separate. This is a cornerstone of American law, the First Amendment to the Constitution. *"Congress shall make no law respecting an establishment of religion, or prohibiting the free exercise thereof..."*

Made in the USA
Columbia, SC
09 December 2020